# Chasing After Trouble

By:
## T.M. DeLawrence

———————

**The nest of flashing red and blue lights illuminated the morning sky as the sun yielded to the dark clouds above**. Every so often, the clouds would celebrate by sprinkling the earth with drizzle. However, an occasional flash of sunlight would be a reminder that the celebration would soon come to an end and another hot summer day would take precedence, despite the clouds' petty victory.

The 1997 Ferrari 355 purred as it came to a stop, away from the gathering crowd and parking lot of emergency vehicles. He turned off the engine and took in the setting before him. Police officers had sealed off the area, trying to keep the early morning joggers, nosy neighbors and reporters at bay. He looked at his watch to confirm the time. Television and newspaper reporters had stationed themselves everywhere hoping to get "the scoop" before the morning paper could hit newsstands throughout the region.

He could feel a lump developing in his throat and his stomach tightening. The environment he was about to involve himself in was never something he anticipated being a part of. He took in a deep breath as the Ferrari's purring ceased. He opened the door and stepped out, allowing the drizzle to sprinkle across his face and skin.  Though he had been awake for a little over a half-hour, the little drops of cool liquid helped in reviving his senses.  He was beginning to smell the morning dew coming from the mulch surrounding the residence. Images were becoming clearer as he began to pick out the variety of colors that permeated the environment.  He could distinctly begin to hear the variety of voice tones and accents of bystanders as they questioned the police and speculated about what happened.

He closed the door to the Italian sports car and made his way up the path to the apartment where police detectives were hurrying in and out.  He seemed to go unnoticed until he reached the yellow crime scene tape forbidding him to go any further.  He lifted the tape and a hand fell on his shoulder.

"Can I help you sir?" asked a voice from behind.

He looked back to find a uniformed officer doing his assigned duty in trying to keep the public's interest to a minimum.

"I'm sorry sir, but this area is for police personnel only.  I'm afraid that I'm going to ask you to step back to the area with the other bystanders."

"Hughes," said a voice from the apartment door.  "It's okay.  Let him through."

He turned to find a young female officer coming from the police-filled apartment to greet him.  She was one of the few people who wore the uniform of the Virginia Beach Police that he could actually call a friend.

Her name was Elizabeth Marie Companstella and he met her when he joined the police academy. Because of her long name, he nicked-named her E equals MC.  He later shortened it to E, because it was easier to say in a sentence or to get her attention.

During their days at "The Academy", she had told him that her father had pushed her to become a police officer in order to continue the family's heritage. Elizabeth was the only woman in her family to take on the role that traditionally fell to the responsibility of the Companstella men.  Throughout the training, Elizabeth surprised many of her male colleagues when she exceeded the department's standard and anomalous expectations.  Her performance would have made the policemen in her family proud.

The uniformed officer named Hughes lifted the yellow tape and he ducked under to meet with Elizabeth.

"Good morning," she greeted. "Mr. Garrett said you were coming."

"What happened E?" he asked, using the pet name he gave her.

Elizabeth shrugged as they started their walk to the apartment.  "It looks like someone broke in the house, and Ms. Taylor caught them in the middle of it."

He took in a deep breath as he held back his sorrow.  It was his second day of employment with Garrett and Taylor, Corporate Law Offices, a company half-owned and ran by Tessa Taylor.  Because his departure from the police department was more accurately described as banishment, Tessa Taylor was there to pick up the pieces and gave him a fresh start as a private investigator. He owed a lot to Tessa, and he was nowhere close to repaying the favor.

"Any leads?" he asked.

"Nothing official yet," Elizabeth replied solemnly as they reached the apartment.

From the doorway, he watched the police department's forensics team taking snapshots of the scenery, trying to piece together various clues. It looked like it was going to be a tough assignment. The apartment had been torn apart. It was as if a tornado had been born in the middle of the living room and unmercifully displayed its insatiable appetite for destruction. The burgundy couch and love seat had been ripped open like gutted fish. The glass coffee table separating them was now many little islands of glass splinters. Looking past the living room through the breakfast bar, he could see the refrigerator door and the kitchen cabinets had been thrown open and their contents exhibited across the counters. He suspected much of the same throughout the apartment. There was an oak desk in the far corner by the kitchen. It had been toppled over, its drawers strewn across the floor with their contents emptied on the carpet. The awards and framed pictures that were once on the wall above the desk sat on the floor cracked open. A computer monitor with a busted screen had somehow managed to travel to the other side of the room where it positioned itself next to a plant that had been uprooted and discarded. At the far wall leading to the bedrooms was the remnants of an aquarium. It had been emptied out onto the carpet, soaking it with a variety of fish and aquarium toys that the detectives were still having a hard time avoiding.  In the center of that mishap was a large black bag as the sum of one's ill-timed actions and a sad reminder of how precious life was.

"I'm sorry," Elizabeth consoled.  "But, we're doing everything we can."

He looked further inside the apartment to find Kevin Garrett sitting by the fireplace, neatly tucked in a corner away from the mass confusion of the city detectives.  The remaining half of the corporate law firm was holding a picture frame.  He decided he would give it his best to console the grief-stricken attorney.

"Keep me posted okay?" he asked as he began to walk off.

Elizabeth nodded.  "I will," she answered.

Kevin Garrett swallowed and wiped a tear from his eye as the investigator sat down beside him.  When he saw him yesterday, Kevin Garrett was a medium build, clean-shaven, neatly dressed lawyer with a baby face that could charm any jury in his favor.  His smile added a touch of genuine congeniality, which was reciprocated daily by each of the secretaries in the corporate office which Kevin fancied to flirt with.  Today, his surf-tanned face was haggard and populated with stubble.  His normally slicked-back dirty blonde hair joined his clothes as they rebelled against the normal tidiness Kevin prided himself on.  His smile had conceded to the angst growing inside him and his eyes painted a picture of regret.  He knew that she and Kevin were close.  They had known each other for almost five years before they created the corporate law firm.

Tessa also spent most of her time with Kevin and his family during the holiday

seasons and when Tessa was in trouble; Kevin was normally there to help her

through it. It must have been torturous for him to be present as the grisly

scenario unfolded.

He looked at the picture Kevin was holding. It was a picture of him and

Tessa in front of the tinted glass building in Virginia Beach's Lynnhaven area.

It was the first day of business for Garrett and Taylor, Corporate Law Offices

and the beginning of a very successful partnership.

"Just seems like yesterday, we were talking about who would have their

name first on the glass window of the office." Kevin smiled and gave a humpf.

"You know, I won that by a coin toss."

"It's gonna be okay." he replied. "The police will get the guy who did this.

And when they do, he'll pay for what he did."

Kevin looked at the black private investigator. His eyes were red from

tears and lack of sleep. His hair was ruffled and his suit was wrinkled. "I want

the bastard dead."

He nodded in agreement. "I know."

Kevin looked at the picture and swept away the tears swelling up. He took

in a deep breath trying to resume his composure. "I know this may seem like a

lot to ask, but I want you to handle this. Please? Do this as a personal favor to

me. I do not want this to end up collecting dust in some file cabinet sitting in the basement of the Virginia Beach Police Department.  I want you to find the person who did this."  The anger in his voice was beginning to emerge from the hurt.  "If you need anything, anything at all, you have my full authorization.  Do whatever it takes."

He stood up and tried to smile, realizing the full complexity of the task assigned to him.  "Well, first I need you to go home and get some sleep.  You're not going to do either one of us any good in the condition you're in now."  He looked around the ransacked apartment.  "Let me worry about this."

He reached out his hand and helped his employer from the corner of the apartment.  "Thank you." Kevin said.

"Don't mention it." he responded.  "Go home.  I'll page you if I turn up anything."

Kevin nodded and looked over at the bulky, black plastic covering the body of an old friend.  "I miss her."

The private investigator stood silent, looking at the figure lying under the plastic.  The lump in his throat seemed tougher to swallow.  He then focused his attention to Tessa's partner, who was taking a long look at the unmoving black bag before slowly walking out of the apartment.  He could see the tears were again forming in the attorney's eyes.  It was hard for the investigator to be objective, because he knew the pain of Kevin's loss.  He knew it well enough that he was continuously reminding himself that he was there to work this as he would any other case assigned to him.

Once Kevin had disappeared within the crowd of people and news photographers, he walked over to the plastic bag and knelt down beside it. He slowly lifted the covering and quickly glanced at the person who interviewed him the day before. He closed his eyes for a moment of silence to say good-bye and to thank her for giving him a second chance. She deserved more than that, but with the police gathering as much evidence as they could; it was all he could do without drawing attention to himself. He opened his eyes and took in a deep breath to clear his mind. It seemed that his first assignment for Garrett and Taylor might be his last.

<u>**Chapter One**</u>:


**The black 355 came to a standstill behind a safari green Jeep Wrangler four-by-four**. Derek Chase emerged from the birthday present from his father and straightened his beige and black tie as he took in the scenery. He had driven to Sandbridge, an area in Virginia Beach well known for its secluded, resort-like atmosphere. He had received a page from Jeff Tanner, a freelance photographer for the local newspaper, The Virginian-Pilot, and someone who had also been a close friend since college.

He and Derek met during their freshman year in college when they played basketball. Because of their competitive nature, they became starters by their sophomore year; and because of Jeff's inside game and Derek's three-point shooting, they were given the nicknames "Backboard" and "Rimshot". They made a powerful combination.

One explanation for their effectiveness was the non-verbal communication they had. "Rimshot" would always know where "Backboard" was in case he did not have an open shot, and vice versa if "Backboard" was too heavily guarded. The statistics the two shared rivaled records set by past Ithaca athletes and the fame they earned surpassed even the greatest of players in the NBA.

The neighborhood was quiet, except for the barking of a nearby dog. Though a few vehicles loitered in the streets, the street was wide enough for two cars to pass. The houses were spaced apart enough allowing for residents to preserve their privacy. He silently complimented the neighborhood as he walked up to Jeff's folly, the safari green Jeep with monster tires. Jeff's Jeep was a vehicle he often feared would eat the Ferrari had it ever needed to share a parking space.

The photographer looked at him and whistled. "You look pretty business-like today wearing a tie and all. Who's the interview with?"

"Garrett and Taylor Law Firm. I'm interviewing for their investigator position."

"Well, good luck mi amigo. From what I hear through the legal grapevine, they're supposed to be top-notched."

"Yeah," Derek responded. "I heard that too. If I get the position, it'll be the first real job I've had since I resigned from the police department."

"Well, ya know what they say about the police department. They're nothing more than pawns in a politician's chess game."

Derek agreed as he nodded. "Yeah. I know."

Jeff switched the conversation and held the roll of film up as if it were a trophy. "Just so you know Compadre, you owe me big time for this one. It took me all morning, but I got 'em." He tossed the roll of film to Derek. He slightly lifted his fitted Ithaca University cap and ran his fingers through his sandy

blonde hair.  He then lowered the brim of his baseball cap over his blue eyes.

"Pretty interesting pictures."

Derek nodded as he looked at the film.  "Thanks Jeff.  I would've

committed suicide if I had to take another picture of a man cheating on his

wife."

Jeff chuckled as he pulled up the sleeves to his white mock turtleneck.  He

folded his big tanned arms and slouched into the driver's seat.  "Then you

oughta love these play by play photos.  The wife's in them too!"

"You're shittin' me!"

"I'm not shittin' you," Jeff replied pointing over to the driveway.  "She got

here maybe an hour after I did.  She went inside and caught our esteemed

husband and the nympho going at it like wild dogs in heat.  They argued for

awhile and then before I knew it, all three of them were doing the wild thang!"

"You almost sound jealous."

"Believe me.  I am."

Derek chuckled.  During his two years as a private investigator, he had

seen some odd things, some of which he could not rationalize.  This oddity

amused him.  His client was a neglected recluse getting a divorce from her

boisterous playboy husband who was hardly home because of business trips that

took him to the other side of the country.  Through a day of intense surveillance, he discovered that the business trips were weekend excursions to a house that was owned by a thirty-seven year old sex-starved nymphomaniac searching for her lost teenage years.  Most of the pictures that were taken by Derek were only pictures of the husband entering or leaving the house.  The shades were normally shut, so he could never catch the affair as it was happening.

Derek figured that the reclusive wife grew tired of waiting for the hard evidence to pass onto her attorneys and took matters into her own hands.  She followed her husband to his mistress's house; and from what Jeff was saying about the pictures he took, the reclusive wife, who wanted to convict her husband of adultery, got more than what she bargained for.

The black detective tossed the roll of film back to Jeff.  "All's well that ends well."

"Don't you want to know how I got these?"  Jeff asked.

"Let me guess," Derek responded as he looked around the neighborhood.  It was still very quiet.  "You hopped the fence and got a little closer?"

"Not in so many ways," Jeff began to explain.  "I remembered what you told me about never being able to see the affair as it was happening because the shades were always drawn shut.  So, my main objective was to get those shades up."  Derek looked on as he pointed over to the large bay window on the side of the house.  The detective noticed that the shades had been drawn.

"So, being the super-genius that I am," Jeff continued.  "I went over before our Don Juan got there and rang the doorbell."  His head flopped against the Jeep's headrest.  His face was in awe as he went on.  "Oh, D let me tell you.  For a woman who's approaching forty, she's built for show and endurance."

"Jeff."

Jeff shook the image out of his mind and looked back at the house.  "Anyway, she comes to the door wearing an outfit that could double as a handkerchief.  I tell her that I'm with Penthouse Magazine scouring the area for candid shots, and ask if she would like to participate."

"She jumped at the chance?"

"Like a frog on a Pogo Stick."

"Tanner," he said, shaking his head.  "You need some serious help."

Jeff smiled.  "Don't we all?"  He remarked as he tucked the roll of film in his shirt pocket.  "I'll have these pictures ready for you this afternoon.  I'll drop 'em by your place later on." and he gave a devilish smile.  "If you don't mind, I'm gonna make doubles for my own collection."

Derek nodded.  "Thanks Jeff."

"Hey no prob.  Just remember, you owe me one."

He chuckled.  "What?  The pictures aren't enough?"

"Close, but not quite," Jeff smiled as he turned the Jeep on. The chassis shook and the 4x4 growled as the diesel engine came to life. "Tell you what. I have a hot date with a stewardess tomorrow night. Let me borrow the Ferrari."

He laughed as he shook his head. "Not on your life."

"C'mon Derek," Jeff pleaded. "You're the only person in Virginia Beach that owns a Ferrari."

"Actually," Derek corrected, "there's twelve of us. Two of us own 355's, three own Testarossas, six own the 308's, and one has an F40, but I think he's selling it. You may want to talk to him."

"I'm being serious! C'mon D?"

"I'm being serious too! No way, no how."

"Not even for the man who got you the pictures of a husband cheating on his wife? The pictures you couldn't get?"

There was a chuckle in Derek's response. "The same pictures you're keeping a copy of and probably pictures I won't even need since the wife's in them too."

It was Jeff turn to chuckle. "You know, she wasn't half bad either. Oh, if I could've been a fly on the wall."

He shook his head. "Jeff, thoughts like that will only get you in trouble."

Jeff's devilish smile appeared on his face as he answered the question. "Why do you think I want to borrow the Ferrari?"

The investigator smiled back. "And that's just the reason why you'll never get the keys."

The free-lance photographer gestured his surrender and chuckled as he shifted the manual transmission of the four-by-four into first gear. "You know me too well."

"We're two peas in the same pod."

The Jeep lurched forward as Jeff's chuckle turned to laughter. "I'll catch you later D. Good luck with the interview," and with that he rumbled off down the street. Derek watched the four-by-four disappear around a corner. He then looked at the house that was a stage for a reconcilement between husband and wife, the beginning of a new friendship between wife and mistress, and the explicit desire for all three to explore their human sexuality together. It was a rare experience envied by Jeff Tanner. He chuckled and shook his head, envisioning the trouble his longtime friend could potentially get into with a fully-fueled Ferrari.

**He straightened his beige and black tie as he stepped out of the 355.** He reached inside and grabbed the black suit jacket from the passenger seat. He slid into it as a soft breeze caressed his face.

He looked around as he closed the door to the Italian import. The parking lot was filled with vehicles. Some looked very expensive, while others looked as if they needed to be towed away.  A small, thick wooded fence separated the office parking lot from the speeding traffic of Lynnhaven Parkway.  Many of the cars zipping by were racing to get on or off of Interstate 264.

Interstate 264, formerly known to locals as Route 44, was the stretch of highway that connected Norfolk, Portsmouth and Suffolk with the Atlantic Oceanfront.  He remembered when there was a twenty-five cent toll-booth that broke the highway in half.  After the city reviewed their revenue, and the many complaints from the populace, Virginia Beach abolished the toll-booth and raised the speed limit to 65.

After intersecting with Interstate 64, which connected Richmond with the southern tip of Virginia, Interstate 264 branched off towards Downtown Norfolk and its Waterside area.  During the summer, he rarely traveled to Waterside.  It was usually congested with its bumper to bumper traffic of tourists and business-dressed pedestrians.  Many of the tourists would be hoping to get a glimpse of one the naval vessels returning from deployment.  Every so often, they would be graced with the presence of an aircraft carrier.

The business people, who seemed to be from every neighboring city, were always hurried.  They took unnecessary chances when crossing the street and bumped into each other without remorse.  It would be amusing to see two well-dressed businessmen in combat using their leather briefcases as weapons when they attempted to enter a building through the same door.  He would fear for the men if they were in a confrontation with a woman. Their high-heeled shoes were as dangerous as they were fashionable. With everybody's quest to be on-time, it seemed that between the hours of 9 and 5, Downtown Norfolk and Waterside were as alive as New York City during New Year's Eve.

The only other time it was crowded during non-business hours were when the local minor league baseball team, the Norfolk Tides, had a home game, and during Harborfest when all of Hampton Roads would turn out for good outdoor cooking, live entertainment and a loud, bright display of fireworks. For an area as small as that section of Norfolk, the events and businesses certainly boasted a strong community following.

He looked at his watch. He had twenty minutes before his interview with Tessa Taylor. His eyes followed the base of the skyscraper until it reached the flashing red light at the top. He knew the building as Lynnhaven One. It was the newest of skyscrapers with only three years of age. With thirty-seven floors and an observation deck, Lynnhaven One took the title of "The Tallest Corporate Building in Virginia Beach". He could see where the observation deck began on the thirty-fifth floor. He had heard that even on a foggy day, employees could see the Atlantic Ocean and the Chesapeake Bay Bridge, which connected Virginia Beach to the Eastern Shore.

The alarm to the Ferrari beeped twice as he tucked the key ring into his pocket. He took in a deep breath and began his walk towards the front entrance of the skyscraper.  He hoped that his interview with the co-owner of Garrett and Taylor Law would give him the opportunity that one day he too could view that picturesque setting from the thirty-fifth floor.

The two glass front doors quickly slid open for him as he walked in.  He took off his shades and looked down at the marble floor to find his reflection staring back at him.  He looked up and was in awe at the large, clear sheet of water coming down from the observation deck.  It funneled down into a large pool surrounded by trees and flowers.  Because of its height, the waterfall sprayed a very thin mist; therefore, anyone who came to close received a little sprinkle.  In the middle of the pool surrounded by this mist, was a monument of a stone fountain, which sprayed an umbrella of water.  It was beautiful.

The architects must have enjoyed creating this and wanted others to enjoy it as well.  A few stone benches encircled the area.  He could see some people taking advantage of these benches.  Some of them seemed to be relaxing with a cup of hot coffee, while others partook in reading a good book.  He too began to relax.  With the waterfall and the sunlight provided from the tinted glass windows, Lynnhaven One's main lobby was an indoor park.

Amongst this beauty was the touch of reality.  There were many people, who were on the clock, walking about with files and briefcases in their hands. The deliverymen from UPS and Federal Express were among them and weaved in between the employees like running backs in a football game.

He stepped over to the elevator and pressed the little white button.  Garrett and Taylor Law Firm was on the thirtieth floor.  He straightened his posture as he waited for the gold doors to open.  He could hear the "made for office" rendition of Stevie Wonder's "I Just Called to Say I Love You" playing softly in the background.  He looked at his reflection in the elevator door and critiqued his attire.

The beige and black designer tie softened the contrast between the black jacket and beige pants.  His gold watch sparkled from the midday sun and his black dress shoes by Bass were polished for success.  He smiled arrogantly.  Though he was most comfortable in a pair of jeans, a polo shirt and a pair of loafers, he felt powerful in a good suit.

The elevator doors opened and two women, who were discussing lunch plans, a uniformed security guard, and a mail courier with a cart full of envelopes, quickly filed out of the elevator.  Derek held the door open as he watched them exit.  Once it was empty he stepped inside and pressed the white button for the thirtieth floor.

He could hear the remake of Stevie Wonder's song fade off into the background and a version of Fifth Dimension's "Beautiful Balloon" took over.  He remembered back to when Marilyn McCoo sang it on the late-seventies television series, *Solid Gold.*  He took in a deep breath as he felt the elevator come to a stop.  He mentally prepared himself for an intense interview.  He knew Tessa Taylor and her background.  Before opening her firm, she was a

hard-nosed Assistant District Attorney, displaying lion-like tenaciousness.  She

prosecuted the cases no one wanted.  After a while, she felt she had seen it all

and decided to go into corporate law, where the players were more ruthless, the

cases were shadier and the stakes were higher.  She attacked businesses with the

type of determination and sacrifice demonstrated by a knight in King Arthur's

court, and used her ambition to propel herself to the most sought-after law firm

in Hampton Roads.

The elevator doors opened and unveiled the glass doors of Garrett and

Taylor Law.  He straightened his posture and stepped out onto the marble floor.

He scanned the bright brass that outlined the entrance to the office and lettering

on the glass door.  It suggested a certain type of prestige one would expect, but

could not afford when searching for a law firm.

He took in another deep breath, quickly rehearsing his answers to various

questions he anticipated to be asked by Ms. Taylor.  He swung the heavy glass

door open and stepped inside towards what he hoped would be a new career

opportunity.

The large half-circle of the reception desk greeted him.  His attention was

quickly diverted to the three shelves in the wall behind it.  Placed on the highest

shelf was a replica of The Scales of Justice.  On either side, sitting majestically

in the lower shelves, were two stone lions.  It looked like they were protecting the statue from all that would defile its mission to right what had been wronged.

He wondered if that perception was the one that was intended. It would serve as

a representation of Garrett and Taylor Law, defenders of those who have been

wronged, and enforcers of all that remains just. His eyebrows rose when a

comparison of King Arthur and Camelot re-entered his mind.

He re-focused his attention to the receptionist in front of him. She had a

light milk chocolate complexion and her head slightly cocked to one side. She

stared at him with her piercing brown eyes, waiting for him to state his business.

The auburn highlights in her shoulder length hair glistened under the office

lights; and her round-framed glasses complimented her slender face that wore a

light shade of pink makeup. He could see her adjusting the top of her business

suit that seemed to be a little tight in the shoulders. From the firm muscle tone

in her arms, he guessed that she was about 110 pounds and would probably be

more comfortable in a tank top and shorts.

"I'm Derek Chase. I have an appointment with Ms. Taylor."

She smiled and glanced down at the appointment book in front of her.

With her long red nails scanning the page, she found his name, and with a pencil

put a check beside it. She picked up the phone beside her and hit a button.

"Ms. Taylor?" she said in a quick, squeaky voice. "Mr. Chase is here."

She paused for a moment and then put the receiver back in its resting spot. She looked at him and smiled. "If you would please have a seat, Ms. Taylor will see you in a few moments."

He smiled as he began his descent into one of the leather chairs that were huddled a few feet in front of the reception area. "Thank you."

She adjusted her business suit once more before grabbing a drink and placing the straw between her red lips. He could see the dark liquid, he suspected to be cola, rise through the straw and disappear. She caught his stare and smiled as she swallowed. "May I get you something to drink?" She asked.

He shook his head. "No thank you."

She put the drink down and leaned towards him. "I have a lunch break at one. We could get together later on."

"Excuse me?"

"You know? You and me going out and doing the restaurant thing."

"I'm sorry," Derek relayed. "I don't quite follow where you're going with this."

"Well," she explained. "You were staring. I thought you might be interested."

"I'm terribly sorry. I did not mean to come across -

"It's okay," she interrupted. "Maybe some other time."

He slowly nodded, acknowledging the situation, as the door to Tessa

Taylor's office opened.  He quickly stood from the leather chair recognizing the

attractive blonde.

"Thank you Saundra," she said looking at the receptionist.  "Mr. Chase,"

she continued.  "I'm ready to see you now."

He smiled as he adjusted his suit jacket.  He walked past the half circle of a

desk and caught a wink of her eye.  He smiled in response and disappeared

within the office.  He was not sure, but he thought he heard a giggle as Ms.

Taylor closed the door behind them.

"That was Saundra Wilkins," Tessa Taylor began as she walked over to her

desk.  He carefully studied her movements.  He silently complimented her

aurora of grace and authority that she carried.  He was more impressed now

than when he first met her.

"She's our intern from Virginia Wesleyan College." she said.

"Wesleyan?" Derek replied.  "I have a friend that does security there."

"Good," Tessa responded.  "Maybe he'll be able to keep an eye on her for

me.  College students these days can be misled so easily."

He nodded in agreement as he thought back to a few moments ago.  He

was not sure if Saundra was being misled or the one who was doing the

misleading.  He concluded that further pursuit would only lead to more trouble

and dismissed the thought from his mind.  He watched Tessa Taylor sit down in a brown leather captain's chair.  She reached for his file and opened it.  He took the opportunity to do a quick scan of his surroundings.

There were awards and university degrees framed on the wall like trophies. A plant that resembled the one in the foyer of his beach house was poised brilliantly as it separated the awards on the wall from the mahogany bookshelves.  Tucked away in one of the bookshelves along with her legal textbooks and manuals was a figurine of the Scales of Justice.  It stood proud as the afternoon sun glistened against the gold statue.

He continued to scan the office.  In the corner closest to the window, another plant stood in attention next to the plush chair.  He glanced over at the window as a bird flew by.  He could see the rooftops of the hotels along "The Strip".  He realized that this office represented the cornerstone of one person's dreams and ambitions coming together as reality.

He looked at the mahogany desk.  It was very neat.  On one side, was her "In/Out" basket and a designer pen and pencil holder.  On the other side was her phone, in which the cord was free of knots, and a few pictures of what he suspected to be her family.  In the middle were only the necessities, his paperwork and a silver pen.  He admired her meticulousness.

Tessa motioned for him to have a seat.  "Please sit down."

"Thank you."

She flipped through a couple of pages and decided that she would start the conversation. "Do you have any brothers or sisters?"

He raised an eyebrow. She was going to start with his personal history first. "I have two older sisters and one younger sister."

She smiled. "It must have been tough growing up with three women."

"It still has its moments," he responded.

"Your mother and father? What do they do for a living?"

"My father now runs my grandfather's import/export business."

"And your mother?" Tessa asked.

"My mother was killed in a car accident when I was three."

She frowned slightly. "I'm sorry to hear that."

"Thank you," he replied. "But it is not necessary. Because I was so young, I never had a chance to spend a lot of time with my mother. So, I do not share the amount of grief as do my older sisters."

"I understand," Tessa stated. "Still, my heart goes out to you and your family."

"Thank you."

Tessa Taylor paused and then closed the dossier. She then sat back in her chair and he watched her demeanor become more professional. "Mr. Chase, let me get straight to the point. I'm not sure if you are the right person for this job. I mean, you were an honor roll student at Ithaca and dropped out a semester before graduating with a master's in criminal justice. You were also a police officer for the City of Virginia Beach, and we both know what happened with that. Honestly, your history says that you seem like a competent person who can get the job done. However, there have been too many unfortunate incidents, which detour you from your goal. And I don't see you hurrying to get back on the right path. To sum it up for you Mr. Chase, at Garrett and Taylor, we expect you to go the distance, giving two hundred percent of yourself all the way, despite the obstacles. Tell me; can you bring that quality to Garrett and Taylor? Please, make an impression on me Mr. Chase."

He took a minute and sat back in the leather chair. He was coming to the conclusion that this interview would soon have the same results as all the others. No company wanted to hire a graduate school dropout and an ex-cop with a less than perfect background.

He looked at the blonde interviewer before him and quickly studied her body. His eyes searched. She was more attractive than when he first met her a year ago. She was a young, very attractive, voluptuous woman that wore little make-up, because she was aware of her natural beauty. Her peach colored face was fresh with energy and her dark green eyes flashed with intensity. Her perfume was sweet as she sat across from him. Her navy blue business suit was powerful, yet it defined her seductiveness. It was no wonder she was the most sought after attorney in Virginia. Her beauty complimented the long list of degrees and awards that decorated her office. He decided that if he were not going to get the job, he would definitely make an impression. He crossed his legs, folded his arms, and smiled. He had the perfect response. "You're either wearing a thong or no panties at all."

"I beg your pardon?"

He continued with his observation. "You're a very bright and intelligent individual as suggested from the neatly framed degrees on the walls. The picture of your family tells me that they are upper/middle class, yet you yourself have very expensive taste since you have a mahogany desk and soft leather chairs in your office. I would guess that you like the beach, since your office overlooks the Atlantic, and with the small amount of plants I would say that you like to be outdoors."

"What does all that have to do with me wearing or not wearing underwear?"

The investigator chuckled. "Nothing at all. I watched you when you escorted me into your office. There were no panty lines in your skirt, but if I had to choose, I would say that you were wearing a thong. You don't look like the type that would go without underwear. But then again, I could be wrong."

Tessa smiled. "Excuse me Mr. Chase, but this could be considered as sexual harassment. I could make sure that you never work in this state again."

"I understand that, but I made an impression. That is what you asked for. Is it not?"

Tessa smiled as she scribbled a note in file. "Mr. Chase, I'm going to do something that I hope you don't make me regret later. I'm going to take a chance on you. I expect you to be here Monday morning at 8 AM sharp. We have to get you familiar with the security set-up and fill out the paperwork for payroll." She then stood up and extended her hand. Derek stood and accepted the handshake. "Welcome to Garrett and Taylor."

He was still in shock when he said. "Thank you Ms. Taylor."

"Please, call me Tessa. Just to clear the air: you were right about a lot of things. I like to be outdoors. My family lives on the outskirts of Boston in a community that is considered upper/middle class, and I am very proud of my accomplishments."

"What about the underwear theory?" he dared to ask.

Tessa folded her arms and smiled devilishly. "Well, Mr. Chase, I guess that is one mystery you'll have a hard time solving."

"Well, if I may further respond to your original question. When there is something I truly want or believe in, I'm not easily detoured."

"I will personally test that statement."

He smiled as the phone on her desk chimed. "Excuse me for a moment," and she hit a button on her phone. "Yes Saundra?"

"Kevin would like to see you."

"Send him in.  Thank you Saundra."

Tessa's office door opened and a well-dressed businessman walked in.  His shirt and dress pants had been professionally ironed and he draped his jacket over his arm.  His briefcase looked brand new.  His long dirty blonde hair was slicked-back and his face had a deep tan.  He looked more like a surfer than a lawyer.  Derek smiled thinking to himself that this was the non-serious side of Garrett and Taylor Law.   The newcomer's smile was genuine as he walked in.

"Tess," he began.  "I just wanted to let you know that I'm on my way to that conference in Richmond, I'll be back later on this afternoon."

"Okay," Tessa responded.  "Give 'em hell."

"Always."

Tessa looked over at the detective she just recently hired.  "I'm sorry," she apologized.  "Kevin Garrett, I'd like you to meet our new investigator, Derek Chase.  Mr. Chase, meet the other half of Garrett and Taylor."

"Welcome aboard," Kevin greeted extending his hand.

Derek stood from his chair and shook his hand.  "Thank you."

Kevin looked at Tessa with a smile and then back at the detective.  "I hear she can be a slave driver, but the benefits aren't too bad."

Derek chuckled as Tessa chose to ignore Kevin's banter.  "I'll make sure I don't get on her bad side."  Derek replied.

She quickly interrupted their conversation. "Kevin, you should probably stop trying to corrupt our new investigator, I think he's on my side already."

The co-owner of the law firm shook his head as he began backing his way out of the door. "Damn, foiled again."

Tessa smiled and shook her head. "Kevin, maybe when you get back you can give Mr. Chase a tour of Lynnhaven One.

"Would be my pleasure."

"Thank you," Tessa responded. "Good luck at your conference. Have fun!"

"Oh most definitely. It was nice meeting you Mr. Chase." He was about to leave when he stopped. "Oh, I almost forgot. I'm meeting the Commonwealth's Attorney for dinner around 7:00 at Le Chambord on Great Neck. Care to join us?"

"Not tonight. I have plans."

"Okay, be good then." And with that he left her office closing the door behind him.

"Seems like a nice guy." Derek commented.

"He is," she confirmed. "I love him to death. It's because of him we are where we are today." With the distraction gone her business like composure resumed. "Well, I have your first assignment," she began as she walked over to the office window. "That is if you want to start right away?"

"The sooner the better," he replied.

Her smile was of satisfaction. "Good, but I'd rather discuss it over dinner. Tell me Mr. Chase, do you like Italian?"

"Happens to be my favorite."

"Very well. Do you know where Aldo's is on Laskin Road?"

"I have a copy of the menu at home," he joked.

"Good. Is six o'clock this evening good for you?" she asked.

"Absolutely."

She smiled. "Then it's a date. I'll be working late today; you can pick me up here at five-thirty."

"Yes ma'am."

"And Mr. Chase," she concluded. "Don't be late. I would hate for you to be tardy for your first assignment."

Derek smiled. She was trying to make him feel comfortable. "Wouldn't dream of it. Besides, if our dinner conversation is anything like this interview, I'm sure it'll be an enjoyable evening."

She responded coyishly. "I hope you're as good as you think you are, if that being the case."

He detected a hint of a challenge and gladly accepted the dare. "It'll give me a chance to prove how determined I can be."

With his commitment a devilish smile went across her face. "Indeed it

shall."

<u>**Chapter Two**</u>:

**"Did anybody ever tell you that you are a very mysterious man?"**

The question took him by surprise as he took a sip of his wine. He smiled

as he blotted the sides of his lips. He looked across the table at his employer and

shook his head. "No." he replied. "I can't say that anybody has, Miss Taylor."

"Please," she said as she quickly took a sip of her wine, "call me Tessa."

"I do apologize Tessa. My father always said that when you sit at the

dinner table with a beautiful woman, you need to address her as either Miss, or

My Lady."

"Your father must have been extraordinary."

He smiled. "My mother thought so."

She leaned closer towards the table. "Tell me about your family." she said

softly. "I mean after all, there's not much that I know about you. Your

personnel file tells me you were a student at Ithaca and you were a Virginia

Beach police officer; and that's where it stops. Call me suspicious, but up until

seven years ago, Derek Chase didn't exist. Besides what I had, I couldn't find

any other employee records, driver's license, former addresses, diplomas,

awards, nothing. I couldn't even find the purchase order for that Ferrari you drive.  Do you know that I traced your social security number?  That looks like

that was also issued about seven years ago."

His smile was genuine.  "I see I'm not the only detective sitting at the

table," he replied.  "To answer your question, I'm not who I say I am."

"Then who are you?"

He saw that she had taken the bait.  "I'm actually from a planet on the

other side of the galaxy, if you hang a right next to the Big Dipper and go

straight for about thirty million light years, my planet is the sixth one on the

right."

She pretended to giggle.  "I'm being serious."

He chuckled as he took another sip of wine.  "Okay," he conceded.

"Honestly, my father travels a lot.  Originally, I was born in a small city in

South America.  When I was four we moved here to Virginia Beach, and since

the age of seven, my sisters and I have been globe hopping.  We didn't return to

the United States until I was twenty-three, which is when I got my driver's

license and new social security number.  Most of my schooling was abroad,

which made it very difficult to get into Ithaca.  I didn't have to work, because

once I started, it was time to hit the road and go to another part of the planet.

Any award I would've received would have been for "The Fastest Suitcase

Packer of the Chase Family."

Her giggle was real this time.

"By the way, I enjoyed my tour of Lynnhaven One," he said attempting to change the subject. "You can see for miles from the Observation Deck. It's absolutely beautiful."

"That's what I hear."

"Well, maybe I can talk you into going up there for a cup of coffee."

"Thank you Derek, but I'm not too big on heights. Not to mention, every time I go up there, it's cloudy and I can't see much. Can I take a rain check?"

"Sure."

"Now, tell me more about yourself."

"What about you?" he asked in hopes of changing the subject.

She sensed his hesitancy. "What would you like to know?" she asked. "You seemed to have me all figured out during our interview today."

She was right. He quickly had to find something to talk about. "Well, what about your family? How do they feel about having a lawyer in their family?"

"They actually have two lawyers. My sister is a lawyer for the Judge Advocate General in Falls Church, Virginia. But to be honest, they're really not keen on the two of us being twelve hours away. My father is very sick and our mother wants us in Boston to help take care of him, but unfortunately, neither one of us have been able to break away," he watched her as she reflected on what she had said. "I'm sure we'll get together and figure something out."

"I'm sorry, I hope-

"No, don't worry about it," she replied. "It's perfectly alright." Her joviality was returning. "Is there anything else you'd like to know?"

Again, he quickly scanned her to find something he could ask about. He found it on her wrist. "That's a beautiful diamond tennis bracelet. Four carats is it?"

"Actually it's six carats. It was last year's Christmas present from Kevin."

"What did you get him?"

"I gave him and his wife cruise tickets to Mexico."

"With benefits like that, I'm going to enjoy working for this company."

She laughed and diverted the attention back to him. "Okay, enough about me, there must be more to Derek Chase than just a spoiled little boy refined in the various cultures of the planet? I still don't know anything about you. Tell me? Are you a Democrat or a Republican? Do you like jazz or heavy metal? Are you a saint or a sinner? And tell me more about your family? You really didn't go into a lot of detail."

"You are inquisitive this evening," he replied. "I didn't know I was on the witness stand again."

"I like to know who's working for me."

He took another sip of his wine and blotted his lips. He looked at her and smiled as he answered. "If you must know, it's safer that I avoid discussing politics.  I prefer jazz over heavy metal, and I like to consider myself a saint

with some devilish virtues."

Tessa laughed at his response.  "And you probably like to wear boxers

rather than briefs."

"That is a conversation we can save for a later date."

She smiled remembering the dialogue they had when he first interviewed

for the position of Investigator at Garrett and Taylor.  "I'll tell if you do."

Derek weighed the consequences and felt it best to change the subject.

"There's not much I can discuss about my family.  As I said before, my father is

in the import/export business.  He manages about eighty percent of my

grandfather's corporations around the world.  As you already know from this

morning, my mother died in a car accident four months after my brother was

born."

"Yes.  I remember.  If you don't mind me asking, could you tell me more

about what happened?"

"No one really knows.  It was a sunny spring afternoon when my mother

was returning from her sister's house.  She was driving along one of the back

roads and lost control of her car.  She broke through the guardrail and went over

the cliff.  My brother was in the car with her.  Both of them were killed in the

crash."

"How awful."

Derek stared at the glass of red wine sitting before him as he wallowed in the past. "Investigators and rescue workers concluded their death to be an accident caused by driver carelessness. But I disagree." He concluded. "Not my mother. She had been driving since she was twelve, not to mention, it was a road she knew very well."

"Hmm. That sounds suspicious."

"The news was devastating to our family and friends. Anybody who knew my mother loved her. Then came the rumors."

"Rumors? What rumors."

Derek's attention quickly reverted back to the present. He looked across the table to find Tessa holding on to his words as if she was in the middle of a cliffhanger. "I'm sure you just didn't bring me here to talk about my life. You said you had an assignment for me?"

"Don't stop," she retorted. "I was just getting ready to crack that shell of yours."

Derek smiled. "It's much safer for you if you don't."


**His heart relaxed as he focused on his work and studied the body**. She was wearing the navy blue suit she wore to dinner from the night before. Her white blouse was bloodstained. It looked like she had been shot once in the chest. Derek looked at her wrist and raised an eyebrow. She was still wearing the six-carat diamond tennis bracelet that Kevin bought her for Christmas.

He re-covered her body with the black plastic body bag as he scanned the living room. He saw Tessa's purse on the table next to some opened letters. He stood up and walked over to the table. He opened her purse and found her wallet. He opened the wallet to find her credit cards and her money safely tucked away in the billfolds. He looked at the opened mail that sat next to the purse and found a new unsigned credit card in the pile. Many questions were beginning to formulate.

"Oh for Pete's sake!" came a deep bellowing voice of disgust. "What the hell is he doing here?"

Derek turned to find Lieutenant Terry Austin walking into the apartment with Sergeant John Steele. When he worked with the Virginia Beach Police, one or both could often be seen at various crime scenes barking out orders and fending off the press. Both were wearing the standard light brown trench coat. The Lieutenant's balding head and gray beard added to the look of fatigue. Sergeant Steele was a little bit younger and bulkier than the Lieutenant. His black hair was slicked back and his clean shaven face gave him the appearance of a Hollywood movie star on display.

"Will someone get him the Hell out of here?" the Lieutenant pleaded. He looked around the room with his arms outstretched. "He's contaminating the crime scene!"

Derek sighed. The history he and Austin shared was not a pretty one and each time they crossed paths, the confrontation was never favorable. Lieutenant Austin thought of him as a rogue looking to jump into anything without weighing the consequences. Meanwhile, Derek thought of the Lieutenant as a hard-nosed, whip cracking general who missed his calling in Hitler's SS Army.

"Lieutenant?" Derek began.

"Listen Chase," the Lieutenant interjected. "You may not have gotten it in that mule head of yours, but you're no longer a cop and this is a police matter. I don't need you turning this into a three ring circus. As far as I'm concerned, this is a simple breaking and entering case. Tessa Taylor came home, found a prowler, there was a struggle and he shot her in the chest."

Derek walked over to the Lieutenant. "Austin, I hate to shatter this perfect scenario; but if this was a simple breaking and entering, why didn't the prowler take her diamond tennis bracelet or the money in her wallet? I found an unsigned credit card on the table. What prowler in his right mind would turn that down?"

"He was scared."

"Bullshit!" Derek exclaimed. "Somebody was looking for something."

"Like what?" the Sergeant asked. His voice was friendly yet very inquisitive and firm. He reminded Derek of a younger version of Humphrey Bogart's Sam Spade. The Sergeant also assisted with Derek's training while he was in the police academy. Though they were not close friends, there was a certain respect between the two.

"How the hell should I know," Derek shrugged towards the Sergeant. "But I'm gonna find out."

"Derek," the Sergeant pleaded. "Why don't you let the police handle this one?"

"And why don't you two just kiss my ass? I happen to be the lead investigator for Garrett and Taylor. I'm in this whether you like it or not."

"Chase," the Lieutenant interjected. "If you so much as breathe anywhere near this case, I will charge you with obstruction of justice and throw you in an electrified, two by two cell encased in barbed-wire."

"Steele?" the detective asked. "The Lieutenant looks a little pale. Are you sure he's getting his daily enema."

Austin smirked. "Chase, haven't you learned anything? You were a good-for- nothing cop and now you're a good-for-nothing investigator. Let the real cops handle this one. Stay out of it."

Derek leaned closer to the Lieutenant. "Not on your life, but I will let you in on a little secret Lieutenant. The academy teachers were right. You really are a jackass."  And with that, Derek walked out of the apartment.

43

<u>**Chapter Three**</u>:

**Derek stepped out of the elevator onto the thirtieth floor of Lynnhaven One, still upset at himself for the previous night.** With the Ferrari's ignorance of city speed limits, it only took ten minutes to drive from Aldo's on Laskin to Marina Shores on Great Neck. She was impressed with the time, commenting that if they had instead dined with Kevin and the Commonwealth's Attorney and drove the speed limit back, it would have taken them fifteen. Again, he mentally chastised himself. Though dusk had not quite fallen at 7:20, walking her to her door would have been the gentleman-like thing to do. Of course, she turned him down when he did offer and was adamant that he went home, stating that he needed his rest for the amount of work she was going to unload on him. Upon retrospect, she might have still been alive if he insisted.

He stepped into the marble hallway in front of the glass door of the corporate law firm Garrett and Taylor. He had changed from his earlier morning attire of jeans and a polo shirt. He was now showered and cleanly shaven, wearing neatly pressed black slacks, shiny black loafers, a tan collar-less shirt, a black vest and black jacket. His shades dangled from his vest as he walked across the marble floor.

He walked through the glass door of the law office and was immediately

reminded of the uneasiness sitting in his stomach.  The mood was solemn.

Employees were slowly walking about remembering the positive and powerful

aurora of one of the two designated champions of Garrett and Taylor's corporate

law enforcement.  Maybe it was the way she conducted herself.  She was

playful, but quite aware of the authority she commanded.  Or maybe it was the

respect she not only had for others, but for the cause of justice.  Garrett and

Taylor Law was known for defending the underdog and took pride in defeating

the power hungry and those who operated above the law.  Regardless, she would

have been a good person to have been acquainted with.

He looked at Tessa's secretary.  Saundra was fighting to hide the sadness

that everybody else who knew Tessa Taylor was showing.  The college student

of Virginia Wesleyan looked up from her computer to find the investigator of

Garrett and Taylor walking up.  She took in a deep breath regaining her

business-like composure.  She moved her hair from her face to the back of her

ear.  He noticed she had been crying.

"Good morning Mr. Chase."

"Good morning Saundra," he began.  His heart went out to her.  "I'm sorry

about Ms. Taylor.  How are you holding up?"

"I'll be okay," she responded.  "Mr. Garrett had called earlier and told me

that you might be stopping by.  I'm here if you need me."

"Thank you," he said. "I don't know how long I'm gonna be, but I'll need to go through all of Tessa's files."

"Doesn't that violate client confidentiality?"

"More than likely, but I'm not in the mood for policies and procedures. And if anybody asks, you never saw me."

The intern nodded as she opened her desk drawer. She pulled out a spare key and stood from her desk. "The police say it's an open and shut case. Do you think it's something more than that?"

"That's what I'm here to find out." Derek replied. "I'll need a list of every employee, client, and potential client for the last three years. We'll start with that. Also, solicit phone records from the phone company and the company's bank statements."

Saundra reached towards her desk and grabbed a pen and a pad of paper. She began scribbling notes. "Files of employees, clients, potential clients, phone records and company bank statements. What are you looking for?"

He shrugged. "Not sure yet. I'm hoping that something in her office will put me in the right direction."

Saundra stepped over and unlocked Tessa's office door. Taking in a deep breath, she slowly pushed it open. The detective looked over her shoulder and a surge of adrenaline quickly started traveling throughout his body. Tessa's office mimicked her beach apartment. It had been distorted from its professional, structured-like surrounding into an unorganized calamity of papers and files strewn across the floor.  However, it wasn't the littering of paper that alarmed him.  It was the ominous figure of the security guard laying face down on the carpet in a pool of blood.

**Derek rummaged through the files littered across Tessa's office**.  He only had minutes to decipher what was pertinent information, before Lieutenant Austin and his crime scene unit were on the scene and sealing off Tessa's office.  As much as he looked forward to proving his point, he didn't have the energy to confront Austin.  So, he quickly looked for clues as his heart raced.  She could have been murdered for any one of the cases she had worked on.  As an Assistant District Attorney, she put hundreds of criminals behind bars.  As a corporate lawyer, many companies lost millions because of her.  Each file he opened had a motive.

The latex gloves he borrowed from the cleaning lady stretched across his fingers as he opened another file.  His curiosity peaked.  The cover letter within the file displayed a company logo of a lion-like animal with wings.  He had seen that logo before, he was sure of it.  He looked over the desk at the body lying on the carpet, particularly at the outfit.  The logo on the letterhead matched the logo of the patch on the shoulder of the security guard's body.  He took a seat in Tessa's leather chair and continued to read the file.

Around three months ago, Tessa had been conducting an investigation against Griffin Securities Inc., a local security company that specialized in providing twenty-four hour, state-of-the-art security for the larger corporations. It seemed that Michael Thatcher, a former police officer for Virginia Beach, now security personnel for Griffin Securities, had been indicted for stealing company secrets from Premiere Tech, one of their clients. Premiere Tech, who specialized in computer programs, had been raided of their blueprints for a new artificial intelligent computer. The irony of the whole thing was that Thatcher was caught on video by the very system he was employed to monitor. Despite this exculpatory evidence, the indictment never went to trial. Thatcher had somehow managed to escape from the authorities and the video had been lost after police had checked it into evidence. Strangely enough, Griffin Security settled out of court for a healthy sum of money.

Derek read the last paragraph of Tessa's report and closed the file taking in a deep breath. Despite the settlement, Premiere Tech took a big financial loss when Valkyrie Industries, one of their competitors, came out with a system similar to what they had been developing. In his opinion, Thatcher had sold the blueprints to Valkyrie Industries, but Thatcher was still nowhere to be found. He had became a ghost. His picture was posted on every police department wall across the planet and he even had a spot on television's *America's Most Wanted*.

In spite of every attempt from law enforcement officials, Michael Thatcher had continued to elude the long arm of the law.

His thoughts were broken up when Saundra walked into Tessa's office. The look on her face was a combination of fatigue and depression.

"Find anything?" she asked.

The detective wondered if Tessa had uncovered new evidence that would lead to another indictment against Griffin Security. Maybe Premiere Tech was not the only company they were stealing from. "I might have something, but I'm not sure yet."

"Well, I have the phone records from the phone company. As soon as the police are done, I'll pick up the bank statements from Crestar. Do you need me to pick up anything? Like dinner or somethin'?"

The thought of food caused his stomach to churn with anticipation, but he fought the urge. He looked at his watch. It was almost two in the afternoon. "No, that's okay." he answered. "I'll pick up something later."

"Okay."

"Thanks for your help Saundra." he responded.

"No problem Mr. Chase." she replied looking at the body on the floor. "It's obvious that this isn't a simple breaking and entering. Something is going on. Please promise me that you'll get the guy who did this."

"Saundra, that's a promise I intend on keeping."

She smiled and walked out of the office.

He looked at piles of manila folders scattered across the floor.  It would take him the rest of the day to go through everything.  He sighed quietly realizing that based on the morning's events, the folder in his hand was his only lead.

He made a decision as he quickly walked out of Tessa's office.  Saundra was not at her desk, probably gone to the lobby to meet the police.  He took out a post-it note from her desk drawer and left a note for her to bring the files and the reports to his beach house.  He also asked for her to meet him there that night and help him go through the files.  He needed to follow up on a lead, which would start him on the path of repaying a large debt to someone who took a chance on him.


**"Ms. Taylor's death is an unfortunate one Mr. Chase," said the President of Griffin Security, as he leaned back in his chair**.  His southern drawl rivaled that of train conductor from New Orleans, loud and robust.  Derek had not been there for more than ten minutes and it was becoming annoying.  "I don't know how much help I can be, but I will try to answer as many questions as possible."

Derek looked past Thomas Janocky III's shoulder through the large window overlooking Waterside with its conglomerate of shops and office buildings strategically positioned next to the docks leading to the shipyards.

He then focused his attention back towards the business man sitting in the large leather executive chair. Thomas Janocky III was a man of a medium size build with gray streaks along the sides of his black hair. His shirt was neatly pressed and the dark blue suspenders complimented the dark blue tie with tiny aqua polka-dots.

"Thank you, Mr. Janocky, for seeing me on such short notice. I'll be as brief as possible," Derek replied. "How would you classify your relationship with Ms. Taylor?"

"An adversarial one, but professional nonetheless, Mr. Chase," Janocky answered. His voice was calm and business-like. "Most of our conversations took place in the conference room in the presence of my office managers and my attorneys."

"Could you tell me what was your reaction when Ms. Taylor indicted Griffin Securities Inc. for corporate sabotage?"

"Your knowledge of local news is impressive Mr. Chase," Janocky said with the same smile as practiced by politicians and used car salesmen. "I was shocked that my company or any person under my employ would partake in such an act of deceitfulness."

"Have you had any contact with Michael Thatcher since the settlement?"

"I wish I would," Janocky replied. "I'd take that varmint and give him a whoopen he'll soon never forget. Griffin Securities takes pride on its good reputation."

Derek glanced around the office to find it similar to Tessa's, not too much personality, but just enough warmth to make you comfortable. "Did you know Ms. Taylor was working on another indictment against your company?"

"Why no," Janocky answered. The expression on his face suggested that he preferred to have been slapped across the cheek by the detective. "I was unaware. But if you think that I may have something to do with Ms. Taylor's death, you're sorely mistaken."

"I wasn't implying that you were," Derek smoothly responded. "I'm researching every possible lead."

"Indeed you are."

"Mr. Janocky," Derek continued. "Ms. Taylor's office was broken into this morning. The police are there now examining the body of a man wearing your company uniform. He had been shot and the office is in shambles. Would you happen to know something about that?"

Janocky gave a gasp. "My word. That's terrible! From time to time we send someone out there to fill in. In case normal building security has someone who might have called in sick. I must find out if we sent someone there last night and inform their family.  The poor sonovabitch was probably doing his job and interrupted the perpetrator, who eventually saw no other recourse but to kill him."

Derek heard the sarcasm coming from his lips.  "I'm sure that was the case."

Janocky cleared his throat and leaned back in his chair.  "I must say Mr. Chase, your researching every possible lead does point to some rather negative implications towards myself and my company.  I do not appreciate that."

He ignored Janocky's observation and looked down at the desk the company's president was sitting at.  He studied the sculpted statue of the quadruped animal with the tail and hindquarters of a lion and the forelimbs, wings and head of an eagle with ears added.

"The Griffin." Derek started.  "Most notable for its vigilance, courage and strength.  It has numerous virtues and no vices.  Has sharp eyes, a keen ear and some would speculate to be a faithful as a dog."

"You continue to amaze me Mr. Chase.  You know your mythology." Janocky said.

Derek snickered under his breath.  "Yes, but because of present circumstances, I'm not sure if that description holds true in this case," and his hazel brown eyes turned from the statue to its owner.  "Wouldn't you agree?"

Janocky failed to comment as he looked over the investigator's shoulder at the secretary that silently walked in. "Well, Mr. Chase, I would love to continue this discussion. It has been enlightening. But, I'm afraid that I do have other engagements that require my attention. Should you have any further questions, please contact my secretary, and she will let you know when I am available."

Derek stood up and nodded. "I will do that Mr. Janocky. Thank you for your time."

The CEO of Griffin Security Inc. also stood up. "You're welcome Mr. Chase. I do hope you apprehend the villain behind Ms. Taylor's death and the unfortunate demise of one of my employees."

The detective's smile hinted satisfaction as he slightly mimicked Janocky's southern drawl. "Indeed I shall. Good day Mr. Janocky," and with that Derek put his shades on and walked out of the office.

Chapter Four

**Derek took a bite of the sausage pizza delivered from Pizza Hut**. He looked over at Saundra on the other side of the beige sectional sofa. She was diligently going through a stack of papers crumpled within a file. She tucked a stretch of her dark hair behind her ear removing it from her line of sight as she scanned the documents. She suddenly sat back in the couch with a sigh.

"Tell me again what I'm looking for?" she asked. The tone in her voice made him conscious of the fact that she was becoming tired.

A slight yawn escaped from Derek warning him that he too was becoming tired. Hours had passed since they first began reviewing the files from Tessa's office. In hopes of finding a good lead, they were trying to summarize all of Tessa's cases over the past few years in one night.

He picked up a folder and rested his back against his side of the sectional sofa encompassing the fireplace. "Something out of the ordinary, like Griffin Securities, that's my only lead so far. Try to find something that would look like a motive."

"Mr. Chase, every one of these files has a motive."

"I know," Derek replied with a sigh as he scanned the pages of the folder in front of him. "I know." He flipped to another page in the file he was holding and sat up. Memories of his past resurfaced from an ocean of nightmares like a breaching whale. He took in a deep breath as his heart began to quicken.

"For a moment, I forgot that Tessa was the Assistant District Attorney in the Letourneau Case."

"What happened with the Letourneau Case?" Saundra asked.

Derek took in a deep breath as he slowly replayed the incidents leading up to the trial. "It was the case that led to my resignation from the police department."

"What happened?"

"Sometimes I find myself asking that same question."

***The police cruiser rolled to a stop in front of the liquor store.*** *Sergeant Letourneau placed the car in park and unbuckled his seatbelt. Derek watched him and smirked.*

*"Shouldn't we wait for the end of our shift before we start hittin' the bottle, huh Sarge?" he said jokingly.*

*The Sergeant mimicked the smirk. "You've been my partner for a month now. That still doesn't give you the right to razz me about my activities after I take off the badge. Besides, the men and women of the police department who work the night shift, like to partake in an early morning cocktail. It helps us sleep better during the day."*

*"Is that so?"*

*"Yeah!" the Sergeant replied. "Not that it's any of your concern Rookie, but this is business. There's a guy with some information about some crooked cops in our precinct. I'm supposed to meet him inside."*

*"Crooked cops? In our precinct? You must be kidding."*

*"Well, that's what I intend on finding out." The Sergeant opened the door grabbing his nightstick from the middle of the two seats. "Stay here; I'll only be a few minutes. Got that Rookie?"*

*"Yes, Sir."*

*The Sergeant closed the door shaking his head. Derek watched him walk around the front of the cruiser and disappear into the liquor store. His attention reverted back to the police radio as he listened in on the different calls being transmitted.*

*He chuckled as he heard one of his counterparts respond to a domestic dispute between a husband and wife. The call advised that the wife had already bitten the man and that an ambulance had been requested. The thoughts of different circumstances leading up to being bit amused him.*

*His attention was quickly diverted when he heard a gunshot. He looked up to find the Sergeant stumbling backwards out of the liquor store firing his weapon. Derek quickly scrambled out of the cruiser as another man stepped out of the liquor store. His weapon trained on the Sergeant.*

*"Freeze!" he yelled quickly withdrawing the standard issue Beretta 9mm pistol. "Drop your weapon!"*

*The man's arm swiveled towards the rookie and Derek squeezed the trigger. He could see the would-be assailant spinning sideways as the bullet caught the perpetrator in the arm. The gun fell harmlessly to the ground.*

*Derek stepped away from the protection of the car door and slowly approached the perpetrator leaning up against the glass doorframe of the liquor store.*

*"Get face down on the ground now!" Derek yelled.*

*"Don't shoot!" the guy yelled. "I'm a fucking cop!"*

*"Bullshit!" Derek yelled. "Get face down on the ground now!"*

*"I'm a cop goddamn it! I'm with Internal Affairs!" He began reaching inside his jacket.*

*"Take your hands out of your pocket and get face down on the ground now! Do it!"*

*The perpetrator looked at the rookie cop and stopped his movements. He slowly withdrew his hand from his jacket and nodded in compliance. "Okay," he said. "I'll get down on the ground! My badge is in my jacket pocket!"*

*"Get face down on the ground now! Spread your hands palms facing up!" Using his free hand, Derek reached for the walkie-talkie microphone on his*

*shoulder.  "Control, this is Atlantic Blue 7 Charlie.  Shots fired on the corner of Pacific and 16<sup>th</sup> Street.  Officer down, send back up and a rescue unit."*

*The radio crackled back.  "Acknowledged Atlantic Blue 7 Charlie."*

*The perpetrator was on his knees as he made another plea.  "I'm a fuckin' cop!  I'm with Internal Affairs; your partner is –*

*Derek flinched as a shot rang out.  He watched the life of the perpetrator drain from his eyes.  The perpetrator's body slowly fell forward picking up momentum until he hit the pavement.  For a moment he stared at the lifeless body and then looked at the Sergeant who was standing a few feet away.  The barrel of his revolver was still exhaling smoke.*

*Weapon still trained on the perpetrator; the rookie cop stepped over towards the lifeless body.  He knelt down and reached for a pulse.  He couldn't find one.  He could hear sirens as he reached around the body through the warm liquid and searched the inside of the jacket pocket.  He had to know.  He had to know if he had shot a fellow police officer.  He pulled out a wallet and flipped it open.  A bloodstained badge confirmed his uncertainty while immediately filling his mind with more questions and doubts.  He looked at the Sergeant, who stood there; weapon still aimed at the fallen officer.*

***Two months had passed since that incident and Derek found himself on the witness stand for the District Attorney's Office.*** *Sergeant Letourneau and* *two other police officers had been arrested by Internal Affairs for money*

*laundering and drug related charges. The perpetrator that identified himself as*

*a police officer had lead the investigation which lured Sergeant Letourneau into*

*a well-planned sting operation. His efforts that night resulted in his death.*

*When Internal Affairs arrived on the scene, they promptly arrested them both*

*and brought them in for questioning. Sergeant Letourneau was later indicted on*

*charges of murder of a police officer, money laundering and an attempt to*

*solicit an illegal narcotic. Through further investigation, Derek had been*

*cleared of the charges. The District Attorney sought his statement as an*

*eyewitness to be one of the many nails in Letourneau's legal coffin.*

*"Officer Chase, could you tell us about what happened the night of July*

*14th, nineteen ninety-eight."*

*He looked at the Assistant District Attorney, Tessa Taylor. Her green eyes*

*were emotionally searching for the truth as they searched through out him. He*

*took in a deep breath and relayed the events of the night in question. "Sergeant*

*Letourneau and I were assigned ocean front patrol. We had stopped at the*

*Vicks Liquor Store on the corner of Pacific and 16th Street. Sergeant*

*Letourneau had informed me that he was meeting an informant who had some*

*information about some corrupt police officers in our precinct."*

*"Corrupt police officers?" she asked. "It's hard to imagine isn't it Officer*

*Chase?"*

*"Yes ma'am, it is."*

*"Could you please tell the court what happened next?"*

*"I was listening to the police radio when I heard a shot coming from the liquor store. I looked up to find Sergeant Letourneau stumbling backwards out of the store. I then saw another man come out of the liquor store after the Sergeant."*

*"When the Sergeant came out of liquor store, did he fire a shot?"*

*"Yes ma'am. He fired one shot."*

*"Did you think when he fired the shot he was defending himself or retreating?"*

*"Objection, Your Honor!" cried the defense attorney. "Speculation."*

*"Sustained."*

*Tessa cocked her head to the side and strategically began a slow pace around the courtroom. "Officer Chase, how long have you been with the Virginia Beach Police Department?"*

*"Not including my time at the academy, I've been a police officer for six months."*

*"Out of those six months, how long have you been assigned to Sergeant Letourneau?"*

*"Only one."*

*"Out of those six months, how many times have you drawn your weapon?"*

*"The night at the liquor store was the first time ma'am."*

*"Have you drawn your weapon since then?"*

*"No, ma'am."*

*"So, why did you draw your weapon that night Officer Chase?"*

*He took in a deep breath as the events replayed in his mind. "I felt that my life and the life of my partner were in jeopardy."*

*"That would be pretty convincing for me. If I saw my partner back peddling out of a liquor store firing his weapon and somebody coming out after him. I would definitely be inclined to defend myself. So what happened next?"*

*"I yelled freeze, and the suspect turned towards me with his weapon raised."*

*"That's when you fired your weapon, correct?"*

*"Yes ma'am. You are correct."*

*"I don't get it Officer Chase," Tessa began. She went back to her table and picked up a file. She opened it as she continued her observation. "When you fired your weapon, you hit the suspect in the shoulder. Why not his chest or his head? I reviewed your academy files. You were the head of your class in marksmanship, both with a pistol and a rifle. You could've nailed him easily. If you felt your life was in danger, why not put the suspect down?"*

*"I was taught by my instructors at the academy that my sidearm and my badge are only tools to enforce the law. It was unwritten, but outwardly known*

*that our law, above all else, is to serve and protect. How I used those tools would determine how well I enforced that law."*

*Tessa gave a quick glimpse of a smile, showing her approval as she continued on. "Okay, so after you shot the suspect, did he identify himself as a police officer?"*

*"Yes he did."*

*"What did you do?"*

*"I told him to get face down on the ground and spread his arms out."*

*"Why? The man has identified himself as a cop."*

*"As I said before, I felt my life, as well as Sergeant Letourneau's, was in danger. I did not want to take any chances. We were taught at the academy to secure the suspect and the area before determining the events leading up to the arrest. It proved to be a more effective way of keeping all parties involved safe."*

*"Did he comply?"*

*"After repeated commands, the suspect dropped to his knees."*

*"What happened then?"*

*"I continued to tell the suspect to lie face down on the ground, but he kept yelling that he was a cop."*

*"Did he say anything about Sergeant Letourneau?"*

*"He was about to, but Sergeant Letourneau fired his weapon."*

*Tessa shook her head and spoke. Her tone was inquisitive and soft, almost friendly. "Sergeant Letourneau fired his weapon. Point blank into the chest of Internal Affairs Officer, Robert Parks, thus killing him almost instantaneously. Tell me, Officer Chase, do you think Sergeant Letourneau fired his weapon because he was in fear of a disarmed suspect on his knees, repeatedly stating that he was a cop? Or do you believe what the rest of us already know?"*

*"Objection Your Honor!" Defense council interjected. "Prosecution is blatantly defaming my client!"*

*"Sustained," the judge retorted. "The jury will disregard the prosecution's last statement," and then he focused his stare harmlessly upon Tessa Taylor. "Be careful Ms. Taylor. Remember that you're in a court of law, not Dateline. Another statement like that and I'll fine you."*

*"Yes, Your Honor," Tessa conceded.*

*"Do you have any more questions, Ms. Taylor?"*

*"No, Your Honor. I have no further questions."*

**The air stiffened as the crowd waited for the jury to return.** *Derek looked over at Sergeant Letourneau. He seemed to have been unmoved by the whole event.*

*"All rise!" ordered the bailiff.*

*The courtroom rose as the judge and the jury entered into the courtroom.*

*Their faces were distraught. The rookie officer believed that they were*

*wrestling with the dilemma of what could make a good cop, with numerous*

*citations and recommendations go bad.*

*"You may be seated," said the judge as he took his seat. He spread the*

*legs of his glasses open and set them on his face as the crowd returned to their*

*seats.*

*"Madam Speaker," started the judge. "Has the jury reached a verdict?"*

*A young woman with red hair stood up. Her cream sweater made her*

*resemble a professor Derek had in college. Her face carried the weight of their*

*decision. "We have, Your Honor."*

*"Please hand the bailiff your verdict."*

*She handed the bailiff the slip of paper and he walked it over to the judge.*

*He opened it and studied the decision made by the impartial citizens. He re-*

*folded the document and handed it back to the bailiff. The bailiff returned the*

*document to the young woman.*

*"Sergeant Letourneau." the judge started. "Will you please stand as the*

*verdict is read by the jury?"*

*The Sergeant and the defense attorney stood. The Sergeant's body was as*

*stiff as an ironing board set to press the wrinkles out of a dress shirt. He*

*solemnly looked at the jury as she read the verdict.*

*"On the charge of manslaughter, we the jury, find the defendant, Sergeant Nicholas Montgomery Letourneau, guilty."*

*The crowd of the courtroom gasped as the cameras of the newspaper photographers flashed in rapid succession. They hoped that the verdict would jar a reaction from the Sergeant. They were wrong. Letourneau stood fast and waited for the punishment.*

*The gavel struck several times before the judge could talk over the courtroom noise. "It is by order of the court, that finding you guilty on the charge of manslaughter, Sergeant Nicholas Letourneau is immediately reprimanded to a minimum security prison for no more than a fifteen year sentence. Court is adjourned!" and the judge struck the gavel again.*

*The courtroom illuminated like the Fourth of July as newspaper photographers fought each other for that one picture that would summarize the entire trial. Sheriff's deputies locked the metal bracelets around the Sergeant's wrists and began to escort him out. Derek watched him as they escorted him past the prosecutor's table. They stopped in front of the rookie police officer.*

*"You did good Rookie, but it doesn't stop with me. This is bigger than anybody could imagine. My advice would be to watch your back. Be seeing you around Rookie."*

*Sergeant Letourneau chuckled as the two deputies revived their efforts to take him into custody. His chuckle turned to laughter as he exited the courtroom with photographers and reporters hounding his every step.*

*The rookie officer fell back into his chair, relieved that the ordeal was coming to an end, but was now questioning the Sergeants parting remarks. Several ideas were beginning to formulate in his mind. His thoughts were interrupted when Tessa placed her hand on his shoulder. It was a comforting gesture. She smiled as if she understood what he was thinking.*

*"Sometimes when you win, you also lose. You gotta take each battle as they come, and grow from them. It's how you survive when you do what we do."*

"It was a messy situation," Derek continued "I'm still trying to get past it. If there was a model police officer, Sergeant Letourneau was it."

"Why'd he do it?"

"Nobody knows. He didn't say anything during the trial. I testified as to what happened and Letourneau was sentenced to fifteen years in a minimum security prison. Two months after the trial, I was politely asked to resign from the police department."

"Why?"

"I don't know. Something about my performance record not meeting standards. It was a trumped up charge, but I could tell something was not right.

Cops that were supposed to be my friends turned their backs on me.  I was given

desk assignments and every time I would take a step forward, something would

knock me two steps backwards.  So, I succumbed to the resignation request."

"Mr. Chase," Saundra started.  "That's awful."

"Please Saundra, call me Derek.  Mr. Chase sounds so formal.  I still have

a little more than twenty years to go before I retire."

"From what I've heard, you've lived a very interesting life already."

Derek smiled as he gave a humpf.  "It's been an everyday roller coaster

ride."  He took another sip from the bottle of beer.  "But now that you know

something about me.  Tell me a little bit about yourself."

"What would you like to know?"

"I don't know.  Start somewhere."

"Well, let's see.  My mom was an insurance agent and my father is a pilot

for United Airlines.  I have two younger brothers and one older sister."

"I'm the only boy in my family.  I have two older sisters and one younger

sister," Derek commented.  "All three can be a pain."

Saundra laughed and continued.  "I'm a senior at Virginia Wesleyan.  I'm

also from the windy city of Chicago, so I guess that makes me a Bulls fan."

"What made you come Virginia?"

"The beach."  She answered.  "I am studying to become a law student.  So

I'm trying to learn as much as I can before I graduate."

"Well, stay with Garrett and Taylor. You'll learn a lot from the company. Who knows, you may be the next Tessa Taylor."

Her smile faded from her face as Derek realized what he said. He lowered his head and silently chastised himself for his verbal comparison. Saundra settled back into the sectional sofa and a tear welled up in her eye.

"I'm sorry Saundra, I-

"It's okay." she said with a sniffle. "I just haven't had a chance to accept what has happened."

Derek moved over to the other side of the sofa and put his arms around Saundra and hugged her. "It's okay. Nobody has." He looked at his watch. "Look, it's getting late, why don't you go home get some rest and I'll call you in the morning and we can go through the rest of these files."

"Okay."

He stood up lifting her from the sectional sofa. "Good." He said as he walked towards the front door. "I'll walk you to your car."

"Thanks Derek. You're really a nice guy."

Derek opened the door with smile. "Good, my secret is still safe." He said as they stepped out of the beach house. Large rocks were set side-by-side outlining a path to the cobblestone driveway. They walked to her car which was parked along the street.

She smiled as she took her keys from her purse.  She fumbled with them trying to select the key to her car and they fell to the ground.

"I'll get 'em." He said as both he and Saundra stooped down to pick up the keys.

Derek grabbed the keys as he heard an engine come to life.  He looked up to find a red Lexus clawing for traction as it began speeding towards them.  The car quickly screeched to a halt in front of them as the car window rolled down.  He quickly pushed Saundra to the ground as he saw the muzzle of a pistol revealing itself.  All of a sudden, he found himself stumbling backwards as three silent pops pounded his chest.

He fell against the fender of Saundra's car and fell hard onto the pavement.  He layed there motionless, struggling to catch his breath as he listened to the screeching of tires.  He fought to catch the blurred image of the Lexus, fishtailing onto an adjoining street, but a black shroud was beginning to overtake him.  The chances of catching the assassin had faded away with his consciousness.

<u>**Chapter Five**</u>:


**He winced in pain as the nurse wrapped the last piece of gauze around his rib cage.** He could feel the bandages squeezing his body together. He groaned as he shifted slightly. The smell of antiseptic was making him light-headed and he closed his eyes from the hospital's bright light, which added fuel to the headache he retained from the collision with the pavement. He looked over in the corner to find E. She was wearing black jeans and a red long-sleeved shirt. The gun sat ominously in the holster on her hip next to her pager. He figured it had already beeped once that night. She clutched onto the bulletproof vest that had just saved his life. He smiled acknowledging her presence. Though she smiled back, her face could not hide the look of concern.

"I suppose hugging you would be out of the question?" she asked.

He looked at her with a half-hearted smirk, but reminded himself that it was comforting to have her there. "You could, but I might snap in half."

Elizabeth smiled shaking her head. Her long black hair waved across her shoulders. She was glad he was still alive.

The door opened and his doctor walked in. Her white overcoat draped over her green hospital scrubs. He could hear her white Nike sneakers grip the clean tiling of the hospital floor. She looked athletic, slender, yet she carried a very toned body.  He figured her as a runner.  Even through the hospital attire he could see her muscular legs.  Her stethoscope hung loosely around her neck.  He could see traces of blonde strands peeking through her dark brown hair that was strung into a ponytail.  He could see the smoothness of her light mocha skin on her face.  Her brown eyes studied the chart she carried.  She looked at him and raised her eyebrows.

"I'm Doctor Gellar," she began.  "I have been reviewing your chart and quite frankly, you're very lucky."

"Must be that Irish blood on my grandmother's side," he said sheepishly.

"If the gunman was any closer, you'd be in the morgue," she added.  "Do you always wear a bulletproof vest?"

He rubbed the back of his neck hoping to relieve some of the headache.  The question to him was trivial.  Because he had been a cop, wearing a vest while working only seemed natural.  For him it was a common practice, and despite its cumbersome features, tonight it proved how useful it could be.  He answered the doctor's question giving her a half-hearted smile.  "It hangs right in the closet next to the tuxedo."

She smiled back.  His cynical humor was appealing.  "You're going to be sore for a couple of days.  The x-rays did show that one of your ribs had a hairline fracture, but for the most part, you'll be fine as long as you stop trying to be Superman."

It was his turn to smile. "His job is a cakewalk compared to mine." He replied as he reached for his shirt. "May I go home now?"

Dr. Gellar sighed. "Well, I had hoped that you would stay overnight for observation. But I suppose that's not going to happen." She folded her arms, squeezing the chart against her chest. "Let me get the release forms for you to sign. I'll be right back."

Her ponytail wagged as she opened the door and walked out. He smiled. She was cute. He had hoped that he would have the chance to meet up with her under different circumstances. He looked over at E who was now leaving the corner for his bedside.

"When I pulled up and saw you being loaded into the ambulance," E began. "I didn't know what to think. You had me worried there for a minute."

"I didn't know you cared that much."

"You'd be surprised at how much I care."

He looked at her. He could see the worry in her hazel eyes. He chose another conversation. "Did they find the red Lexus?"

E shrugged. "No, but we have an A.P.B. out on it and we have detectives looking over the house."

The door to the examination room opened. To his dismay, Lieutenant Austin stepped in rather than Dr. Gellar. Derek gave a moan and Austin's blue eyes glared at the detective.  He rubbed the stubble around his chin contemplating what he would say to the detective.

"Something told me it'd be you." Austin began.  "Why is it that I always seem to get caught up in your mess?"

"Karma?" Derek said smartly.

Austin gave a huff.  His face accented his fatigue.  It was chiseled like that of a gargoyle protecting a castle.  His peers and the officers in his command respected him.  Though he hated to admit it, there was some admiration from the private investigator sitting on the hospital table.  Austin was the role model for the perfect cop.

He reviewed Austin's attire.  Tonight, Austin was wearing his tan trench coat, a pair of dark slacks, and a white polo.  On his feet was a pair of Dockers that were scuffed along the edges.  Derek figured that some unfortunate rookie was selected to call him at home and wake him up.  He knew that the rookie would get an ass-chewing once Austin had his morning coffee.

The Lieutenant began his interrogation.  "Would you mind telling me why my men are at your house sniffing around for evidence on a case you shouldn't even be a part of."

"I don't know," answered the detective.  "Maybe it's the trail of doughnuts I left in the middle of the driveway?"

"Let me make this very clear," he began.  "This was and has been a police matter.  We will handle this.  If you want to be helpful I suggest you stay out of our way."

Derek slid into his denim button-down shirt as Dr. Gellar stepped into the room.  There was a form attached to the clipboard.  "I'll stay out of your way if you stay out of mine."

"Do you have a hearing problem?" Austin asked.

"Look Austin.  I don't need you badgering me about the way I do things.  I don't work for you anymore, remember?"

"And I live a year longer each time I'm reminded of it," he mumbled.  "You're reckless, Chase.  It's just a matter of time before it catches up to you."  He then lifted his finger and pointed at the detective.  "I'm warning you for the last time.  Stay out of it!  This is police business!"

"When someone decides they want to use me for target practice, I would say this is my business."

Austin held up his hands in frustration.  He walked to the door of the examination room and opened it.  "Do whatcha want, but if you get in my way, I'll be the one using you for target practice," and with that, he left.

Dr. Gellar handed the clipboard over to Derek.  "Sure you won't change your mind and stay overnight for observation?"

He took the clipboard and signed the paperwork. "Thanks Doc, but hospitals make me sick," he said as he handed the clipboard back to her. He happened to catch her brown eyes. She was very attractive. He allowed his impulses to continue. "Tell you what? My home number is on there; how about dinner sometime this week and you can evaluate my progress then?"

She smiled at the thought as she took back the clipboard. "I don't normally patch up people so I can have dinner with them." She paused. "I'm afraid I'm gonna have to decline your gracious invitation.  As far as evaluating you, I believe you'll recover without any permanent damage, say for a bruised ego.  In the meanwhile, no strenuous activities."

"Scouts honor," he replied.

She gave a silent humpf. "I bet you were a scout.  Goodnight Mr. Chase."

He smiled as he slowly started buttoning his shirt. "Goodnight Doc."

"Do you flirt with every woman you meet?" E asked.

"Just the cute ones," he answered as he stood up.  Soreness coursed through his body. "You'll get with me tomorrow for lunch and you can tell me what Forensics finds out?"

She smiled. "Yeah, I think I can manage that." Her hand gestured towards the vest. "I'll see if I can sneak you another one of these too."

"Thanks E.  I owe you one."

"You owe me two," she interjected. She reached into her jeans pocket and dangled the keys to the Ferrari in front of him. "I also took the liberty of driving the Ferrari over. Thought you might need it."

He took the keys from her and kissed her again on the cheek.

"What would I ever do without you?" he asked.

E took in a deep breath and sighed coyishly. "I shudder the thought."

Despite all attempts to detour him, he now had a third confirmation that Tessa's death was not accidental. Somebody did not want him snooping around. Instead, his motivation had been given more fuel to thrive on. He had a theory and hoped ballistics would be able to take the bullets from his vest and clue him in on the type of gun used. Hopefully it would match the same weapon used on Tessa and the security guard. The customized Lexus was a lead he could follow up on tomorrow morning. He knew of only one organization in Virginia Beach that kept tabs on every customized vehicle in the Hampton Roads area. Only his visit this time would be more than just a grooming necessity.

**Designer hair grease and scented hair spray easily succeeded in assimilating its environment as Derek walked into Buzz Cutts Barber Shop.** The new track from P. Diddy played loudly enough to give the impression that the artist was performing live. With a smile he scanned the barbershop. There were six of them wearing their blue smocks with the Buzz Cutts logo. They tended to the customers in their chairs blocking out all other distractions. Much like a beauty salon, the barbers at Buzz Cutts heard it all and would often give advice. They were not only hairstylists, but psychiatrists as well.

Working his way from the far corner, he saw the person he considered an older brother. He was shaving the back of his customer's head. The customer went on about his business reading the daily newspaper. The barber was a fairly broad-shouldered, dark-skinned man with a snow white goatee. The curly hair that cascaded down the sides of his head matched the facial hair. His light blue barbershop uniform was pressed and his shoes were polished. It was the same way he presented himself when Derek first had his hair cut twenty-eight years ago. His name was Clarence "Slappy" Cutter, one of the remaining founders and now sole proprietor of Buzz Cutts.

Slappy started Buzz Cutts in 1965.  There were three founding members, his Uncle James Cutter, Slappy's father Joseph Cutter and then Slappy.  Slappy was twenty-seven then and he was an eager entrepreneur looking for a chance to succeed.  Now, at fifty-eight years of age, he credited his success to the perseverance instilled by his father and his uncle.  The inheritance led to four other locations branching out to the different areas of Hampton Roads.

The detective remembered when his father took him from the suburbs of Virginia Beach to the urban jungle of Norfolk every other Saturday morning to be professionally groomed by Slappy or Slappy's father.  Derek hated it at first, and would cry in the chair like any other four year old.  However, after time and many lollipops later, it became a grooming necessity he grew accustomed to.  Since then, Derek was a loyal customer of Buzz Cutts.

Next to Slappy was Jamal Thompson.  Besides Slappy, he was the oldest barber there.  His caramel colored skin and well-built body got him the label of "Pretty Boy".  Before becoming a barber, he was in the Army as a Gunnery Sergeant and was called to do a tour of duty in the Gulf War.  For the most part Jamal was quiet, but everybody could feel the roar of the warrior underneath.

In the middle were the two brothers, Paxton and Arturo Glidden.  They were known throughout the surrounding neighborhood as "G-Love" and "G-Money" respectively.

"G-Love" was famous for being the ladies' man.  His tanned baby face was the hypnotizing agent for the opposite sex.  Even while he was at work, women would come in and further stroke his ego by making plans with him for that night.  While most men had hit their sexual peak at eighteen, "G-Love" boasted that at twenty-eight his was just beginning.

"G-Money", on the other hand, was sharp as a brass tack.  His bald head sparkled, as did his black leather shoes.  Like Slappy, "G-Money" wore a tie every day.  The money he made from the barbershop went into purchasing stock.  The dividends he earned were triple to what he invested.  "G-Money" had a knack for knowing what to buy, when to buy it, and most importantly, when to sell it.  He was the one who had helped Slappy expand to four other locations.  "G-Money", like "G-Love", flaunted his attributes by driving around in a customized BMW.  Together, they were the most popular and requested barbers Buzz Cutts had to offer.

"Yo!  Whadup dawg?" a barber cried out.

Derek recognized the barber as Andre Lover, Slappy's protégé and resident comedian.  Today, his chocolate colored face was full of youthful energy.  Slappy bragged that when Andre went off to college after the summer, he was one hell of a player for Old Dominion University's basketball team.  However, Andre was still from the wrong side of the tracks.  His father was in jail for armed robbery and his mother could care less if he existed.  As he did with most of his young employees, Slappy took it upon himself to be a positive black male parental figure. Buzz Cutts was not only a barbershop, but also a haven for those who needed a second chance.

"Whadup Dre?" Derek responded as he extended his hand. Andre accepted the greeting and shook it firmly.

"Ya know. Just illin' to be chillin'. So what brings you to this part of the hood?"

"Had to check in with my homies." Derek replied.

Andre laughed. "Homies huh? Shit! Man, you drive a Ferrari 355, live in a phat crib on da beach, dress like a superstar. Your pockets are practically overflowing with money and you wanna come to da hood and check in with the homies? Man you ain't right."

"Well, you can't say I ain't lookin' out for my brotha-man."

"I feel ya. You still cool with me D."

"Ditto my brotha," and Derek extended his hand again. "I'll check with you later. Don't forget, you owe me a one-on-one."

"School's always in session! You just gotta be willin' ta learn."

"We'll see. You forget. I played basketball too."

"Yeah, but back when you played ball, the hoops were still made of straw. I don't wanna embarrass you."

As a heed, Derek pointed his finger with a smile, "I can still teach you a thing or two." he said, only to get a humpf and a smile from Andre as the barber returned his attention to his customer.

Closest to the door next to Andre, was a hefty size Hispanic by the name of Omar Gonzales.  He nodded at the detective as he focused on the patron sitting in his chair.

"Que pasa?" Derek asked.

"Nada bro," Omar responded as he outlined his customer's sideburns. "Just trying to make ends meet."

Omar was a former sheriff's deputy for the city of Hampton.  He not only worked as a barber, but was also Buzz Cutts' watchdog.  Earlier in his career, he was shot in the line of duty when a prisoner tried to escape.  He had used his body to shield the warden and took a bullet in the arm.  Realizing how close he came to death, he resigned and started working as a bouncer for "Jumpers" Dance Club at the beach.  He brought his little son in for a haircut one day and noticed the Help Wanted sign.  He needed the extra cash and asked Slappy for a job.  Slappy reviewed his qualifications and both agreed that his services at Buzz Cutts would be more than just cutting hair.  Omar installed the alarm system for Buzz Cutts, as well as its state of the art surveillance equipment.  Anything that was seen or heard in Buzz Cutts was recorded for security purposes.  Unspoken or not, Omar was Buzz Cutt's secret police and his rule was law.

"Well, I could use a partner," Derek hinted.

"Nah man," came the Hispanic accent. "Slappy'll have my head and besides, you one tough homey already."

"That's because I'm afraid of people like you."

"Yeah, and my mother's a Leprechaun on the East Side."

The investigator chuckled. "Hey Omar, you used to be in law enforcement; have you ever heard of Griffin Security?"

Omar nodded. "Si. Supposed to be high tech and stuff. They provide security for a lot of companies up and down the East Coast. Some of my cop buddies say they're numero uno. They hire a lot of people that used to be cops or were in the military."

"How come you're not working for 'em?" Derek asked with a smile.

"And miss out on a gold mine such as this?" Omar laughed. "No way man, I've been shot at enough in my lifetime. And besides, G-Money's workin' on makin' us rich. Tryin' to get us in the stock market and shit."

"Keep listenin' to G-Money and you'll lose more than your hair."

"That ain't even right D," G-Money barked out.

"Derek!" Slappy yelled out acknowledging the detective's presence. "Stop botherin' my employees and get your ass over here. See if I can talk you into taking me up on that job offer? Could always use a good barber!"

"Maybe some other time," he answered as he walked past Omar.  He neared the barber's chair and looked around to notice that the Buzz Cutts was unusually crowded.  "You guys do seem busy today?"

"It's that time of the season ya know.  Beginnin' of summer.  People wanna be stylin' and profilin'.  Be this way for anutha week or so."

Derek nodded in agreement.  "Hey Slappy, I need your help," he began erasing the grin from his face.  His tone became business-like.

"What's on your mind?"

"Do you know who owns a red customized Lexus?"

Slappy raised an eyebrow.  He looked over at one of his co-workers wearing one of the barbershop uniforms.  He was finishing up and wiping the hair from the face of his client.

"Hey Money?" Slappy yelled.  The uniformed barber looked up as he removed the drape from his customer.  "Do you know anybody who drives a red customized Lexus?"

G-Money scratched the top of his baldhead.  "I only know of two customized Lexus's.  Both are red, the first was totaled in a car accident and the other hasn't been around in a while."

"Who owns them?"

"The guy who owned the one that was totaled died in the accident.  It was a damn shame because he was a college guy.  He was speeding on the highway and lost control.  Pronounced dead on arrival.  The other belongs to, uh, what's his face?  What the hell is his name?  Um-

"You mean Titus?" Andre interjected as he outlined the back of his client's head.

"Yeah," Slappy replied.  "That's the boy!  Him and his vintage Afro.  Every so often, he comes up in this parking lot with that booma-daboom noise, peeling his tires and such.  Why you lookin' for him?"

"Well, the person who felt the need to use my chest for target practice drove a red customized Lexus." Derek answered sarcastically.

Omar spoke up.  "That don't sound like Titus, he's not into drive-by's.  He's into drugs and such."

"Where can I find Titus?"

"Normally, Titus finds you," Jamal interjected.  His voice was deep and bellowing.  It carried throughout the barbershop.  "He's the big man for this local gang called the Park Place Posse.  They hang out on the corner of 21st and Colonial Avenue.  They're some misguided individuals."

"Misguided?" G-Love asked.  "Those hoodlums are downright killers!"

"Yo D," Andre yelled.  "If you're going to visit the Park Place Posse, I suggest you find a SWAT team, because nobody that goes in alone has ever come out alive."

"Andre," Derek began. "Fifty bucks says not only do I come out alive, but I'll convince Titus to come in for a haircut."

"You gotta death wish or something?" Andre asked. "Titus ain't cuttin' the fro. That's his trademark man!"

"You in or what?"

Andre reached in his pocket and pulled out a fifty. He walked over and slammed it on Slappy's workspace. "You might as well give me the money now, because you won't be coming back later."

Derek reached into his back pocket, pulled a crisp fifty-dollar bill out from his wallet, and handed it to Slappy. "Oh, rest assured my brotha, I'll be back."

"Okay Terminator." Andre said with a smile. "Betta follow my advice and get some backup, or the next time we see you, it'll be tonight on the six o'clock news."

"You almost sound like you're volunteering to join me in this little escapade?"

"Fuck dat," Andre responded. "You on ya own!"

Derek chuckled as Andre walked back to his customer. He took in a deep breath as he began going over the different scenarios he could be faced with.

"I hope you know what you're doin'," Slappy mumbled.

"I do too Slappy," Derek replied. "I do too."

**The Ferrari idled softly as it rolled to a standstill on the corner of 21st Street and Colonial Avenue**. He looked across the street to a parking lot of customized cars. He could hear and feel the base emitting from the corner in front of him. He scanned for the red Lexus, but could not find it in the surplus of personalized vehicles. However, he did see a young black male with an Afro that fit the description given to him at the barbershop.

He ceased the engine of the sports car, counting the individuals across the street. He counted nine. He knew that his training in martial arts taught him to take on multiple attackers, but he never had to put it to use. His heart began to quicken and he could feel himself getting anxious.

*The first step to climbing a mountain is to see yourself at the top.* He quickly thought. It was a phrase his Jujitsu instructor used when Derek encountered a difficult obstacle. Through usage of that philosophy, he realized that one's chances for success were greater, if one already saw themselves accomplishing the task at hand.

He stepped out of the car pulling his shades from his face. He took in a deep breath. It made his ribs ache, but he ignored it as he crossed the street. The music seemed to be vibrating the ground with every step he took as he moved closer to the gang of delinquents. He stepped on the sidewalk and did a strategic scan of his surroundings.

The gang was stationed in front of a small 7-11 convenience store.  They were sitting on the customized cars in the parking lot.  He did not see anything he could use for a weapon, like a trash can lid or a discarded stick.  He mentally reviewed defensive and offensive moves from his martial arts training as he stepped within four feet of the Park Place Posse and stood.

*Let's start climbing.*

One of the Posse members turned and caught Derek's stare.  A Philadelphia Eagles handkerchief was wrapped around his head.  He slid off the hood of the Jeep Cherokee that was generating the loud music. He recognized it as gangster rap.  The Posse member's jeans hung loosely from his waist and the checkered shirt was tucked in on one side of his body.

"Can we help ya with sumtin' homey?"

The investigator could see the gold cappings on the Posse member's teeth. He focused his sight on Titus who had drifted deeper within the group. "I'm here to speak with Titus."

Another gang member stepped up next to the first.  He was taller and stockier.  His skin was lighter than Derek's coffee complexion and his dreadlocks flapped loosely as he stepped up.  The cuffs in his jeans devoured the top of his boots and his T-shirt hung loosely from his body.  Derek could see the other gang members moving closer to him.  He felt like a wounded seal in a sea of sharks.

"Do you have an appointment?"

"No," answered the detective. He could feel the group surrounding him. "But, I think he'll wanna see me."

The gang member with the gold cappings jerked his head. "Yo, Titus! Homey here would like to speak witcha, but he ain't got no appointment!"

"Kick 'em to the curb!" Titus ordered.

"Sorry my brotha," said the taller one. "But you's got to be goin'."

Derek sighed. "Well, my brotha, you're just gonna have to kick my ass, cause I ain't movin'."

"If that's what it's got to be," replied the gang member with the gold cappings. "Take 'em out fellas!"

Derek glanced over his left shoulder as a gang member ran up to him. He looked like a linebacker for a high school football team. He jumped and side-kicked the Posse member in the midsection. The attacker tumbled backwards as fast as he came. Derek ducked as the fist of the taller gang member flew over his head and retaliated with a reverse punch to the midsection. He could feel one of the gang member's rib buckle under the blow. He stood up, grabbing the taller gang member by his dreadlocks, and directed him into another Posse member wearing a Miami Dolphins windbreaker.

A Posse member wearing a red checkered shirt sent a lazy front kick towards the black detective. Derek easily blocked the kick with the swinging of his arm and blocked the oncoming combination punch from the attacker. He then countered with a rapid flurry of punches to the face and throat. He executed a jump front kick lifting the attacker through the air and onto his back unconscious. The smaller gang member grabbed Derek from behind. He gritted his teeth as pain streaked through his torso. He caught a glimpse of two Posse members running up, both fairly built. One was wearing a blue T-shirt and the other looked like a stand-in for Mike Tyson. Both were displaying the gold cappings as they snarled. The detective blocked out the pain and lifted his body in the air, kicking them both backwards. He then used his downward momentum, turning sideways just before his feet hit the sidewalk, and flipped the smaller gang member onto his back. Derek sent a reverse punch to the posse member's face knocking him and the gold capping out.

He quickly stood as the gang member sporting the Miami Dolphin's windbreaker ran up. The Posse member threw a punch and Derek blocked grabbing the assailant's wrist and locking the arm. He then sent his free arm underneath the Posse member's captive arm and sent it upwards. He could feel the bones breaking as easily as the wooden blocks he practiced on. He spun underneath the Posse member's body and yanked his arm back. The Posse member flipped onto his back like a caught fish.

"You broke my fuckin' arm!" the Posse member screamed.

Derek stepped to the side as an attacker with a gold capping and dreadlocks ran up. He sent his arm out and caught the attacker in the throat, clothes-lining the Posse member. He fell to the ground unconscious from the wind being knocked out of him. He turned sending a foot to the face of the Posse member with the broken arm trying to get up from the sidewalk. The attacker limply fell back to his resting-place.

He took a quick inventory of the Park Place Posse. Five of the Posse members were down and the other two was gathering their thoughts. He went on the offensive as he ran towards the two. He stepped on the hood of a customized Honda Accord and jumped towards one of the Posse members. He did a roundhouse kick catching the Posse member in the blue t-shirt in the face. The kick lifted the Posse member in the air, spinning him like a propeller. The young gangster fell on the ground with a thud unconscious.

The other Posse member resembling Mike Tyson slowly moved towards Titus and the remaining gangster who omitted himself from the skirmish. He protectively stood next to Titus. His outfit consisted of a Colorado Rockies baseball jersey and jeans that hung off the waist and draped over his construction boots. The Mike Tyson look-alike clutched his stomach from being kicked earlier. He was breathing heavily. Derek watched him like a piece of meat. His martial art instructors would have been proud of his performance. The seal had now become the predator.

The Posse member took in a deep breath as he reached around his back. Derek instantly withdrew his Glock from the shoulder holster.  From the corner of his eye, he could see the other Posse member, who stood next to Titus reaching behind the baseball jersey.  Derek quickly unveiled the matching Glock from the holster tucked in the small of his back.

"Now as far as I see it," Derek began.  "My appointment is with Titus and Titus only.  You can stay here, and end up like your buddies, or you can leave while you still can."

The Posse members looked at one another and slowly walked away from Titus.  They got into a customized BMW and squealed off.  The investigator then focused his attention to Titus.  He motioned for the gang leader to walk over as he put one of the pistols away.  Titus slowly moved from his spot.

"Why you sweatin' me man?"

He stepped up to Titus and grabbed him by the neck.  He then shoved him face first onto the hood of the Jeep Cherokee.  He put the Glock up against Titus's head and cocked the weapon.

"I need to know why you were takin' pot shots at me last night."

Titus tried to move his head, but Derek's grip was firm.  "Man, I don't know what the hell you're talkin' about!  I don't even know your ass!"

"Then who was drivin' your Lexus?"

"Beats the fuck out me!" Titus yelled. Derek lifted Titus's head a little then slammed it back down on the hood of the Jeep Cherokee. Titus's Afro offered no protection from the hard metal. The detective's grip was tightening against the base of Titus's neck. "Man, I don't know! My ride was impounded last week!"

"Your car was impounded?" Derek asked. His grip loosened a little, but he still kept Titus's head against the hood of the customized Jeep. "That's bullshit!" He yelled as he re-tightened his grip.

He could now hear the pleading in Titus's voice. "Naw man! I swear! The police caught me dealin', and they took my shit!" Titus tried to lift his head, but Derek forced back onto the hood of the vehicle. "Look man, I'm tellin' the truth!"

"You know what Titus? I got a fully loaded Glock nine-millimeter resting against your head. Do you know that'll blow a nice little hole through that peanut you call a brain?"

"Man, I'm tellin' you the truth! The car was impounded last week! I swear to you! What can I do to make you believe me?"

Derek took a moment to gather his thoughts. Titus could be telling the truth. Giving the gang leader the benefit of the doubt, he uncocked the weapon and loosened his grip around Titus's neck. He quickly jerked the gang leader from the hood of the customized Jeep. The Afro was now slightly flattened on one side of Titus's head. "You know what Titus? I gonna give you the benefit of the doubt." He said. "So, I'm gonna let you go with a warning, if you're lyin', there'll be no place you can hide. I will hunt you down and -

Titus quickly interrupted Derek's sentence. "I'm tellin you the truth man! The cops took my ride! What can I do to make you believe me man?" He pleaded.

He raised an eyebrow remembering the bet he made with Andre at Buzz Cutts. "Titus, you know what? There is somethin' you can do for me."

**Chapter Seven**:

**"The autopsy report was completed late last night,"** Elizabeth said as she handed Derek the Coroner's file. "I want you to know that I had to pull some heavy strings to get this."

Derek took off his shades as he took the file. He took in a deep breath. His encounter with Titus and the Park Place Posse aggravated his cracked rib. He slightly winced in pain as he took a quick glance around the outdoor restaurant named Amigos. For a lunch hour, it did not seem busy. He noticed that the waiters were spending more time with the patrons and ensuring better service.

Elizabeth took a bite of her chicken quesadilla as he opened the file. She quickly chewed and swallowed. "Coroner estimates 7:30 as the time of death."

*Ten minutes.* He thought as he again began to mentally reprimand himself. *Ten damn minutes.*

"She was shot at point blank range, in the chest right through the left ventricle. Ballistics found a nine millimeter casing on the carpet."

"Nine millimeter, huh?" Derek responded. "How come none of the neighbors reported hearing gunshots?"

"None of them could," answered the black female police officer. "There was a domestic disturbance report that came in earlier that evening. One of the neighbors was having a big party at the time of Tessa's death. The loud music drowned out any noise coming from Tessa's apartment. If it wasn't for her front door being wide open and a nosey neighbor, she'd still be there."

He sat in silence for a moment speculating the scenarios. "It doesn't make sense. I can understand the burglar high-tailing it out of there because he just shot Tessa. It's a spur of the moment thing and he gets scared. What I don't get, is no one hears the gunshot because of the loud music, if it was a burglar, why not take what you can? She was wearing a diamond tennis bracelet; there was money in her wallet and an unsigned credit card on the counter."

Elizabeth pondered his remarks. "It doesn't make sense to me either."

"Because, it wasn't breaking and entering," Derek retorted. "Somebody was looking for something they thought Tessa had."

"Any idea what it could've been?"

The investigator shook his head. "I don't know, but they looked around her office too. Before you guys came, I did some looking of my own and couldn't find anything either. With the dead security guard laying face down in her office, it looks like somebody may have beaten me to it; but I would need to search Tessa's apartment to be sure."

"Good luck.  The Lieutenant has the crime scene locked up so tight, you'd be arrested a block before you got to the apartment complex."

"I like to think I'm a little more resourceful than that." he commented as Elizabeth took another bite of her Mexican entree.  Many times he had to sneak his way in and out of crime scenes.  There was not anything the Lieutenant could seal off that Derek could not get into.

"What about the autopsy of the security guard?"

"The medical examiner is doing that now.  Should know something this evening."

"Did you find out anything from the bullets that almost killed me?"  He asked.

She swallowed a bite of the spicy quesadilla.  "Yes, I did."  She answered.  "I know you were hoping that your would-be assassin was Tessa's killer, but I'm afraid I cannot support your theory.  The bullets don't match.  The bullets from your vest were from a forty-four."

"So you're telling me that someone used a nine millimeter pistol to kill Tessa and now his buddy, Dirty Harry is trying to kill me?"  Derek asked sarcastically.  He was trying to make light of the situation.

"Well, it could be something like that."  Elizabeth retorted back.  "After all, you and Tessa had rubbed some people the wrong way."

"There's a news flash." He replied as he closed the file and handed it back to Elizabeth.

"Oh, there's something else I need to tell you about Tessa's autopsy." she interjected. "Tessa was about two months pregnant."

"Tessa was pregnant?" he asked. "Based on what I've seen so far at Garrett and Taylor, I'm surprised she had time for a social life."

Elizabeth smiled coyishly. "You make time for the things you love."

Derek smiled back and refocused on the case. "I got another question for you," he began. He thought back to what Titus told him earlier about the customized Lexus that was confiscated. "Who has authority to requisition an impounded vehicle?"

Elizabeth took another bite of the lunch Derek offered to pay for. "Anybody does, as long as they have the Lieutenant's signed approval. Why?"

"Well, the person who shot me was driving a customized Lexus which belongs to a gang leader named Titus. I talked with Titus and he told me that his car had been confiscated during a drug bust a couple of weeks ago."

"I'll check it out." She said as a waiter walked up. He filled the glass of water she was nursing. "By the way, isn't Titus the leader of the Park Place Posse? How did you manage to get information from him?"

The light-skin investigator silently chuckled remembering the expression on Andre's face when he escorted Titus into Slappy's Barbershop. Titus advised that he wanted to change his image and that he wanted to be bald.  He

demanded that Andre would be the one to cut his hair.  Titus also warned Andre

that if there was so much as a bristle left, the Posse would publicly shear him

like a sheep.  Derek took Andre's fifty and with a devilish grin, advised him to

do a good job, or he would be the one on the six o'clock news.

"I grew up in tough neighborhoods."  He joked.  "I had friends like Titus."

Elizabeth raised an eyebrow.  "Aw, c'mon?  I know you better than that

Derek Chase," she said.  "You probably pried it out of him."

"Yeah, you know the whole truth about me."  Derek responded.  He took a

sip of ice water.  "Thanks for sticking around."

She smiled.  "So, your father is in a business that you don't necessarily

agree with; and your family history is not picture perfect.  Find me a family that

doesn't have similar problems.  Even though your situation is a little more

unique, you're no different than the rest of us."  She took a sip of her drink and

leaned closer across the table.  "Let me tell you something Derek Chase.

Regardless of your past, you have something special inside; and I think that's

why I continuously put my badge on the line for you.  It would be safe to

assume that I like you Derek.  After last night, I realized just how much."

He examined the police officer that used friendly competition to push him

through the police academy.  He could see the softness in her coffee toned skin

and the black police uniform hugged the different curvatures of her athletic body.  His mind began to wander precariously.  Her brown eyes reflected a sense of intimate delicacy.  For the first time, he looked at her with a strange sense of desire.  His cellular phone beeped, interrupting the conversation and a brief thought of impurity.

"We'll have to continue this conversation later."

"Maybe tonight," she smiled.  "Say over a glass of wine and some soft music?"

It was Derek's turn to raise an eyebrow.  "Say seven-thirty." he responded as he pulled the phone out of his jacket pocket.  "At my place."  He flipped the cellular phone open and answered the call.  "This is Chase."

Elizabeth looked on as he silently remained on the phone.  She had indeed known the black detective for a long time, but she never yearned for something more than friendship until now.  Maybe that special attribute he possessed was tugging at something more than just her heart strings.

"I'm on my way," Derek responded as he hung up.  He pulled the fifty he won from Andre from his pocket and placed it on the glass table.  "I need to go." He began as he stood up.  "I'll see you tonight?"

She nodded.  "I'm looking forward to it."

Derek smiled.  "Thanks for the ballistics report."

"You're welcome," she said and she reached down underneath the table and pulled out a new bulletproof vest.  "Oh, and don't forget this."

He took the vest and kissed her on the cheek. "You're always watching my back."

"Somebody's got to." She replied. "Be safe."

He snickered. "And miss the opportunity to live on the edge? Never!" and he walked out of the Mexican restaurant.

Elizabeth sat back in her chair and watched him leave. She knew that his above average instincts and reactions to different situations made him a very competent investigator. She just hoped that his instincts and reactions would lead him back to her that night.


**Sydney Taylor cordially smiled as Kevin introduced her**. Like her sister, she was very attractive. Her hair was long and black, unlike the inherited blonde tint Tessa had. Her Navy uniform confirmed the curves of a voluptuous woman and hinted at the possibility that she had an athletic muscle tone. Despite the make-up that accented her tanned face, her expression was business-like.

"Sydney Taylor, this is Derek Chase."

He accepted her handshake as she began. "It's a pleasure to meet you. I'm sorry it has to be under these circumstances."

"I understand," he consoled. "You have my deepest sympathy."

"Thank you," she replied.  Her voice was soft and he guessed maybe an octave lower than Tessa's.  He studied her face.  It was almost as if he were looking at a mirror image of Tessa.  "Mr. Garrett informs me that you are pursuing the case to find out who murdered my sister?"

"That is correct."

"Have you made any progress?"

"Yes, I have, but nothing concrete.  I wouldn't want to get your hopes up unnecessarily."

"Of course not."

"I will promise you Ms. Taylor that I will find the person or people responsible for this and hold them accountable."

"Thank you, Mr. Chase.  I know you will do your best."

"Excuse me," Saundra interrupted.  "Mr. Chase, I have the information you requested."

"Thank you Saundra, in a moment," and he returned his attention to Tessa's sister.  "Again Ms. Taylor," he began as he extended his hand.  "It was a pleasure meeting you and I hope to have some information for you soon."

"Thank you Mr. Chase.  I do appreciate all that you're doing."

Derek smiled as he stepped away and walked over to Saundra.  He glanced over his shoulder as Kevin placed his arms around Sydney Taylor's shoulder and escorted her away

"After last night, with all that happened," Saundra began. "I couldn't sleep. So, I went through some more of the case files. Guess what I turned up?"

Derek opened up the files and quickly perused through it. He saw the information Saundra was referring to. "You found some information on Michael Thatcher?"

Saundra folded her arms and nodded. "I had some help from one of my friends at Wesleyan. He's a computer geek and everything, but that's beside the point. We were able to tap into the police department's computer system."

"Tell me you have a current address for this guy?"

"As a matter of fact, we do. It appears that he's a resident of Virginia Beach."

"Did you say Virginia Beach?"

Saundra nodded. "He's at Princess Anne Memorial Park Cemetery. Michael Thatcher mysteriously died two months ago, and that's not even the icing on the cake. Guess who his roommate was at Boston College?"

Derek shook his head.

"Terry Austin."

"Lieutenant Austin knew Thatcher?" he asked in disbelief. His fingers were ripping through the papers in the file looking for written evidence to substantiate what Saundra was conveying.

"Not only did he know Thatcher, but he also knew Ms. Taylor. Boston College is her alma mater."


**The Ferrari sat silently in the rear of the Virginia Beach Police Department's parking lot**. Derek had tucked it neatly beside a police van as to avoid detection. He waited for Austin to exit the building.

Could Austin be involved in Tessa's murder? If so, what did Tessa have that somebody would kill for? Could have been something that involved Griffin Securities? Or something altogether different? Derek found that he was beginning to ask more questions than what he had answers to.

Austin walked out of the precinct and quickly got into the gray Crown Victoria. Derek started the engine of the Italian import and eased the throttle into first as the unmarked police car backed out of its parking space.

*Well, let's see what kind of skeletons are hiding in the Lieutenant's closet.* Derek thought as the four-door sedan began rolling out of the police parking lot and onto the street. The Ferrari eased out of its resting spot and discreetly followed after the police lieutenant.


**Following Austin proved to be the more boring part of Derek's day.** After he left the police department, Austin picked up his dry cleaning, stopped at a fast food restaurant and then drove down to the oceanfront where he sat on the corner of Atlantic Avenue and Seventh Street. Forty-five minutes had passed since the Ferrari had pulled into the dirt parking lot across the street. Without causing too much attention to himself, he had a good view of Austin and the activities surrounding him.

The detective scanned Atlantic Avenue to see it over-populated by tourists. Women in bikinis were skating along the sidewalk as surfers carried their boards to the oceanfront. Street vendors stood outside of their stores advertising the merchandise they had on sale, while customized cars cruised "The Strip". Their music echoed throughout the beach.

He re-focused his attention on the Crown Victoria as a pair of bikini-clad skaters rocketed by. Austin sat in his car unmoving. *What is he waiting for? Who is he waiting for?* Derek asked himself.

Fifteen minutes passed before a dark blue Ford Taurus pulled up behind the unmarked police car. A man wearing jeans and a sports jacket stepped out of the new vehicle and walked towards Austin's vehicle. Derek grabbed his binoculars and spied upon the newcomer. From the information in the folder he read earlier, it looked like Michael Thatcher. But that was impossible, because Michael Thatcher was dead.

He looked on with eyes of a hawk trying to commit every detail and movement to memory. Austin had stepped out of his vehicle and the two men shook hands. Austin then reached back inside the unmarked police car and pulled out a long red file.  He handed it to Thatcher who opened it up and studied it.  Thatcher closed the folder with a nod and then reached into his jacket pocket, withdrawing a disk.

*Now what could that be?*  He asked himself as the Lieutenant accepted the disk.  They cordially shook hands and Austin returned to the driver's seat of the unmarked police car.  His car slowly rolled back into the flow of traffic.  Derek made a mental note to himself, to find out what was on the disk that was now in Austin's possession.  Thatcher returned to the Ford Taurus as Derek re-ignited the engine of the black sports car.  For the moment, it was best to follow after the man assumed to be dead and the file he was carrying.  There was no telling where Thatcher would disappear to and how long it would be before he resurfaced.  Of course, he knew that he would have ample opportunities to resume his inquiry of the Lieutenant.  Their rapport practically made that inevitable.

His heart began to quicken as the Ferrari slowly rolled forward.  The number of questions he had were multiplying with each thought as he pulled out of the parking lot after the blue sedan.  He had hoped that Thatcher and whatever was in that red folder would be able to answer a few of those questions.

## <u>Chapter Eight</u>:

**The Ferrari stayed three cars behind the Ford Taurus as it traveled down Shore Drive, the two-lane road outlining the oceanfront from Virginia Beach to Norfolk.** The Virginia Beach end of Shore Drive was surrounded by various vegetation. It made it a very scenic and relaxing drive during the day. At night, it was dark and desolate, where even the headlights of a car were shrouded by the night sky.

As one traveled towards Norfolk, the vegetation progressed into the Great Neck area, which was considered the upper/middle class suburbs of Virginia Beach. Once past Great Neck, Shore Drive crossed into Norfolk and became more industrialized with the establishment of naval bases and an easy access to Norfolk International Airport. The Norfolk side of Shore Drive ended just before the Hampton Bridge-Tunnel in the former Ocean View area. Due to the renovation of the once drug-filled, pornographic nature of Ocean View, Norfolk City Officials decided to expand the name Shore Drive through the area and increase commerce by tourists and locals alike. The decision was both positive and profitable.

He followed the blue sedan through the scenic part of Shore Drive, questioning Thatcher's rendezvous with Austin. His distrust of the police department resurfaced as he relived the images of Sergeant Letourneau and the incident with the undercover officer from Internal Affairs.  He wondered why a good officer with four commendations and an impeccable record would suddenly become a rogue cop.

He thought up a few hypotheses, but quickly succumbed to the anticipation of meeting up with Elizabeth for an evening dinner later that night.  A strange desire welled up inside him.  The opportunity to explore any type of romantic encounter eluded him and he forgot what it was like to be wanted by another.  He was nervous and excited at the same time.  He felt like a giddy schoolboy who just experienced his first kiss.

A smile escaped him as he followed the Ford.  He forced his mind to focus on the task at hand.  He glanced in the rearview mirror to see a burgundy sedan moving in fast behind him.  It looked like an unmarked Crown Victoria.  He looked back towards the Taurus to see the sedan move in front of another car.  Derek lowered the accelerator to maintain his following distance.

Flickering lights from his rearview mirror stole his attention away from Thatcher's vehicle.  He looked to find the burgundy sedan speeding up behind him.  He saw the red and blue lights flashing in the grille of the car.  His suspicions that it was an unmarked police cruiser were confirmed.  He moved to the right lane to let the police car pass.

The cruiser pulled up beside him and Derek looked over at the two men in the car. They both were wearing shades and the expression on the face of the passenger was blank. As the cruiser edged up ahead, the passenger slowly turned his head and looked over at Derek. His face was stern and his hair had been cut like a cadet in the military. Derek stared back wondering what call came over the radio as the unmarked cruiser edged past him.

He re-focused his attention on Thatcher as the Ford Taurus pulled in front of a yellow Volkswagen Beetle. His eyes went wide as the unmarked cruiser suddenly swerved in front of him. He slammed on the clutch, throwing the throttle into third gear. He swerved to the right and bounced onto a small dirt lot on the side of the road. He slammed on the brakes sending a cloud of dirt in the air. The unmarked cruiser pulled into the dirt lot after the black import and screeched to a halt in front of the Ferrari.

Derek caught his breath as his heart continued to beat hard against his chest. He looked at the unmarked cruiser in front of him and saw the two men step out of the car. Both men resembled government law enforcement officials, rather than the plain-clothes detectives Derek were expecting. Both men were wearing dark suits and shades. The blank facial expression Derek noticed on the passenger was shared by the driver.

Derek got out of the Ferrari with his heart still racing. "What the hell is the matter with you?" he yelled. "You could've killed me!"

"Mr. Chase," said the passenger. "I'm detective Lawson and this is detective Harden. We need you to come down to the precinct and answer a few questions regarding Tessa Taylor."

"What was the matter with the phone?" he asked. "You didn't have to run me off the road!"

"Sorry Mr. Chase," said the driver.

The high pitched chime of a cellular phone caught the three of them off guard. With his left hand, the driver reached in his jacket pocket and revealed the phone. He flipped it opened and put it to his ear. Derek spied the tattoo of a bullet with a dagger through it on the detective's wrist. He was sure he had seen that tattoo before.

"Yes," he answered. "We will be bringing in Mr. Chase for questioning."

*Questioning?* Derek thought. *Am I a suspect now?* He raised an eyebrow in confusion. "Is this something where I should notify my lawyer?"

"That won't be necessary Mr. Chase," said the passenger who was claiming to be a detective. "We just want to ask you some routine questions."

The driver closed the flip phone and placed it back into the confines of his jacket pocket. "We just want to eliminate any loose ends."

*Eliminate loose ends?* He thought. His stomach was tightening. "Okay," Derek answered. "Let me just get something out of my car," and he turned towards the door of the Ferrari. A hand from behind grabbed his arm.

"There's no time for that," said the passenger.

Derek's head turned and found the well-dressed detective pointing a gun at his chest. He looked over at the driver who had also unveiled a pistol. He quickly analyzed the situation to find that he was being set up. His mind quickly calculated different strategies to get out of the situation.

"You're right," Derek retorted. "I won't need my lawyer for this after all."

The passenger of the unmarked cruiser yanked Derek from the door of the Ferrari and shoved him towards the driver. He followed closely behind the black detective with his gun pointed towards the investigator's back. The driver re-holstered his weapon and opened the rear door of the unmarked cruiser. Derek knew that once he got inside the sedan, he would be taking a one way trip. He had to make his stand now.

He stopped at the door and quickly glanced at the two men pretending to be detectives. With as much power as he could muster he sent his foot towards the man behind him and caught him full in the mid-section. The back kick lifted the man in the air and onto the ground knocking the gun out of his hand.

Derek then quickly yanked the door causing the driver to briefly lose his balance. It was all he needed to send an elbow to the driver's jaw. The man's shades flew from his face through the air as he stumbled sideways from the blow. The phony detective quickly regained his balance and reached for his weapon. Derek quickly went on the offensive grabbing the driver from behind.

He put his arm around the driver's neck and grabbed the hand reaching for the gun.  Derek helped the driver withdraw his weapon and pointed it towards the passenger who was reaching for his discarded weapon.  Derek squeezed the driver's finger that was on the trigger and coughed off a couple of shots catching the passenger full in the chest.  Derek saw the bullets' impact as blood exploded from his chest.  The passenger pretending to be detective Lawson fell backwards on the ground unmoving.

The driver sent an elbow to Derek's midsection re-aggravating the cracked rib and knocking the wind out of the private investigator.  Derek stumbled backwards as his breath returned.  He could see the phony detective taking a step forward and swinging his hand with the gun to take aim at his target.  Derek sent a crescent kick towards the weapon knocking it out of the assailant's hand.  The assailant countered with a sidekick of his own, once again catching Derek in the midsection.  The black investigator bounced against the side of the unmarked cruiser coughing.  He ducked as a foot flew towards his face.  He then sent a front kick sending the driver backwards.

Derek took in a deep breath as the driver regained his balance and charged.  He sent a kick towards Derek head; Derek blocked and retaliated with a punch.  The driver blocked and sent his foot towards Derek's ankles.  Derek quickly jumped in the air and sent both his feet towards the driver connecting with his chest.  The force lifted the driver into the air and onto his back as Derek landed on the hood of the unmarked cruiser.

The assailant slowly stood to his feet as Derek rolled off the hood of the unmarked police car.  It was his turn to attack.  He stood in front of the driver in an offensive pose.  The driver reached into his jacket and unveiled a combat knife.

He charged towards Derek, thrusting the knife forward.  Derek sidestepped as the assailant sent the knife after him.  He could feel the blade piercing the clothes and his arm.  He winced and quickly backed up.  In hand-to-hand combat, Derek had won confrontations without a scratch.  This incident put him in an unfamiliar situation.

*This has to end now.*  He looked at the driver who had a smile on his face.  The driver knew that he had the upper hand and it would be a matter of time before he could claim victory over the private detective.

He charged again towards Derek thrusting the knife forward.  Derek again sidestepped the attack; however, this time he quickly grabbed the driver's wrist.  He sent his right foot up and with all of his strength, did a roundhouse kick to the stomach.  The driver buckled.  Derek held onto the wrist and lifted the driver's arm in the air.  He spun under the assailant's arm and sent the knife into the driver's stomach.  The driver doubled over and Derek grabbed his head and snapped his neck.  The driver pretending to be detective Harden limply fell onto

the ground like a discarded sack of potatoes.

He breathed heavily as he backed up towards the Ferrari.  He clutched his

bleeding arm as he looked at the two dead bodies of the men who he suspected

had every anticipation of killing him.  He forced himself to relax as he reached

inside the Ferrari for the cellular phone.  His investigation of Tessa's murder had

gotten someone's attention, and for whoever it was, they were now proceeding

with actions to make sure it remained a mystery.


**Sergeant Steele walked up to Derek, who was being treated for the**

**knife wound by the ambulance attendants**.  The expression on his clean-

shaven face was not a favorable one.  The sergeant's slicked-back blonde hair

was ruffled from the soft summer breeze and he had traded his trench coat he

wore the morning before for a casual blazer.

Derek winced as the ambulance attendant wrapped the last piece of gauze

around his arm.  "We need to take you to the hospital."  The attendant remarked.

"You need to have that wound stitched up."

"I heal fast," Derek retorted.  He quickly looked up at the sergeant and

gave a sheepish grin.

The sergeant smirked at him and then looked back at the nest of flashing blue lights. He saw the two heavy black body bags being loaded in the City Coroner's van. He then focused his attention back to the investigator.

"Do you wreak havoc wherever you go?" Sergeant Steele asked. The tone in his voice suggested that he was trying to make light of the situation.

"No," Derek answered. "Sometimes, it comes to me."

Steele jerked his thumb towards the coroner's van. "I ran a check on the plates. It's not one of ours."

Derek hopped off the edge of the ambulance and slid his shirt over his head. "I figured that when they wanted to kill me," Derek replied as he started walking to the Ferrari. "So, who were they?"

"Don't know," Steele answered. "Neither stiff had any identification and both of them had the same tattoo on their wrist. I have to run a check against local gang signs. The funny things is that, they both look familiar. I think they used to be cops."

"Used to be cops?"

Steele could hear the frustration in the detective's voice. "Now Chase, don't go jumping to conclusions."

"I'm investigating my boss's murder. The same person who happens to be the lawyer who helped put an officer behind bars. She just happens to be investigating a security firm that hires ex-cops, one of which was found dead in her office.  And today, I find your boss, a police lieutenant, talking with a man who has been missing for the last three months.  To top it all off, two men, who claimed to be detectives, just tried to kill me.  You tell me they used to be cops.  What conclusion am I to jump to?”

“Derek,” the Sergeant began.  “I’m sure that there’s a perfectly good explanation for all of this.”

“Yeah, it’s called a corrupt police department that has full reign over the system.  You forget Steele, I’ve been there, done that.”

Steele sighed.  “I know what happened a few years ago wasn’t your fault, but don’t start diggin’ stuff up that you want to keep buried.”

Derek closed the door to the Ferrari and ignited the Italian-made import.  The roar of the engine exemplified the mood he was in.  “I’m already past that.”

The Sergeant stepped back as the tires of the Ferrari clawed for traction.  Dirt and gravel flew up in the air as the black vehicle quickly maneuvered through the maze of police cars.  Steele took in a deep breath and sighed as the Ferrari bounced on the pavement and rumbled down Shore Drive.  He looked back over at the attendants who were loading the last of the body bags into the black Coroner’s van.  Whether it was intended or not, Derek’s past had came back to haunt him and the former cop was now looking for retribution.  Steele hoped that once the score was settled, the skeletons would be buried forever.

Chapter Nine

**The limousine driver opened the car door as Thomas Janocky walked across the parking garage.** They both turned with the screeching of tires echoing throughout the structure. They could see the black 355 coming around the corner and accelerating towards them. The door to the import opened as the car came to an abrupt standstill a few feet away from the open limo door. Janocky's face went pale as Derek stepped out of the Ferrari with a weapon aimed at his head.

"I do say Mr. Chase," Janocky began. His drawl emphasized the look of surprise on his face. "I am beginning to wonder what exactly it is you want from me."

"I want the truth." Derek answered as he walked around the front of the Ferrari.

"What truth?" Janocky asked. "I've told you all that I know."

"Is that a fact?" Derek asked as he cocked the pistol. "I'm sure there must have been something you left out."

"What are you trying to imply Mr. Chase?"

"Two men impersonating detectives just tried to kill me. I have a strong notion that if I was to check your personnel files, I'd find their resumes."

"That's absurd!"

"Care to prove otherwise?"

His ears caught the sound of a weapon being cocked behind his back. Before he could react, he was frozen by the familiar voice that began to bellow throughout the parking garage. "You always had a flare for the dramatic, eh, Rookie? Drop the gun and kick it away."

Derek uncocked the weapon and slowly lowered the gun to the ground. He raised his hands as he resumed his full height and gently kicked the gun across the parking lot a few feet away from him.

"Mr. Chase," Janocky interrupted. "I believe you already know my Chief Security Advisor and personal bodyguard, Nick Letourneau."

Derek took in a deep breath. "I should've known that it would've only been a matter of time before I ran into you again."

Nick Letourneau stepped in front of Derek and smiled. His face was haggard and his hair was mostly gray, almost white in some spots. He seemed hardened from his term in prison. Derek mocked the ex-cop's smile. "I'm getting the sense that you're not happy to see me." Letourneau said as he began frisking the detective.

"I'm not," the detective replied. "Early parole?"

Letourneau chuckled as he withdrew the pistol from the small of Derek's back. "You can say that," he said as he tossed the weapon. "Janocky heard about my situation and sent his lawyers to do some plea bargaining on my behalf."

"Another fine example of how our justice system works."

"Listen Rookie," Letourneau began. "The system fucked us both. Let's work together; we can change this city. Make the system work for us for a change."

It was Derek's turn to chuckle. "I think I'm gonna pass on this one. Maybe some other time."

Letourneau smiled and shook his head. "You always thought you were a righteous cop. Look where it got you? I'm offering the chance to take back what's yours."

"I won't lose my soul for it."

"Think about it Mr. Chase," Janocky interjected. "With a man of your background and connections, this could be the opportunity of a lifetime."

"I'm afraid you don't know me all that well."

"On the contrary. I know more about you than you realize. You see I conducted a little investigation on my own. I know your father, Thomas Washington, is the son-in-law to Enrique Denteveron. When your grandfather passed, your father inherited seventy-eight percent of the business, and some of the people in your grandfather's organization were not too pleased with that decision. So, when your father decided to move the company headquarters from

Columbia to the United States, it was more for personal reasons than for business politics.  Join us Mr. Chase, and together we can assure the security of your grandfather's corporation and his name.  We might even be able to find out who murdered your mother."

"You think by bringing my family into this will change my mind?" Derek laughed.  "My father has done well thus far without you or me.  And as for my mother's killer, I'm quite capable of determining that on my own.  So once again, the answer is no."

Letourneau and Janocky looked at the detective realizing that the look in his eyes was not to be swayed.  Letourneau gave a humpf.  "You're a stubborn bastard."  He uncocked his weapon and secured it in the shoulder holster within the confines of his suit jacket.  "Okay Rookie, go it alone.  But I'm warning you, stay away from Janocky."

"And if I don't?"

Letourneau remained quiet and just smiled.

Janocky broke the silence between them.  "Well gentlemen, enough said.  This enjoyable meeting has concluded," he interjected.  "Good day Mr. Chase," he said as he disappeared inside the limo.

Letourneau stared at Derek a while longer.  His tone was courteous.  "Remember what I said.  Don't interfere." With that said, he followed after Janocky and got into the limousine.  The car pulled off and rolled out of the parking garage leaving the investigator with the realization that his situation became that more complicated.


**Derek took a bite of the roast pork fried rice from the local Chinese restaurant**. The taste was greasy and sweet from the duck sauce. As he chewed, he looked over at Elizabeth with a smile. The candlelight flickered in her eyes as she looked back and smiled. With the exception of the stereo system playing an intimate blend of saxophone music, their dinner had been a quiet one.

"I'm sorry about the ballistics report, forensics has been extremely busy."

"Don't worry about it. I can get it later."

"I'll get it to you as soon as I can," she said as she gracefully picked up a mouthful of Chinese vegetables with her chopsticks. Derek looked on with admiration as he took another fork full of the roast pork fried rice.

"When I was twelve, my dad took me to China for one of his many business trips. He unsuccessfully tried to teach me how to use those things."

Elizabeth swallowed and a smile went across her face. "Something tells me that was one messy lesson."

They chuckled together. "You can say that again. Half of my dinner was in the plate and the other half was in my lap. By the time I was done eating, I looked like an over-sized egg roll."

Their chuckling turned to laughter. "My babysitter was Chinese, Lynn Mi. Every Thursday for lunch, my dad would come home from his patrol and Lynn Mi would make an oriental meal of some sort. She forced us to eat it traditionally. Not to mention she hid all of the kitchen utensils anyway."

"I can see how that can be a conducive learning strategy," Derek retorted as he took another fork full of his dinner and swallowed. "Since those business trips with my dad, I've given up on trying to eat with chopsticks."

She swallowed another bite of her Chinese vegetables. "Maybe it's time you had another teacher." She took one last sip from her red wine before taking the napkin from her lap. She wiped the corners of her lips and stood up.

He sat motionless as his eyes scanned the dinner guest. His khaki colored dress pants and white collar-less shirt did not do justice for Elizabeth's sleeve-less, black, satin dress. He looked like he was ready to go to the night clubs, while she was dressed for the opera. When he first opened the door to greet her, he was taken aback by the outfit. He teased her slightly saying that she did not have to dress up for the occasion, but she told him that was all she had in her closet that was not at the dry cleaners.

She made her way behind him and took the fork out of his hand. She replaced it with a set of unused chopsticks. "First step is knowing how to hold them."

"Careful," he warned. "This could get messy."

Elizabeth smiled as she continued on with the lesson.  She gently positioned his fingers accordingly on the foreign utensil.  "Just remember to use your index finger and your thumb to guide the chopsticks."

Derek scanned the plate of pork fried rice for the biggest piece of meat he could find.  He found one hiding under a portion of fried egg yolk.  He attempted to secure the food with the chopsticks, but only succeeded in chasing it around the plate.

Elizabeth could not help giggling as he discarded the chopsticks in defeat.  "They always say practice makes perfect," she said.

Derek smiled.  "At the rate I'm going, your children's children will know how to use chopsticks before I do."

"Sometimes, you need to have the desire to want to do something," she advised.  Her voice then softened.  "You'd be surprised at what you can do when you want something bad enough."

He looked up at her as she stood behind him.  He wiped the corners of his mouth with his napkin and stood up from the table.  He took a step into her personal space and took her hand.  Her skin was soft and her perfume was sweet and invigorating.

"You know Elizabeth," he began.  "That almost sounded like a subtle hint."

"Elizabeth?" she asked.  "No witty nicknames, Mr. Chase?"

"Not tonight."

She smiled. "Well, you're the detective. All the evidence is there in front of you. All you have to do is look for the obvious."

They leaned closer towards each other and their lips merged. They hungrily kissed each other as her arms separated from his hands. They slowly traced the curvatures of his back as she embraced him. His hands worked their way from her shoulders to her buttocks as he pressed up against her firm body. His hands then followed her spine upwards to her neck. He cradled the back of her head letting her long black hair run through his fingers. She could feel his body responding to hers. Their lips parted and they looked at each other.

"This could get complicated," she warned.

"Well, Ms. Companstella." He smiled. "You're the police officer, handle the situation."

She looked into his eyes and threw caution to the wind. Her lips joined with his, determined to fulfill a fantasy long awaited. She quickly moved her hands to his chest and unbuttoned his shirt. His fingers slowly unzipped the black dress. He kissed along her neck, using his tongue to taste her skin as she slid the shirt from his shoulders. Her hands then outlined the curves and the muscles in his chest. They followed the path to his belt and unbuckled it. She undid his pants in hopes that all animalistic instincts would take over.

Derek slid the dress off her shoulders and watched it fall loosely to the floor. He looked at her body. She was more beautiful than he had imagined. He kissed her on the lips. Their tongues quickly darted in and out, teasing each other while exploring their kiss and hungry for a night of pure ecstasy. He cradled her back and swept her legs from underneath her. They kissed as he led her to the bedroom. It would be a night they would never forget.

He gently laid her on the bed and he followed after her. He could feel her hands sliding his underwear from his body. He used his legs to further escape from the clothing.

Their arms wrapped around one another as his manhood brushed up between her inner thighs. She moaned as he kissed her along the neck. Her hair tickled his chin as his tongue caressed the spot right under her ear. Her nails dug into his shoulder as his manhood grew closer to its target. He could feel her hand sliding in between his legs and caressing him. She used it to touch the outside of her private area. Their kissing became ravenous as he could feel himself wanting more. Her body was warm and inviting when she allowed him inside her inner sanctum. A low moan came from both their lips. It was firm as he repositioned himself to go deeper inside. She lifted her hips to accommodate the change as he slowly and rhythmically began sliding inside her. She moaned as her body continued to keep in rhythm with his.

His hand cupped her breast and caressed her hard nipple as he kissed her along the neck. His tongue followed his fingers as he traced the outline of her areola. Her fingers clutched his butt as she kissed him along the neck and the shoulder.

He rolled onto his back as she followed him. After a moment of re-adjusting she raised upright and began moving back and forth, her hands on his chest. He held her by her waist as the pressure began building up inside. He could feel himself swelling. Her fingers ran through the hair on his chest as she moaned. Her movements became faster as he could feel juices running down his thigh. He slightly gritted his teeth as he could feel pressure building at the base of his groin. His body accommodated as he tried to match her rhythm.

They both let out a low moan as they exploded together. Their pace slowed as their bodies quivered. He stayed inside her as she layed on top of him. She kissed him gently on the lips as he held her. For a moment, their fantasy had been complete and they said nothing. They just laid there together and enjoyed each other company.


**She slept peacefully snuggling up against his warm chest**. He held her firmly as he re-played the night's happenings. They made love twice that night, the second time more intoxicating and relentless than the first. Derek committed every detail of Elizabeth's body and how she moved to memory.

He thought of her words and her kisses, remembering that it had been a long time since somebody made him feel like a special part of their life. He took in a deep breath as his hand caressed her shoulder. Her skin was so soft that it almost felt like silk. He realized that she was softer than her appearance let on as he lightly kissed her on the forehead.

*Well, you're the detective. All the evidence is there in front of you. All you have to do is look for the obvious.*

He would have jumped out of bed if it had not been for the fact that Elizabeth was using him for a pillow. He needed to get back to Tessa's apartment and look around. The first time he went there he was bullied out by Lieutenant Austin. There was clearly enough evidence to support that this was not a prowler that Tessa happened to stumble upon. Somebody was looking for something. Derek was hoping on the possibility that Tessa returned home before they could find it.

He gently rolled Elizabeth to the other side of the bed. He watched her as she curled up next to a neighboring pillow. He smiled when she spread the satin sheet over her bare back. His mind quickly returned to the task at hand as he slid out of the bed. He hastily jumped into a pair of jeans and a black t-shirt. He then put on a pair of socks and his black mountain boots.

Quickly, he left his room, quietly closing the door behind him. If he woke her, she would attempt to talk him out of it and wait until morning, or she would ask to come along.  In either case, he did not have the time to discuss politics

and procedures.  He gently opened the door to the garage and walked over to the

Ferrari, a car that had once sat in the garage for a month because his pride

refused to drive it.

He remembered when his father came down to Virginia Beach for his 27$^{th}$

birthday.  Derek had went out with his sisters for lunch and when he returned,

the Ferrari was sitting in the cobblestone driveway with a big bow around it.

His father was standing beside it with a sheepish grin as he dangled the keys in

front of him.

*The waves crashed against the surf as his father stood. A slight breeze*

*ruffled the lapel on his suit jacket as he watched a school of dolphins frolic in*

*the water. The burly, chocolate man looked back at the beach house to find his*

*three daughters suddenly scurrying for a place to hide, but allowing them access*

*to still witness the conflict between father and son.  He then turned back towards*

*the Atlantic Ocean.  He seemed more focused on the school of dolphins than his*

*angry son.*

*"So you think you can just come down for my birthday, hand me the keys to*

*a two hundred thousand dollar sports car, and I'm just gonna forget about the*

*shit you've put me through?"*

*"I'm only trying to provide for my son.  I want you to have the best."*

*"What's best for me is for you to stay out of my life! When I was growing*

*up, I did what you wanted and it continued when I went to college! I don't know*

*where I fit into your grand scheme of things, but I do know this. I don't want*

*your life!"*

*His father sighed. "Your mother would be so upset right now."*

*That comment infuriated him. He spun his father around to face him and*

*sent a fist directly to his father's jaw. The blow caused the patriarch to stumble*

*backwards "How dare you bring her into this!" Derek exclaimed.*

*His father rubbed his jaw and regained his footing. "I suppose I did*

*deserve that."*

*"You deserved that and a hell of a lot more! It's because of you she's no*

*longer with us. Had you put the family needs in front of your own selfish*

*ambitions, she'd be alive today!"*

*It was his father's turn to strike. Derek spun to his knee from the force of*

*his father's fist connecting with his jaw. His father's words were that of*

*retaliation. "Don't ever let me hear you say my family doesn't come first. I*

*have worked my ass off for this family. And I did it happily because I loved your*

*mother more than I loved life itself. When she died, I died too! All I have is you*

*and your sisters. I'll be damned if I'm gonna let anybody take you away from*

*me!" He regained his composure, taking in a deep breath and listening to the*

*waves. He looked at his son now standing defiantly before him. His tone softened. "I'm sorry if you feel that I interfered with your life, but I had my reasons, and I don't have to explain them to you or anybody else," and his father started walking off. "No matter what has happened in the past, you are still my son and I love you."*

*He stood there and watched the burly patriarch start his ascent to the beach house. His sisters were now perched on the deck. They had beheld the confrontation between them. His two older sisters slowly disappeared inside the beach house, but the youngest stood there and watched him for a while before coming down the stairs and joining him on the beach.*

*"He's only trying to protect us." She began.*

*"I know, but we should still be able to make our own choices."*

*"Yes, you're right." She agreed. "But give him some time, okay. Remember, we're still healing too."*

The garage door opened as he ignited the engine to the Italian sports car. If he was right, the killer would be back at Tessa's apartment to search for whatever it was that Tessa had. He had to get there first, or forever find himself asking what was so important that someone would kill for it. With an empty street, he could make it to Tessa's apartment in seven minutes. He speculated about the possibility of someone already there searching for the very lead that could point to Tessa's killer.

*No matter.* He thought. He was going to see this through to the very end.

Chapter Ten

**The Ferrari silently rolled to a standstill between a moving van and a Chevy convertible.** Derek thought it was best to park on the opposite side of the apartment complex and sneak in on foot as to avoid detection from the Lieutenant's watch dogs.

He could feel fatigue setting in as he slowly slid out of the import. He longed for a hot shower and a good night's sleep. He promised himself that once Tessa's killer was brought to justice, he'd take a week's vacation and recover.

He quickly hustled across the complex to the section which housed Tessa's apartment. He crouched down behind a dusty pick-up truck and surveyed the area. He located two uniformed officers in an unmarked police car a few parking spaces down from the apartment. He was sure that a back-up patrol vehicle was nearby circling the area. He smiled at the Lieutenant's attempt to seal off the crime scene.

He then centered his attention towards the apartment a few feet away from him and stealthily began to move between the parked vehicles, nearing the path that led to Tessa's apartment. He glanced at the unmarked cruiser to find that one of the officers had fallen asleep and the other was reading a magazine.

Derek shook his head in disappointment. If it had been him and Sergeant Letourneau in that unmarked vehicle, the Sergeant would be on foot surveying the area close to the crime scene while he sat in the police car. His assignment would be to watch the apartment. He would be like a vulture sitting high on a cliff, as its next meal slowly crawled along the hot desert earth below.

Despite the pain in his mid-section, he crouched down and quickly scampered to the path leading to the apartment. Once in the shadows, he stopped and placed his back against the brick wall. He quietly exhaled to relieve the tension in his ribs. Catching his breath, he peered out from the shadows to find that he left the two police officers undisturbed.

He diverted his attention from the police officers to Tessa's apartment door. It was still littered with the yellow crime scene tape. Sliding his back against the wall, he hastily moved through the shadows towards the door. He frequently checked behind him to make sure he was not being pursued. If he was caught breaking into a crime scene, the Lieutenant would personally oversee the construction of Derek's prison cell.

He reached the apartment door and withdrew his lock-picking utensil from his back pocket. He took another glance over his shoulder find everything still very quiet. He focused on the door and looked at the lock pick. It was a gift given to him by Andre at Slappy's. It was guaranteed to be the one burglary utensil that could open any lock that used a key.  Derek was going to put that

guarantee to the test.

He placed his hand on the knob of the apartment door and turned it to

verify that it was locked.  Surprisingly, the knob rotated without resistance.  His

eyebrows raised.  The Lieutenant was strict about securing a crime scene.

Everything had to be locked up so nothing could be disturbed until all

investigations were exhausted.  He was surprised that Austin's strict procedures

were finally compromised.

He quietly pushed the door and it opened.  He returned the lock picking

utensil to his back pocket.  He would have to test Andre's guarantee another

day.  He took another glance over his shoulder and silently made his way into

Tessa's apartment.

He stood to his normal height of six feet and slowly closed the door to the

apartment.  He could smell faint traces of Tessa's perfume.  It had assimilated

with the mustiness and the dryness that death had so proudly left behind.

His eyes scanned the room to see if anything out of the ordinary would

make itself known.  It looked like the police had went through the apartment

with a fine tooth comb.

*Well, you're the detective.* His mind relayed. *All the evidence is there in

front of you.  All you have to do is look for the obvious.*

He then saw something blink out of the corner of his eye.  He turned

towards the table by the sofa and found the answering machine light blinking.

He walked over and found that Tessa had three messages waiting.  He went to

play the messages but a noise from the bedroom startled him.  He quietly opened

the casing and removed the micro-cassette.  He stood up and slowly walked

towards the bedroom.

Inside the bedroom he found another dark clad figure searching through the

contents on Tessa's drawer.  His hunch was right!  Someone was looking for

something and had killed Tessa when she accidentally stumbled across them.

Afraid they would be caught, they left only to return when all was quiet.  It

would explain why the front door to the apartment was unlocked.

Anger escalated into adrenaline.  "Didn't find it the first time?"

The dark clad figure spun around.  Derek could see the surprise in the eyes

behind the ski mask.  Out of fear, the figure threw the lamp at the detective.

Derek dodged the lamp as it shattered up against the wall behind him.

The figure charged, catching the investigator in the mid-section and

slamming him hard against the wall.  Derek sank to the floor as the intruder tried

to run out of the room.  Derek quickly swung his leg, catching the intruder's

ankle.  The prowler fell into the living room as the detective scrambled to his

feet.

The prowler quickly rose from the floor and took a defensive pose as the detective stood in the doorway. The adrenaline flowing through his body isolated the pain and yearned for the fight.

The prowler charged and sent a high round house towards his head. He blocked and sent a back-fist into the face of the prowler. The prowler stumbled backwards not expecting the quick retaliation. However, the intruder resumed a fighting stance. Derek imitated the gesture.

The prowler charged again and sent his knee in the air. The detective positioned himself defensively expecting a front kick, but was quickly stunned by a back-fist to the jaw. He quickly ducked as the intruder swung his leg. The attack shattered a designer vase sitting on the counter near the glass patio doors. It wasn't long before they began trading combinations of kicks and punches.

The detective threw a punch and the prowler caught his arm and spun flipping the detective hard onto the carpeted floor. The intruder went for the finishing blow, but Derek defensively sent his leg up kicking the prowler in the head. He scrambled to his feet as the prowler fell backwards onto the shattered glass of the vase. The intruder suddenly grabbed his arm. The detective noticed that a shard of the broken vase had ripped through the fatigues and flesh resulting in a deep wound on their right arm.

The trespasser quickly tried to get to his feet, but Derek could not let that happen. He charged, catching the intruder in the midsection. The prowler, recognizing what Derek was trying to accomplish, used the backwards momentum and rolled onto his back, launching the private investigator into the air and through the glass patio doors.

Derek hit the stone patio with a thud as glass fell around him. He rolled across the concrete moaning as the pain and soreness echoed throughout his body. He could hear the shouts from Virginia Beach's finest quickly approaching. Realizing the trouble that was going to overtake him, he took the cassette from the answering machine and tossed it in the bushes. He would return and find it later. The tape cassette could prove to be nothing or it could have the one clue he needed to finding Tessa's murderer. Regardless, he could not let the Virginia Beach Police Department find it. They would find whatever it was on the tape irrelevant, and file it with the other unsolved cases in Virginia Beach.

He could hear sirens in the background. He had to get out of there or have the Lieutenant picking his teeth with Derek's arrest papers. His muscles ached as he struggled to get up. He clutched his rib cage as glass fell from his body and sprinkled against the concrete patio. He heard the officers getting closer. Once on his feet, he staggered a few yards and stopped cold as a nine millimeter pistol greeted him.

"Freeze!" said the cop. "I won't say it twice!"

"You got the wrong man!" Derek pleaded.

"Yeah," the cop replied. "We'll talk about it when we get back to the precinct."

Derek took in a deep breath as his physique slowly began damage control. He slowly raised his hands as another officer ran up from behind. He could hear the metallic bracelets snap into place around his wrist as his Miranda Rights recited in the background. It would not be long before Lieutenant Austin started construction on Derek's prison cell.

**Only three other people shared the holding cell where Derek sat.** Two were scantily dressed prostitutes picked up from the beach. He guessed the young blonde to be about 19. She wore a white bikini top with tight red shorts that could have doubled for a thong. Her braided companion, who was wearing a sleeveless, see-through bodice with a mini-skirt, was not much older. Derek often found himself looking away in disgust as the skirt covered as much space as a napkin on an elephant's back. They reached out through the jail bars advising the officers in the room that they were out there just having a good time, and if they were released they would be forever indebted and would repeatedly repay the favor. However, the plea fell upon deaf ears as the uniformed and plain clothes officers continued about their affairs.

The third person, who sat at the other side of the holding cell, arrived shortly after Derek did. He was a young Hispanic male that tried to elude the police in a stolen vehicle after they tried pulling him over for having a busted

taillight. The chase lasted for fifteen minutes on Shore Drive, with the souped-

up vehicle having a large lead ahead of the police. The suspect would have

surely escaped had it not ended with him side-swiping a van. The van was

transporting Navy personnel returning from a training mission. What the Navy

was doing at three in the morning evaded the police, but they were grateful that

they detained the individual until officers arrived on the scene.

Derek glanced at the young Hispanic with regret. The kid not only faced

charges from the police, but could also face charges for putting the lives of

military personnel in jeopardy. Derek shared the same hypothesis with the

police officers that arrested the misguided youth. They taunted the young

Hispanic by informing him that they believed that he side-swiped a bunch of

Navy SEALs returning from a covert mission, and was lucky that all they did

was detain him. Since that revelation, the teenager quietly sat huddled in the

corner trying to withdraw into himself.

"He what?"

Derek immediately recognized Austin's bellowing. He was still recovering

from his encounter with the dark clad figure. The headache from landing on the

concrete patio only intensified as the Lieutenant appeared from around the

corner with the key to the holding cell.

"If I had my way, your cell would be a fraction of this."

Derek rubbed the back of his neck. "Your sympathy for the misguided moves me."

"C'mon," the Lieutenant ordered. Derek could hear the frustration in Austin's voice. Derek stood; he could feel the fatigue uniting with the soreness in his muscles. He desperately wanted that hot shower and a good night's sleep. Austin grabbed him by the arm and yanked him out of the holding cell. "Your saving grace is waiting."

The prostitutes propositioned the Lieutenant as he slammed the cage door shut. He ignored their solicitations as he escorted the detective to the front lobby where Sydney, Tessa's sister, was waiting. Her black hair was ruffled and her Naval Academy sweatshirt and jeans were wrinkled. Derek could see that the weariness in her brown eyes were a carbon copy of the Lieutenant's.

"I don't like bailing people out of jail." she relayed.

"I'm surprised you were awake."

"I wasn't." she answered rubbing his eyes. "I had just went to bed five minutes before you called. I've been up all night trying to organize and distribute Tessa's case load."

"I suppose breakfast is out of the question?" Derek said with a half-hearted smile.

Sydney raised an eyebrow. Without answering the question, she turned and started for the stairs leading towards the exit of the precinct. Just as she began to take her first stair, she lost her footing. Derek quickly reached out and grabbed her arm to keep her from falling. Sydney yelped in pain as she regained her balance. Their eyes met realizing the significance of the incident. Derek released the arm that was beginning to bleed through the cotton sweatshirt. It was her right arm. They stared at each other wondering if he would divulge her secret.

"Are you okay, Ms. Taylor?" Austin asked.

"I'm fine," she replied even though her tone suggested that she was unsure. "Just fine," and she quickly turned and went down the stairs.

"Listen Chase," Austin began as the detective followed her movement. She looked up at him and nodded towards the exit. "This is your final warning. Stay out of this one. It is a police matter and we will handle it. Do I make myself clear?"

Derek turned and looked at the Lieutenant with contempt. His silence relayed his answer and with that, he followed Sydney out of the precinct. Instinctively, both men knew that they would run into each other again.

**Denny's seemed unusually crowded for five-thirty in the morning.** There was a group of college students in a corner laughing about the party they had just came from. A trio of truckers were a few seats down shoveling in their food as if they were on a time schedule. They did their best to ignore the drunken students. The Virginia Beach Sheriff's deputy that sat at the bar continued to read the morning paper keeping one eye out on his surroundings.

The detective took a sip of his ice water. His headache had became a mild sensation in the back of his head. The cold liquid felt good going down his throat. He swallowed as he watched Sydney take a bite of her scrambled eggs. She had not said a word since she posted bail at the precinct.

"How's your arm?" he asked looking at the small bloodstain of the sleeve of the sweatshirt.

"It'll be okay."

"You should have it looked at."

"Why do you care?"

Derek cocked his head to the side. "It's not every day I get to eat breakfast with somebody who's able to throw me out of a glass patio door." He quickly changed the conversation. "I'd like to know just what the hell you were doing at Tessa's apartment?"

"The same thing you were," she answered defensively. "I was looking for the person who killed my sister."

He took another sip of his ice water and sat back against the stiff leather cushion of the restaurant. She took in a deep breath and look at him. Her tone was not as defensive as she continued.

"When I was thirteen, our parents got divorced. Tessa and I promised each other that no matter what, we'd look out for each other. Eventually, our parents were able to work things out and got back together, but that promise we made to each other remained. I loved my sister dearly and I was crushed when I found out what happened. I swore I'd find out who was responsible or die trying."

"Why didn't you tell me?"

"Put yourself in my shoes. I don't know anybody. I don't know who to trust. Anybody could've have murdered my sister. She left me a message a week before she was killed. She said she was working on something big, but didn't say what it was. All she said was that it would be something that could endanger her career. When I heard about her death, I immediately flew to Virginia. I went to her office and went through her files. I happened to stumble across Griffin Securities, so I did some snooping around there, but didn't find anything; but I'm sure they're hiding something. They had too much activity going on at night. They almost caught me, but I got away. I went back to Tessa's office, but there was a guy from Griffin Securities already there going through Tessa's files. There was a scuffle and I shot him."

"Hold on a sec," Derek interrupted as he pieced together the information she was disclosing. "You were in Tessa's office and you killed the security guard."

"Yes I was, but listen to me," Sydney resumed.  Her tone was commanding and aggressive.  "I think Griffin Securities is behind my sister's death."

He nodded in agreement.  "Yeah, but what proof do you have?"

Sydney smiled.  "I worked for Naval Intelligence for five years.  I'll find proof."

Derek looked at her.  He was intrigued, but wary of her intentions.  He took another sip of his ice water and stood up from the table.  "How do I know you didn't kill Tessa, and now you're covering your tracks?"

"I know that I haven't been totally upfront, but she was my sister.  I need to know what happened to her."

He watched the fire burn in her eyes.  He did not trust her, but he would accept her story for now.  He shook his head with a smile as he withdrew his wallet.  "Seems I might need a scorecard with all the players we have.  If you want my help, it'll be easier for me if you stay out of my way.  I will find out who murdered your sister, believe that," and with that he dropped a twenty on the table and walked out of the restaurant.

<u>**Chapter Eleven**</u>:


**He looked at his watch as his eyes fluttered open**.  It was eleven o'clock in the morning.  He cursed for letting himself sleep that late.  He scanned his surroundings to find that he had slept on the sectional sofa in the living room.

He slowly sat up on the sofa as he found a note from Elizabeth on the glass coffee table beside him.  He opened the letter tainted with her perfume.  She was thankful for dinner and had a wonderful evening until the time he left to go gallivanting in the night streets, like some vigilante knight in shining armor.  In her post-script, she advised that it would take a little more than witty remarks and Chinese food before he was pardoned.

He looked at his watch.  It was five minutes after eleven.  He rubbed the back of his neck to find that his body had slightly recovered from the engagements he had the day before.  He quickly reminded himself that Tessa's funeral was today at one.  He looked out the bay window to find a gray sky.  It seemed that Mother Nature was also saddened by the upcoming event.


**Light drizzle fell from the sky like tears as family and friends gathered around Tessa's casket**.  It seemed as if it were expressing its sorrow that another good spirit would have to come home.  It was a sentiment that was shared by all present.

Derek swallowed hard, trying to remove the lump that had developed in his throat as the priest said a prayer for the departed.  He looked over at Kevin who stood beside him and saw the tear rolling down his cheek.  His wife, Heather, comforted his loss by squeezing his hand as she wiped a tear from her eye.

The detective looked past Kevin and his wife to find Saundra's black dress absorbing the light rain as she solemnly stood.  Her eyes were red from the tears she cried earlier.  Part of her make-up was smudged across her face.  She held a white orchid close to her chest as a last reminder of the person who she admired.  He could see the conviction in her eyes that she would surpass her mentor's expectations.

As the priest completed his prayer, the private investigator looked across the casket at Tessa's family.  Her father sat motionless in his wheelchair.  His black hat fit snugly around his bald head, bending the tips of his ears.  His eyes had not moved from the casket.  He tightly held his wife's hand as she wept.  She agitated the string of pearls along her neck as she quietly sobbed.  Even the black veil could not hide the continuous waterfall of tears from her eyes.  She quickly wiped them from her cheeks without disturbing the two white orchids in her hand.

Derek remembered his dinner conversation with Tessa. She had informed

him that her family had been upset with her moving to Virginia and not staying

home in Boston to tend after her father, who had been struck by a car and

confined to a wheelchair. Tessa had tried to stay in touch, but all

communication had been rejected by her parents. The only person who accepted

the long distance calls and returned the gesture of sending holiday cards was her

sister, Sydney Taylor.

He found Sydney holding a big, black umbrella above her parents.

She was staring at him. Her eyes burned with intensity; and though she did

not express it, the private investigator could sense her loss. Their eyes met once

more and Sydney directed her attention back to her family.

His gaze deviated from Tessa's family to the others in attendance. In the

far corner, stood District Attorney Taggert with Sergeant Steele and Lieutenant

Austin. They stared at the coffin remembering their encounters with Tessa

Taylor as they solemnly stood with their trench coats analogously draped over

their arms.

Taggert had worked with Tessa during the Letourneau Trial. Her

dedication to obtaining the facts and cross-reference examination helped in

securing a conviction against Nick Letourneau. Taggert envied the confidence

Tessa display during the trial and the tenacity she demonstrated in pursuing the

case. Their working relationship was a good one, but the legal red tape within the City's modus operandi stifled her ability to obtain the justice she desperately fought for.  Tessa resigned from the District Attorney's office, targeting the corporate realm as another avenue of seeking justice in the courtroom.  Their only chance for communication was when there was an exchange of information, and even so, their conversation would be a transient one.

Derek raised an eyebrow.  Taggert was there because he knew and worked with Tessa.  His entourage, Sergeant Steele and Lieutenant Austin, did not know Tessa personally.  He conjectured they were there as a courtesy to the District Attorney.   However, their solemn faces demonstrated they were indeed mourning for another legionnaire on the side of justice.

To conclude the burial services, the priest completed his prayer by waving the sign of the cross above the casket.  His white robe softly flapped as he stepped back from grave.  Tessa's mother, escorted by Sydney went over to the coffin and placed the two orchids on the casket.  Sydney imitated her mother's act, placing the orchid across the bow of the coffin.  The two of them stood for a moment in reflection of the person that meant so much in their lives.

As they retreated from the box, Derek and Kevin stepped up and rested the stem of the orchid across the dark box.  The lump in Derek's throat tightened as he stepped back.  He could hear Kevin beside him fighting back the tears.  Kevin took Tessa's sudden and tragic death hard.  From what the detective had heard, Kevin and Tessa shared everything from courtroom cases to gossipy secrets. It was a path of inseparable friendship that one person now had to walk alone.

Derek looked up to find Sergeant Steele and Lieutenant Austin escorting the District Attorney away from the grave site. He placed a hand on his friend's shoulder for whatever comfort he could offer.

"She's moved on to a better place," Kevin said. His voice was soft and broken. He cleared his throat and took in a deep breath as his wife stepped up. "It's time for me to accept that."

Derek nodded. "It's time for all of us to accept it." He looked at Heather who had wiped another tear from her cheek. She smiled at Derek's gesture and put her arm around her husband. "If you need me," he began, "let me know. Okay?"

Kevin nodded as his wife began to escort him to their vehicle at the edge of the cemetery. Derek watched them briefly, hoping that Kevin would take his earlier advice and take some time off to privately deal with his feelings.

Saundra stepped up as he turned back towards the coffin. He could see the anguish in her eyes and outstretched his arms. She accepted the gesture and hugged him tightly. He could feel her heart beating hard against his chest. Her spirit broke and she wept. He could feel his heart fall.

"I know," he said, comforting her. "I know."

She looked at him and straightened her composure. "Are you any closer to finding out who did this?" The demeanor that rivaled Tessa's was slowly returning.

Derek took in a deep breath and left his arm around her shoulder as he began to escort her to her car. It was conveniently stationed behind the Ferrari. He would attempt to sum up two days of events in one sentence. He was no closer to knowing who killed Tessa then as he was when he first started. Still, he needed to reassure Saundra that the perpetrator would be caught soon.

"I do have a few leads to follow up on," he said.

"Is there anything I can do to help?"

He nodded. He glanced over Saundra's shoulder to find Sergeant Steele making his way towards the detective as Lieutenant Austin escorted District Attorney Taggert to his limousine. The incident from the night before replayed in Derek's mind. If there was even a rumor that he was within a ten mile radius of Marina Shores, Austin would attempt to lock him up in a cell no bigger than pet carrier and throw away the key. Saundra would be able to retrieve the cassette from Tessa's answering machine without drawing suspicion from Austin's watchdogs.

He leaned closer to her ear and advised Saundra of the assignment he had for her. She agreed and advised she would return to his beach house as soon as the cassette was in her possession. She thanked him for his comfort and hurried off to complete her task. Derek placed his hands in his pockets, hoping that the police officers from last night overlooked the area around Tessa's apartment.

"Chase?"

Derek looked over his shoulder to find Sergeant Steele walking up to him. He thanked himself for taking aspirins with a glass of orange juice for breakfast rather than the usual toast and glass of water. It would help deafen Steele's voice. Derek continued to make his way to the Italian import. "Austin send you over here to reinforce his prime directive?"

"C'mon Derek," Steele responded. "You know me better than that."

"That's why I'm asking."

Steele sighed. "Look Derek," he began. "Why don't you let the police handle this one? I know you think this is personal and you want to be involved, but if you keep pokin' your nose in this, the Lieutenant is going to dedicate the rest of his police career to making your life a living hell."

Derek watched the Lieutenant open the door for the District Attorney. Austin caught his glance and flashed a stern look towards the detective as he began his way to the driver's side of the unmarked Crown Victoria. "If I don't get to him first."

"What do you mean?" Steele asked.

Derek thought back to the exchange of information between Austin and Thatcher. "I would keep closer tabs on your superior officer."

The Sergeant chuckled. "Austin, a dirty cop? Surely, you can come up with a better one than that."

"I saw him on 'The Strip' exchanging information with Michael Thatcher, the wanted man from Griffin Securities. I don't know what they were talking about, but I will find out."

"Michael Thatcher?" Steele asked. "We questioned him when that incident with Griffin Securities occurred. I remember that there was a big rush to open and close the case. In fact, the file is sitting in a dusty box in the basement because of inconclusive evidence, not to mention the fact the man is dead. You must be mistaken. Austin couldn't have met with Thatcher. It's impossible!"

"I know what I saw," Derek stated. "Tell me this. Who was the lead investigator when Griffin Securities was indicted for corporate espionage? " he inquired.

Steele looked over at Austin who had opened the door to the unmarked cruiser. "It was the Lieutenant."

He could see the sergeant contemplating the inference he made and it was the black detective's turn to chuckle. "May I suggest you dust off that box and do some investigating on your own?"

"Yeah," Steele quietly said. "I'll do that."

"Keep me posted," and Derek walked off towards the Ferrari.

He reached the door to the Italian import in ten paces.  He opened it, looking forward to going home and waiting for the meeting with Saundra and the cassette from the answering machine.  He was anxious to learn what was on the tape and hoped that a ground breaking clue would expose itself.  For now, he felt that his endeavors to find Tessa's assailant were lacking.

"Mr. Chase?"

He looked up to find Sydney Taylor standing on the other side of the Ferrari.  He looked past her shoulder to find her parents being escorted into the limousine.

"How may I help you, Ms. Taylor?"

"I want to help you find out who killed my sister."

Derek raised an eyebrow.  "Why should I let you?"

"Because it's the right thing to do," and she paused.  "And I can't do this alone."

He took in a deep breath contemplating his consequences.  "Meet me at my house in two hours.  Let's see what we've got and go from there, okay?"

"Thank you."

"Don't thank me yet, I'm still not sure if I trust you."

She nodded accepting what he had said.  "I'll see you in two hours," and she walked off to join her parents in the limousine.

He slid into the leather seat of the 355 and ignited the engine.  The car

vibrated as he closed the door and placed the throttle in first.  He lowered the

accelerator and a small cloud of dirt and gravel was swept from the ground and

into the air as the import rumbled off, thundering past the exit of the cemetery.

He was going to find her murderer using whatever resource he had available.

**Chapter Twelve**:

**"What are you hoping to find on this cassette?"**

Derek popped the answering machine cassette in the tape player. "I don't

know yet." He answered. "It could be nothing at all, but I have to explore all

avenues."

Saundra smiled in revelation. "You're no further along this case than

when you first started. Are you?"

He looked up and took in a deep breath. "No. I'm not," he admitted. "It

doesn't make any sense at all. Everything I have come across so far leads me in

a different direction."

"Well," Sydney interjected. "I know that if Tessa was here, she would say

that she didn't employ you to work cases where the solution just fell in your lap.

She'd tell you to stop your bitchin' and get your ass in gear! She pays you to be

an investigator, so investigate!"

He glanced at Saundra and then stared at Sydney. A chuckle escaped from

his lips. "Yeah, I guess she would say that." He responded as he hit the play

button on the tape player.

The machine crackled to life as it beeped. *"Hey Tess. It's Kevin. It's*

*about a quarter of seven. I just wanted to remind you that we need to get together tomorrow and review this case load that seems to be piling up. I'm leaving the office now, getting ready to go meet Taggert for dinner. That's it. See you tomorrow. Bye Tess."*

The tape clicked as it paused between messages. It beeped again and another voice filled the living room of the beach house. *"Hello Miss Taylor. This is Doctor Jared. I have the results you requested. I hope this information will help you with the paternity case that you are working on. Should you need any further assistance, please do not hesitate to call me. Thank you, and have a good day."*

Derek glanced at Saundra and then back at the tape player. "Do you know anything about a paternity case?" He asked.

She shook her head. "No." She answered. "As far as I knew, I didn't think a corporate law firm would handle a paternity case."

"They don't." Derek responded. He then lowered his eyes and thought back to the conversation he had with E earlier. "I wonder if she was trying to find out who the father of her baby was."

"What?" the ladies asked in unison.

He raised an eyebrow realizing that he asked that question out loud. He forgot that he had not told them what he had learned. "Tessa's autopsy report came back. She was pregnant."

"My sister was pregnant?"

He nodded at Sydney. "She was about two months."

The JAG officer slumped in her seat in disbelief as Saundra continued her inquiries. "Okay, but what does Tessa being pregnant have to do with her being murdered?"

"I don't know," he answered. "Probably nothing, but just in case, will you double check Tessa's files, and see if you can find anything?"

She nodded as the tape player beeped a third time. *"Hello Tessa, it's Michael Thatcher. I need to meet with you as soon as possible. It's urgent and I'd rather not discuss it over the phone. Please page me at five, two, three, fourteen, seventy-seven as soon as you get this message. Thank you."*

Saundra sat back as the tape player completed its message review by beeping three times. "He sounded like he was in trouble."

The detective nodded. "But what kind of trouble was he in? That's the million dollar question."

"Well, I guess we'll just have to ask him then, won't we?"

The phone chimed and the detective reached over the sectional sofa and yanked the portable phone from its resting place. "Hello," he answered.

She watched him as he sat silently, listening to the voice on the other end. From the dismayed expression on his face, she could see that the message being broadcasted was not a good one. He acknowledged the caller and slowly returned the receiver to the recharger stationed on the end table. He took in a deep breath as he slumped into the cushions of the sofa.

"What's the matter?" Sydney asked.

"That was Sergeant Steele," He answered. "It seems someone else had a million dollar question for Michael Thatcher. They just found him in his car sitting at the bottom of Stumpy Lake."

**The drizzle had turned into mist as the sky grew darker**. The Ferrari gradually nestled itself between a news van and a police cruiser. Stumpy Lake was an under-developed wetland that straddled Virginia Beach and Chesapeake borders, but was owned by the city of Norfolk. The 1,400 acre property, complete with golf course, had been in an eight year dispute. Virginia Beach offered to buy the wetlands from Norfolk, but the neighboring city was already under contract with a local land developer. For days, local news stations bombarded Hampton Roads with the custody battle of Stumpy Lake, but the issue soon fell wayside to other breaking news. Nevertheless, Stumpy Lake would again serve as the background for another heart-rending news bulletin.

He looked through the windshield to find the reporter standing in a spot where the camera could capture the whole grisly setting. The engine ceased as the doors swung open. Sergeant Steele walked up as he and Sydney exited the expensive sports car. Saundra had remained at the beach house to further review Tessa's case files, hoping to find another lead.

Steele continuously shook his head which gave the investigator the impression that his presence on the scene was not a desirable one. "I only called to keep you informed." he bellowed. "I didn't mean for you to come down for a sneak peak. If the Lieutenant even gets wind of you being here, he'll barbecue my badge."

Derek slapped Steele against his shoulder. "Don't worry Steele," he said as he escorted Sydney past the crime scene tape. "The Lieutenant is carnivorous. I don't think badges are to his liking."

Steele growled and gave a huff as he followed after the detective. "Speak for yourself," he replied. "You don't have one anymore."

He ignored the Sergeant's comment and tried to forget about the days he wore a uniform and the loss he felt when he had to take it off. Instead, he pressed onward towards the hi-powered tow truck. It was dragging Thatcher's Ford Taurus from the murky lake.

"What happened," Sydney asked. She was watching the City Coroner fold the yellow sheet over the wet and pale face of Michael Thatcher.

Steele lit a cigarette, took a drag and blew a white stream of smoke in the air. "The divers found him clutching a bottle of Jack Daniels. My theory is that he was drunk, accidentally knocked the car in neutral, rolled into the lake and drowned."

"That's crazy," Sydney exclaimed. "Michael never touched a drop of alcohol in his life. He had liver problems."

Derek's looked at her as she shared that bit of information. He figured she probably knew Thatcher since he and her sister went to the same college. However, his distrust was growing more and more. He tucked the information away in his mind mentally noting to question her later. His gaze then returned to the Ford as the winch pulled it onto the muddy earth.

The Sergeant took another drag off the cigarette and blew another stream of smoke in the air. "Everybody's gotta start sometime."

The detective listened to their discussion of the deceased's recent bad habit as something about the bumper of the Ford Taurus caught his eye. He walked up to the rear of the vehicle as the winch grinded to a stop. He knelt down and studied the bumper. He found the driver's side smashed in with little traces of red paint scattered across the damage. A familiar red Lexus began to play into the scenario.

"Steele."

Seeing Derek kneeling at the bumper of the Ford, and thinking of the possibility of a contaminated crime scene, the Sergeant ended his discussion with Sydney. He took one last drag from his cigarette and threw it down into the damp earth. As he quickly walked over to the detective, the smoke he exhaled made him look like an angry locomotive.

"Are you trying to give me high blood pressure?" Steele asked. "What are you doing?"

The black investigator motioned for the Sergeant to take a closer look at the bumper. "I don't think this was an accident. Take a look at this."

The Sergeant looked at the dented bumper and shrugged his shoulders. "So? It's a smashed-in bumper. There are over a thousand cars in the Hampton Roads area that have smashed-in bumpers. What's your point?"

Derek turned towards the Sergeant. "You must have failed that test at "The Academy" where you have a thirty second glance of a crime scene, and then have to describe it fifteen minutes later."

"So I took the damn test twice," Steele said defensively. "What does that matter?"

Derek chuckled within himself as he pointed towards the collapsed bumper. "See these little speckles of red paint?"

Steele nodded as the detective traced the splotches of red paint within the damaged bumper. "Yeah. So?"

Derek stood to his normal height. "I bet the title on the Ferrari that they match the paint on the red Lexus that was at my house the other night.

Somebody poured that pint of liquor down Thatcher's throat, and then pushed him and his car into the lake to make it look like an accident."

Steele returned to his normal height. "Let's say, you're right about this whole thing. Thatcher was murdered and somebody wanted to make it look like an accident. Why? Why go through all this trouble?"

The detective was about to answer until he heard someone cry for help behind him. The City Coroner had slipped on a wet piece of grass and fell, bringing the covered stretcher down with him. The body of Thatcher had slid off the stretcher and onto the damp earth. It limply rolled face up a few feet in front of Derek and Sergeant Steele. The flaccid arm had splashed into a puddle, but the muddy water failed in hiding the evidence before them. Both men could quickly view the tattoo on Thatcher's wrist. I was the same tattoo that were on the wrists of the men who tried to kill Derek the day before.

"Oh shit." Steele mumbled.

Derek glanced at the Sergeant and then back at the logo. He had the perfect answer for Steele's question. He just hoped this time the police sergeant would take him seriously.

"I would have to say it had something to do with that."

Chapter Thirteen

**The Ferrari's engine murmured as the import thundered past the GTE Amphitheater**. It appeared that a concert was on its finishing act. Even though they could hear the faint sound of drums and an electric guitar, there was a stream of cars lined up at the adjoining stop light hoping to beat the traffic. The light went red as the Ferrari rocketed past, uninhibited by such constraints.

He could feel her eyes watching him. Since leaving the crime scene, he had been silent. He replayed the events leading up to the moment of quietness. What was she hiding? He looked at her only to find her eyes staring back.

"How well did you know Thatcher?" he asked looking back at the road.

"He was a junior and I was a freshman at Boston College. We dated for about three months before we realized that we had nothing in common except that we went to the same college. We decided just to stay good friends. I introduced him to Tess and the three of us have been close ever since. I then heard he disappeared and was later pronounced dead. I was shocked to hear his voice on the answering machine. It's hard for me to imagine that he could be involved in Tessa's murder."

"I'm still trying to make sense of it myself," he mumbled. "It would have been nice to know that Thatcher was a family friend and not just another obscure piece of this jig-saw puzzle."

"I'm sorry," Sydney apologized. "I didn't realize that it was that important."

"I would expect something different coming from a hotshot JAG lawyer like yourself. How am I to trust you if you don't tell me everything you know no matter how small it may seem?"

"Again, I'm sorry. I need to remind myself that I'm not in a courtroom."

"Well," Derek began as the 355 rumbled past the courthouse. "Whatever Thatcher was involved in, I'm sure it had to do with Griffin Securities. We just need to find out what it was he needed to talk to her about. I'm sure we can do that better if you work with me."

"I'm used to working by myself. I never had a partner before."

"Then we have something in common," he stated remembering the past. "Because the last thing I want is another partner."


**Derek switched on the foyer light as he and Sydney walked into the beach house**. He smiled as he found Saundra sprawled out on the sectional sofa. Her head rested against a pillow as her hand held onto a file.

"Let me go make some tea," Sydney stated. "Why don't you get her a blanket?"

He smiled as he walked to a linen closet around the corner and pulled out a blanket. He gently covered Saundra, spreading it out evenly in case she turned in her sleep. He then took a seat in the couch. A moment later, Sydney walked out of the kitchen with a steaming hot cup of tea. She cupped it in her hands as she took a seat next to him. She gave a slight yawn. It was getting late and all of them needed their rest.

"These last couple of days," she began. "I can't remember taking a moment just to relax."

He agreed. "I thought you JAG lawyers were conditioned for long nights."

Sydney took another sip of tea. "We are, but I had more than my share of long nights before I was in JAG."

"Over-indulgence in college fraternity parties or covert operations in Navy Intelligence?"

"Both." She said with a smile. "It's difficult to keep a social life and graduate Summa Cum Laude. During ROTC, I was selected to oversee S.E.A.L. operations in the Gulf War. Spy satellite stuff and gathering intel. I can recall this one lieutenant who had the hots for me. Every so often, when he came back from a mission, we'd go to the firing range and he'd teach me a thing or two about being a sniper."

"Some guys will do anything these days," he interjected.

"Actually, I became a better sniper than he was.  Once he realized that, he never spoke to me again.  Oh well, his loss."

He chuckled quietly.  "Sounds like he got out in a nick of time if you ask me."

"Funny."

"How'd you get involved in JAG?"

"Took me awhile, but the Navy likes persistence.  I started out as a clerk filing cases during summer internships.  I became quite familiar with the Navy's way of law.  About two and a half years later, I was able to sit second chair.  Now, I serve as lead counsel."

"My commendations."

"Thank you," she said.  "But I understand you're the one with the interesting life."

"How so?"

"I did some background checks.  Your family history reads like a gritty paperback novel."

"You did a background check on me?" he said surprised.  "Resourceful aren't you?"

She took one last sip of the tea before setting the mug on the table in front of her. "I need to know who I'm working with. I can understand why my sister hired you. She knew she could rely on you."

"If that wasn't a failed attempt." he replied.

"Chase, it wasn't your fault. Tess hired you because she knew she could trust you. She knew you were black-balled by the bureaucracy of the police department. From what I read, you were a damn good cop. Good cops make great detectives. She knew that, and so should you."

He reflected on her words as she stood up and stretched. She gave a quiet yawn as not to disturb Saundra who had shifted in the couch. "Though I still disagree, thank you."

"Don't worry about it," she said as she began walking towards the front door. "Look, about tonight. I'm sorry if I wasn't forthcoming with my relationship with Michael. You can trust me."

He gave a hint of a smile. "I better," he said as he opened the door. "If you know my family history, then you know what I'm capable of."

"I know," she said as she looked at her watch. "It's getting late. I need to go home. Goodnight Mr. Chase."

He watched her walk across the cobblestone driveway and get in her car. She slowly backed out of the driveway and onto the street. He closed the door thinking about his family. He wondered if Sydney could uncover any new information regarding his mother death?  He took in a deep breath as he started for the study on the other side of the beach house.  He knew it was getting late, but his curiosity fueled his insomnia.  He would break away from Tessa's murder to ponder upon another.

Derek crossed the room quickly and once inside the study, closed the door behind him.  The screensaver on his computer displayed a life-like video of an aquarium.  The fish quickly scattered as his desktop suddenly appeared after hitting the space bar.  He sat down and his fingers quickly went to work and danced across the keyboard pulling up the internet.  The computer beeped and then went to a dial tone.

He looked above the computer at the bookshelf and reached for the family scrapbook, which his dad left behind when he moved the family to Connecticut.  He quickly flipped it open and perused the pages as his modem began dialing.  He came across a South American newspaper clipping of a woman who accidentally drove off the road killing her and her baby boy.  He took in a deep breath re-living his past.

*The wooden plane zig-zagged and swerved through the air as the front door rang.  He landed the wooden flyer on the floor beside his other toys as the maid answered the door.  He looked up and saw Uncle Slappy.*

*"Uncle Slappy!" he yelled and he left the plane running for the front door.*

*"Hey there!" Slappy said smiling. He knelt down and lifted the boy in the air and into his arms. "How's my favorite nephew doing?"*

*"Fine."*

*"Are you still practicing your karate?"*

*He nodded. "Yes sir! I'm on basic form four now."*

*"Good," Slappy responded. "Keep it up. One day you can participate in the tournaments."*

*"Not if I can help it," came a voice. "Even if I have to fight Roo myself." He looked behind him and saw his father coming out of the study. He was smoking his pipe. Compared to Slappy, his father was a much bigger man whose very essence commanded respect. "How are you doing Slappy? Are you and Reggie enjoying your vacation at my expense?"*

*"I wish it were under better circumstances," Slappy responded. His tone was more serious than earlier. He lowered Derek to the ground and smacked his rear. "Derek, why don't you go into the kitchen and let me have a few moments alone with your father."*

*"Yes sir," and with that Derek scurried away into the kitchen. He quickly stopped and peered around the corner.*

*"What's going on Slappy?"*

*Slappy took in a deep breath and lowered his head. "Tom, we heard some talk in the town about Kara. I'm afraid there's been an accident."*

*His father's knees almost gave way upon hearing those words. He stumbled towards the door frame. He clutched his heart. "Oh my God."*

*"Her car went over a cliff; the local police are still going through the wreckage. They need you to identify the body."*

*"Where's Reggie?"*

*"He's there now, making sure the locals are not fucking things up. They think it may be retaliation to her father's decision to put you in charge of the company."*

*"What about the baby?"*

*Slappy shook his head.*

*Derek stood out from the door frame and cocked his head to the side. It looked like his father was crying. He had never seen his father cry. "Daddy?" he asked. "Why are you crying?"*

*His father turned to find his son in the door frame. He took in a deep breath and went over to his son and knelt down. "Your father is very sad."*

*"Is it because of mommy?"*

*His father nodded. "Mommy is taking a little trip right now."*

*"Is she coming back?"*

*His father shook his head. He could sense the pain his father was going through and it scared him. "Not now, but one day, we'll see her again. I promise."*

*"Tom," Slappy started. "We gotta go."*

*His father looked over at Slappy with a solemn face. He took in a deep breath and swallowed as he looked back at his son. He hugged his little boy as tears rolled down his eyes. "I need you to be strong for your sisters. It's up to you and me from now on. Do you understand me?"*

*Derek nodded.*

*His father forced a smile. "Good boy, now go play and I'll be home soon."*

*"Yes sir."*

He could feel a tear welling up in his eye as his heart continued to sink deeper in the pit of his stomach. No matter how many times he read the article, it still brought up that memory. It was the only time he saw a moment of frailty from his father. His father was a powerful man and since his wife's death, he commanded it. He also had a feeling of loss and revenge. How he wished to share one last moment with his mother. There were so many things he would tell her, but most importantly, how much he loved her.

Regaining his composure he turned the page to the next article, stating how his father was a suspect for the murder of his mother and his grandfather. He knew his father was innocent. For him, his mother's death was still a mystery. Somehow, she lost control of her car and went over a cliff. The police department for the small town of San Pulerio ruled that the accident was due to poor weather conditions. Though it rained that night, it was hard for Derek and his family to believe, because his mother's wreckage was found that afternoon; and he remembered the day as being warm and clear.

He believed that somehow, someone convinced the police not to pursue the issue any further than they did. Through some investigation of his own, he discovered that the police report was incomplete; there was no mention of a second set of tire tracks and broken glass, possibly from a tail-light, a few hundred yards away from where his mother's car went off the cliff. There were rumors that the local elders were upset with his grandfather, Enrique Denteveron, and took revenge by killing the one thing he cherished more than anything else, his daughter.

Enrique Denteveron, after many years of single-handedly making San Pulerio one of the richest provinces in Columbia, decided it was time to step down. The local elders, who were the board of trustees, had already chosen a replacement, a local returning from Europe by the name of Diego Tosillio. Enrique went against the elders' wishes and elected the one man who was a key factor in making San Pulerio a respected province, Thomas Washington, an outsider.

Washington was the driving factor in enforcing what Enrique wanted. Through working with Enrique, he met and fell in love with his daughter Kara. They became husband and wife and soon began having children. Enrique could not be more delighted. He was getting old and would hope that the family name or at least the blood line would continue. When Enrique fell ill to a South American virus, it left him in a wheelchair and forced him to step back from the day to day decisions of his company. He relied on his son-in-law to rule.

Thomas did everything he could to keep the company afloat, but because of some bad investments by the local elders, he was forced in an alliance with their neighboring competitor. The board of trustees were infuriated. However, Enrique understood and forgave his son-in-law. He knew that Thomas was doing what was best for the Denteveron family and San Pulerio. Thomas was the one thing keeping San Pulerio alive. He was the perfect candidate to take his place at the head of the company table.

Following Kara's accident, there were rumors that the local elders were lashing out at Enrique and were trying to eliminate his successor, but murdered his daughter instead. Thomas confronted the local elders and they decreed throughout San Pulerio that the Denteveron name would be spared from any further recourse. They also asked that Thomas step down from his position and let Diego take over. Thomas proposed a compromise. Those with the Denteveron name would be respected as a pillar of the community, but he would not step down. The board of trustees refused the proposal. The denial prompted Derek's father to respond with a challenge to the elders advising them that if anybody was willing, they could try and remove him.

After that gauntlet, Thomas quickly sent his children with his American maid, Maria Chase, back to the United States. Knowing what was at stake, Maria promptly changed the children's last name to Chase in hopes that it would keep them safe. In retaliation to the trustee's denial, Thomas moved the company's headquarters from San Pulerio to a small, suburban Connecticut community in North America. This incensed the local elders and they vowed that one day, there would be consequences. Considering the loss of his beloved, Derek's father relished the idea.

His mind replaced thoughts of his family history to speculate about what his father would do if they had came after him and his family. He knew his father was in Viet Nam with Special Forces. Slappy often talked about his father being the biggest and baddest sonovabitch to ever carry an M-16 and how his unit was always called on to do the task no one else wanted. Could one of those missions have something to do with his mother's death? He snickered; it seemed everybody knew something about his father and his mother's death besides himself. There were two parties who had clues to solving his puzzle. The first being the party that murdered his mother and baby brother, and he was not on good speaking terms with the other. He made a mental note to bounce his speculations off Slappy. The barbershop owner was the one who had to tell his father about his mother's accident.

He also became concerned. How did Janocky know about his family and his mother's death? What information did he have? Janocky's list of employees was extensive and could include personnel from the military and all branches of law enforcement from around the world. There was no telling what scenarios could play out if his suspicions about Janocky were true. Derek had to prepare for anything.

He hit the button to the speakerphone next to the computer and dialed. The phone rang three times before a faint, groggy voice picked up. "Hello?"

"How's my little sister?"

The was a long pause before she answered. "Sleeping soundly until her brother decided to wake her up. Do you know what time it is Derek? What's wrong?"

He smiled. "I'm sorry to wake you Crystal, but I need your help. I think the family is in trouble."

He could hear her trying to wake up. "Wha-? What do you mean the family is in trouble?"

"I don't know how to explain this, but I think there may be more to our mother's death than what dad is letting on."

This time he heard the exasperation in her voice. "You called me at one in the morning to tell me something you've been telling me for years. Derek, go to bed."

"Crystal," he urged. "I'm being serious. Something is wrong, I can feel it. There's too much out there for nobody to know nothing. Just keep your eyes open for anything, no matter how insignificant it may seem. Do it for me okay?"

She sighed. "Why me?"

"Allyson told me what you were up to."

"Shit!" She exclaimed. "So you know?"

"Yes and I don't approve, but it's your life, and I'm not going to interfere."

"Thank you. I appreciate that."

"Just do this for me. You're privy to things I'm not, and if shit does hit the fan, dad will have somebody there that he can count on."

There was a moment of silence on the other end. "Okay. I'll hold down the fort and let you know if anything out of the ordinary happens. Just take care of yourself down there. I've already lost one brother; I don't need to lose another."

"I don't wanna lose me either," he said with a smile. "Thanks for taking care of things. Now go back to sleep."

"Don't mention it. Love you D."

"Love you too Crystal. Goodnight," and he disconnected the call. His mind was at ease. Crystal had a good head on her shoulders and her position would allow ample access to all family events and functions, particularly ones pertaining to their father.  However, something in the back of his mind was

screaming at him.  There was something terribly out of place, and until he knew

what it was, there would be many sleepless nights.

<u>**Chapter Fourteen**</u>:


**He took another bite of his bagel as he read the morning paper**. He gave a glance at Saundra who was slowly walking through the doorway. He watched her yawn before going back to the paper.

"Sleep well last night?" he asked, taking a sip of orange juice.

"Yes, I did," she answered as she took a seat at the island bar in the middle of the kitchen. He poured her a glass of orange juice and offered her a bagel. "I didn't expect that couch to be that comfortable."

"Nobody does," he replied. "When Sydney and I got back we didn't have the heart to wake you. Plus, you've been really pushing yourself since this whole thing started." He took a sip of his orange juice. "Did you find anything out about Tessa's paternity case?"

"No," she answered as she began spreading cream cheese over her bagel. "I'm going to call Dr. Jared's office later today."

"Good. Let me know what you find out."

She took a bite of the bagel and a sip of her orange juice before asking her next question. "Did the police have any speculation as to what happened to Michael Thatcher?"

He gave her a slight smile. "No, they're in denial, but I think it definitely has something to do with Griffin Securities. Just need to figure out what."

She quickly gulped another swallow of her juice. "Funny, you should mention Griffin Securities. After I couldn't find anything on the paternity case, I started thinking about Michael Thatcher and his involvement in this whole thing. I think I may have found something that would interest you."

"And what might that be?"

"Well, remember when Thatcher stole the blueprints for that new computer system created by Premiere Tech? We believed he sold the blue prints to Valkyrie Industries because they came out with a program shortly thereafter, correct?"

"That seems to be the theory."

"I called one of my computer savvy friends at Wesleyan and asked him to do a background check on Valkyrie Industries. The company is a subsidiary company for Janocky Incorporated." She divulged as he raised an eyebrow. "Not only that, but Valkyries Industries also provides the security software for Griffin Securities."

"That means Janocky used his security firm to steal software from Premiere Tech and let his subsidiary company profit from producing a program similar to the one that was stolen."

"And he used the insurance money to settle out of court with Premiere Tech," Saundra concluded after taking a sip of her orange juice. "Because the profits generated from Valkyrie Industries would replace that within a few weeks after the software hit the market."

He smiled at her deductive reasoning. "You're getting pretty good at this private eye thing."

"Thank you, but I'm sure the police must have figured this out too. I'm surprised they didn't pursue the issue any further than what they did."

"Not if the lead investigator was a dirty cop," Derek interjected. "Remember, Michael Thatcher was a cop before he went to Griffin Securities. It wouldn't be hard for Griffin Securities to have the police department in their back pocket."

"So how do we prove our case?"

"We need to find that video from Premiere Tech. If it was just a video of Thatcher stealing the blueprints, it would have never disappeared. I'm willing to bet there's more evidence on that video than we've been led to believe."

"But the police lost the video when it was checked into evidence, where could it have possibly gone?"

"Good question. Let me rattle a few cages and see what falls out."

"What are you planning to do?"

"Play a little poker with Janocky and hope he calls my bluff."

**Janocky's fingers tapped against his desk as he sat back in his leather chair**. He was finding the conversation with the black detective to be stimulating. As an occasional gesture of unconcern, he would glance at his watch.

"Really Mr. Chase," Janocky interjected. His tone was very calm and deliberate. "First, you insinuated that I had something to do with Ms. Taylor's unfortunate parting, and now you are inferring that I may have been involved in corporate espionage? Stop me if I am wrong, but does that not sound far-fetched?"

"Actually, I don't believe it's uncharacteristic for a business person of your stature to prefer a hostile takeover rather than a corporate merger, but that's just my opinion." Derek responded.

"Again, you insult me, Mr. Chase," Janocky replied standing up. He walked over to the window overlooking the shipyard and the conglomerate of smaller office buildings of Waterside. "The truth is, Valkyrie Industries was already in the final stages of preparing its software. It wasn't until we swayed Howard Ibelle, one of the developers from Premiere Tech, to work for us that we were finally able to present it to the public. Unfortunately, he passed away a short time after the product was released. But let me ask you; why steal the software when you have the genius that created it?  If there was any corporate espionage, it was from Premiere Tech shooting themselves in the foot."

Derek raised his eyebrows as he stood up from his chair.  "So, you have no reason to believe that Michael Thatcher was murdered?"

Janocky turned from the office window.  His look was serious.  "Michael Thatcher was murdered?  I heard he had too much to drink and accidentally drove his car into a lake."

The detective studied the business man.  "I forgot how deep your connections are with the local police.  You probably know more about Thatcher's death than the homicide detectives."  Something was tugging at him and telling him that there was more about Thomas Janocky III than met the eye.  "Be that as it may, I'm still not convinced of Thatcher's sudden alcoholism.  I just hope that when I view the video tape, I'll find something to prove that it was murder. "

Janocky's eyebrows went up.  "You found the video tape?  The one the police lost?"

"Yes," Derek answered.  "I'm on my way to pick it up now.  I just hope there's nothing on it that would further incriminate Griffin Securities."

Janocky seemed miffed when he responded to the detectives comment.  "I assure you, Mr. Thatcher acted alone."

Derek chuckled as he shook his finger at the business man. "You know, there's something about you that just doesn't fit. I can't put my finger on it, but I'm sure you are as dirty as a fifth ace in a poker game."

"Whether you like me, or hate me," Janocky started as he walked over to his desk. He picked up the phone and pressed a button on the keypad. He then hung up and smiled. His white teeth resembled fangs of a shark. "You have nothing to tie me or Griffin Securities in with any of this."

"Not yet," Derek answered. "But I will."

The door opened up behind him and the detective glanced over his shoulder to find Nick Letourneau walking into the office. Behind him was another burly man.

"Mr. Letourneau," Janocky said. "Would you and Mr. Bosworth please escort Mr. Chase out of the building?"

"Rookie," Nick sighed as he and Mr. Bosworth walked up on either side of the detective. "I thought we had this conversation already. I see we're gonna have to do this the hard way."

Nick, who was on Derek's left, reached for the detective's arm. Seeing his opportunity, the investigator quickly sent his right elbow up catching Mr. Bosworth's nose. The burly man quickly fell to the floor clasping his nose in pain. Nick quickly grabbed the detective's arm hoping to restrain the investigator, but Derek quickly reversed the hold, and with all the force he could muster, slammed the former cop's face hard against Janocky's desk. Letourneau slowly sank to the floor unmoving.

Derek straightened his jacket as he looked down at his convoy. He then looked at Janocky with a devilish smile. "Thank you, but I'm sure I can find my way out. Good day Mr. Janocky."


**The Ferrari idled softly as it rumbled down Interstate 264 towards the beach**. At one o'clock in the afternoon, traffic did not seem as heavy as it was earlier that morning when he traveled to Waterside.

Derek took in a deep breath of the bold, sweet scented interior of the Ferrari. He found himself asking more questions. First, if Janocky did have the man that created Premiere Tech's software, why have Thatcher steal it? And besides being classmates at college, what was Thatcher's current connection with Lieutenant Austin? They were working together on something; he just had to find out what.

He reached for the cellular phone resting in between the leather seats of the Italian import. He dialed the police precinct, hoping that Elizabeth would stay true to her daily routine of sitting at her desk and processing paperwork during her lunch break.

Her voice was like soft music when she answered the phone.  With his sincerest voice, he greeted her with an apology for leaving her in the middle of the night.

He could hear the humpf on the other line and smiled.  She was not as upset as he thought she would be.  She relayed that she understood why he had to leave and justified it because she knew that his investigation was also a personal one.

He glanced into the rearview mirror as he changed lanes.  A red vehicle shifted lanes with him.  He ignored it as he relayed to Elizabeth his plan to sneak into the Lieutenant's office and search through his files regarding Michael Thatcher and the Premiere Tech investigation.

She laughed at his intentions.  She advised that if the Lieutenant caught him, he would not have to worry about his investigation, but would instead be planning his escape from a maximum security prison located in the far icy regions of the South Pole.  She also advised that if the Lieutenant discovered that she aided Derek in his quest, she would be assigned to traffic duty for so long, that her children's grand-children would be born blowing traffic whistles.

The red vehicle closed in on the Ferrari as Derek checked his rear-view mirror.  Realizing that there was not enough space to pass, it drifted back behind a large sport utility vehicle following closely behind the Ferrari.

He concluded his conversation with Elizabeth by explaining to her that no matter how hard the Lieutenant tried, Derek would always remain a thorn in his side. He advised that he would be at the precinct soon, but first, he had to play a game of tag.

Derek placed the cellular phone back into its resting place and took another look in the rear-view mirror. The red vehicle had slithered into another lane and was gaining on the foreign sports car. He then recognized the car as the customized Lexus. Janocky called his bluff.

He downshifted the throttle of the Ferrari and changed lanes. The RPM's screamed as he slammed his foot against the accelerator. The Ferrari leaped forward with a sudden rush of speed pushing his body into the leather seat. He checked the mirror again to find the Lexus had taken pursuit.

He up-shifted as the Ferrari jumped ahead of the Lexus. He noticed the speedometer was quickly climbing to a hundred. He quickly glanced in the rear view mirror to find the Lexus slowly gaining on him. He jerked the wheel and changed lanes, nearly clipping the front bumper of a Corvette. He then changed lanes again and rocketed towards the Independence Boulevard South off-ramp. He figured his chances of turning the tables would be better in the traffic of downtown Virginia Beach. He checked the rear view again to find it almost impossible for the Lexus to duplicate his actions.

However, the driver of the Lexus attempted to imitate the Ferrari's maneuver, but had overshot the exit. The Lexus screeched to a halt and quickly went into reverse from the lane it was in and started for the exit ramp. Derek could faintly hear the screeching of tires coming to a halt, and the sudden crunching of metal and glass coming together. He looked in the rear view mirror to find the Lexus had avoided any collision and was now moving forward, quickly barreling down the exit ramp after him.

Derek downshifted and slowed near the end of the exit ramp. The Lexus was almost upon him. The Ferrari bounced into the heavy oncoming traffic of Independence Boulevard and he suddenly yanked the steering wheel to the left into the approaching vehicles. The Italian import spun in a circle. He could see the onslaught of different automobiles quickly coming to a halt to avoid a collision. His drastic maneuver put the Lexus in a position where it zoomed by the black sports car, and became the target of Italian engineering.

*Tag! You're it.* He thought as the car came to a standstill from the 360.

He shifted the throttle into first and the engine howled. The tires of the Ferrari clawed for traction, kicking loose pieces of gravel into the air. He could faintly hear the other driver's swearing, outraged at the sudden interruption of normal everyday traffic. They displayed their dismay with the simultaneous blaring of horns as the Ferrari thundered off after the Lexus.

The red Lexus quickly threaded its way through traffic as the Ferrari closed in. It was desperate to escape. Unsuspecting vehicles would suddenly slam on the brakes as the luxury sports car squeezed in front them. Derek imitated the maneuvers with less difficulty. It had taken a moment for the vehicles that came to an abrupt stop, to re-commence their forward momentum.

The Lexus shot forward as it entered an open lane. The black Italian import quickly followed after it, as would a mongoose after a king cobra. Never were there two adversaries that relied on speed and power, as well as cunning and initiative. It was a game of mental and physical chess in which both opponents were equals.

However, the same would not hold true for the Ferrari and the Lexus. Even with the obtrusive traffic on Independence Boulevard, the Ferrari was steadily gaining ground on the red luxury sports car. It was of no consequence as to why the manufacturer won so many racing championships.

Derek, once again, kept the integrity of Ferrari's accomplishments as the sports car eased its way into a blind spot on the driver's side of the Lexus. He tried to get a glimpse of the driver, but the tinted windows of the Lexus denied him.

His foot pressed the accelerator deeper into the plush carpeting of the floorboard. The speedometer of the Ferrari was nearing a hundred miles per hour. The Ferrari edged its way in front of the Lexus as both cars neared the busy intersection of Lynnhaven Parkway which connected the quiet rural areas of Virginia Beach with the highly popular and continuously expanding shopping district of Lynnhaven Mall and the growing prosperity of corporate Virginia Beach. His heart had raced before, but now it was slamming hard against his chest, realizing the imminent danger he was in. One mistake or unseen obstacle could cost him his life.

The Ferrari jilted towards the Lexus in an attempt to cut the fleeing vehicle off. The tires of the luxury sports car squealed as it turned and bounced onto a neighborhood street. The detective bounced slightly in his seat as the Ferrari skidded to a halt as it overshot the side road. A small white cloud emitted from the pavement as the Ferrari backed up. He could smell smoke from the clutch as he jammed the throttle in first. The Ferrari would need a day of babying at the dealership after the workout Derek was putting it through.

He could see the Lexus rumble down the quiet neighborhood street as he started after it. He threw the car into third as the Ferrari violated the posted residential speed limit by going thirty miles faster. If he could catch the driver of the Lexus, he would gladly pay for any speeding ticket given to him.

He thundered through the residential area noticing the yellow diamond shape sign. The path the Lexus had chosen was a dead end. His devilish smile went across his face as he snickered. This game of tag would soon be over; his adversary had made a costly mistake.

He then saw a garbage truck slowly grumble into the intersection in front of the Lexus. It quickly winced and loudly sighed as it came to an abrupt halt. The Lexus hastily swerved around the front of the hulking city vehicle and avoided being side-swiped.

The garbage truck resumed its course and Derek stomped on the brakes. The Ferrari's back-end slightly fish-tailed as it came to a stop. Derek yelled obscenities as he peppered the driver with the annoying yelping of the Italian-made horn. Surprised at the second appearance of another vehicle, the garbage truck again came to a halt with a wince and a sigh. Again, the detective loudly voiced his frustration, but his efforts to expedite the mammoth steel frame from the intersection were in vain, and made him the recipient of an obscene hand gesture.

Derek withdrew his weapon from his shoulder holster and pointed it at the driver. He informed the city employee to move the garbage truck or be buried inside it. Out of fear, the operator changed gears and the garbage truck lurched forward. The Ferrari clawed for traction and went around the rear of the city maintenance vehicle in pursuit of the red luxury sports car.

He found it two blocks later, parked behind a Datsun sitting on cement blocks. The Ferrari skidded to a halt behind the Lexus. The detective quickly exited the sports car with his weapon withdrawn and aimed at the Lexus. He quickly glanced at the surrounding neighborhood looking to see if someone was fleeing from the vehicle.  He saw nothing of the sort.  His only distraction were the birds chirping in the neighborhood trees.

The gun was poised for any surprises as his heart raced.  He swung the driver's door of the Lexus open and waved the gun inside.  It was empty.  He quickly stepped back and with his weapon raised, slowly moved in a circle scanning the neighborhood again to find it undisturbed.  He lowered his weapon and kicked the door the Lexus.  It slammed shut as he cursed to himself.  His obscure quarry had escaped once again.

Chapter Fifteen

**"The Lexus you chased is the same Lexus that was seized in the drug raid Titus was telling you about.  They're dusting it now for prints."**

The detective lowered his head and continued to push the standard issue sanitation cart along the corridor as a uniformed police officer walked by.  His disguise as a janitor, with the dusty grey overalls and cap had most personnel in the precinct fooled.  "Did Lieutenant Austin sign the requisition form?"

Elizabeth nodded and handed him a copy of the form.  He glanced at it and stuffed it inside his overalls.  "You're not really serious about the Lieutenant as a suspect in Tessa's murder?"

"Dead serious," he answered.  "I think it may have something to do with the Premiere Tech investigation.  I mean, after all, the man went to college with Tessa Taylor and Michael Thatcher.  Not to mention Thatcher, who was presumed to be dead, is seen at the oceanfront exchanging information with the Lieutenant.  I don't know how everything fits together, but I'm sure I will be a few steps closer once I have a look through the Lieutenant's files."

Elizabeth looked at her watch.  "Well, you have less than ten minutes before the Lieutenant returns from lunch.  He's been here all morning and afternoon bitchin' about Ms. Taylor's murder.  He feels we're not doing enough

to find the parties responsible."

"He's been here all morning and afternoon?  You sure?"

Elizabeth nodded.  "Yep.  He's in such a bad mood that I hate the thought

of him catching you looking through his files."

"He'll never catch me."

"I'm sure you were thinking that when you were arrested for violating a

crime scene."

He glared at Elizabeth with a sheepish smile.  "You found out about that,

huh?"

Elizabeth smiled.  "I saw the report."

"That was different," he defended.  "I was distracted by a surprise mystery

guest.  Threw off my entire game plan."

"Well, I hope this game plan fares much better than the last."

"With this disguise?  I'll be in and out before they even know it."

Elizabeth raised a curious eyebrow.  "Where did you get that anyway?"

Derek smiled.  "Joe in Facilities Management loaned it to me.  It comes in

handy from time to time.  It especially works in office buildings and police

departments."

Elizabeth took in a deep breath as they reached the door to the Lieutenant's office. "You're on your own from this point on. I'll meet you downstairs in fifteen minutes and I'll have the results from Forensics regarding the Lexus."

Derek withdrew the maintenance keys from the belt clip and unlocked the Lieutenant's door. "Thanks E," he said as he opened the office door. Elizabeth nodded and walked off. Derek took another glance over his shoulder. Concluding that no one was observing his actions, he stepped in the office pulling the maintenance cart in behind him. He then closed the door and locked it.

The Lieutenant's office was decorated with pictures from his days as a Major in the United States Army's Military Police during the Vietnam War. Next to those pictures were commendations and awards for bravery. There were also medals and awards from the City of Virginia Beach distinguishing his efficiency as a police officer.

Derek maneuvered behind the Lieutenant's desk. Three pictures of his wife and children outlined the edges of the desk, along with the engraved name plate and designer pen and pencil set. His desk calendar was a day behind and there were scattered memos and files strewn about.

He quickly scanned through the files, finding nothing more than other officer's caseloads waiting for the proper authorization before they could be filed or further pursued. The scattered messages were follow-up calls from judges, suspects and witnesses.  Nothing he could use as a key to unlocking the case he was working on.

He looked up realizing that the Lieutenant's office was much smaller than he had imagined.  Compared to Tessa's office that could overlook the Virginia Beach coastline on a good clear day, the Lieutenant's office was like a foxhole in a war.  He could easily secure and defend his position, away from the everyday chaos that plagued his precinct.

The detective looked at his watch.  He had to hurry, his luck with the Lieutenant had not been good thus far; and he too was trying not to imagine what Austin would do to him if he was caught snooping around the Lieutenant's files.

Three file cabinets sat across the room between a fake office tree and a wall with a window overlooking the parking lot.  He quickly went over to find the metallic drawers locked.  He withdrew the gift given to him by the barbers of Buzz Cutts.  It was a lock-picking utensil.  It was guaranteed to open any lock.  He applied it to the jagged hole.  With a quick and quiet click, the metal drawer lock popped out and allowed him to open the file cabinet.

*I am going to thank those guys the next time I see them.*

It took him a minute to quickly peruse the files.  His heart was beginning to beat hard across his chest.  The files in the first cabinet was merely cases the

Lieutenant had worked previously.  He closed the file cabinet and quickly picked the lock to the second set of metallic drawers.

He scanned through the files and something caught his eye.  In the midst of the manila folders was a thick red file.  He was sure it was the red file he saw Thatcher give Austin.  It was labeled Griffin Securities.  He withdrew the large folder held intact by a rubber band.

The police officer, now turned detective, opened the file to find pictures of Letourneau and Janocky.  There were reports and legal documents from Premiere Tech as well as Valkyrie Industries.  Nestled between the reports was a document by Austin comparing information.  He rummaged throughout the file and found a listing of names of former military and police personnel, none of which were familiar to him.  He saw pictures of Nick Letourneau and the media clippings of the case that put him behind bars.  He found a note from Tessa advising that she would meet Austin and Thatcher at a restaurant for lunch.  It was scheduled for the day after she was murdered.  With the evidence Austin had gathered, Derek knew they were meeting to discuss Griffin Securities, but was it a set-up?  Was Tessa getting too close?  Or was it something else?  He thought back to what Janocky had said about having the creator of the software under his employ at Valkyrie Industries and the document Austin had comparing the software between the two companies.  Maybe he was wrong and the three of them were working to build a case against Griffin Securities.  Maybe the proof was on the video cassette that mysteriously disappeared from police evidence. It would certainly explain why he was being followed by the Lexus and Janocky's surprised reaction when he mentioned it. He gave a short sigh giving in to his dilemma. The possibility that Austin killed his college classmate had crossed Derek's mind. Austin did sign the requisition for the red Lexus and could have pushed Thatcher's car into Stumpy Lake. His reasoning could have been to eliminate the possibility of Thatcher trying to double-cross him. But, he had to re-think that because of Elizabeth's observation. If Austin was at the precinct all morning and afternoon, who was driving the Lexus?

He returned the red file to its resting place and closed the drawer to the cabinet. He glanced at his watch hoping the Lieutenant's lunch was later than normal. He grabbed the sanitation cart and quietly opened the door to the Lieutenant's office. Seeing the corridor empty, he quickly made his way out and locked the office door. He then began to push the cart down the hallway.

The detective quickly maneuvered the maintenance cart around the corner and without warning, it slammed hard into the Lieutenant. Surprised, the Lieutenant staggered backwards trying to regain his balance. He looked like he had been body-checked by a hockey player.

The detective's heart jumped into his throat. He looked downwards toward the cart as the Lieutenant regained his balance and his composure. "So sorry, sir!" he stuttered in the deepest voice he could muster, hoping the Lieutenant would not recognize him.

"How many times do I have to tell you people, to watch where the Hell you're going?" Austin yelled. "One of these days, somebody is going to take a gun and shoot one of you guys in the ass!"

"So sorry sir," replied the disguised detective. "It won't happen again!"

"It better not or I'll make sure the next maintenance job you have will be following the officers on horseback and scooping the horse shit they leave behind! Do you understand?"

Derek nodded and hurried on before the Lieutenant could muster another statement. He smiled realizing that if Lieutenant Austin discovered who he really was; scooping horse shit would be a relatively mild punishment.

**Elizabeth looked on as Derek shook Joe's hand in appreciation for letting him use the facilities uniform.** They chuckled as the detective relayed Austin's threat towards the maintenance employees. Joe smiled, responding that if Austin was not too careful, he might one day be sitting on a "kamikaze commode". Their laughter soon turned mischievous as they went their separate ways.

"Do you like causing mischief?" Elizabeth asked.

"Only when others can benefit by it." Derek responded. "Did they find anything on the Lexus?"

Elizabeth shook her head. "The bumper was recently repainted. They did some test and found traces grey paint."

"Well, that proves one theory." Derek retorted.

"Other than that," the police officer continued. "They came up empty. No fibers, no finger prints, nothing. Whoever was driving wants to remain anonymous. Did you find anything in the Lieutenant's office?"

"A few things, but now I'm asking more questions than what I have answers to."

"Well, I'll have them go through the car again. Maybe, we missed something the first time around."

"Thanks E. I owe you one."

She smiled devilishly. "You owe me more than you think. Now get outta here before you run into the Lieutenant again. It is not a wise career move to tempt fate twice."

He kissed her on the cheek and walked off towards the Ferrari a few feet away. She watched him get inside and heard the 355's engine come to life. The tires squealed as the sleek, black beast maneuvered its way out of the police garage. It bounced out of the driveway and sharply turned the corner into the busy Virginia Beach streets.  She hoped that its owner was one step closer to

unraveling the mystery that consumed his very essence.

Chapter Sixteen

**The shooting range seemed like good way to relieve the stress of day to day life**. At least it was for Sydney Taylor. She was flat on her stomach poised for a shot. He could see the intensity as she peered through the scope and aimed the rifle at its target a few hundred yards away. Derek removed his sunglasses as he stepped within a few feet of her.

A slight breeze caressed the area occasionally blowing small pieces of paper along the field. To keep her hair out of her face, she had weaved her hair into a ponytail and threaded it through her baseball cap. Despite the breeze ruffling the material of her slightly-baggy blue and white jumpsuit, her body was rigid. Suddenly, it jerked slightly as she fired a shot. She released the empty shell with the bolt, locked it back into place and fired again. She quickly repeated the process three more times. He could see the satisfaction on her face as she looked through the scope to evaluate her performance.

"Shooter, Sydney Taylor," came the loud speaker. "Round two score, forty-eight points."

Shortly thereafter, another shooter a few yards away began firing as Derek walked up and knelt down beside her. He watched her reload the rifle. "You weren't joking when you said you dated a sniper?"

She looked up and smiled.

He chuckled. "Remind me not to get on your bad side."

She readjusted the yellow safety glasses as she continued to reload the weapon. "Any new leads?" She asked as she cocked the bolt in place.

"Maybe," he answered. "How well do you know Terry Austin?"

"Lieutenant Terry Austin? I know that he went to college with my sister and Michael Thatcher. Why?"

"I'm not sure yet. I know he's involved, but can't exactly figure out how. I do know that there's an important video cassette out there that someone is willing to kill for. I'm hoping once I find that, I might be able to make some sense of this case."

Sydney looked up at him as the loud speaker broadcasted the score of the second shooter. It was the same score as Sydney's. A third shooter tried his luck firing at the target. "Any ideas where we need to start looking for that video cassette?"

"I looked at one possible place already and it wasn't there, not sure where else it could be?"

"Well, it was stolen from police evidence, right?"

"Yes, but I remember reading in the paper that they searched every nook and cranny of that precinct, as well as interrogated everybody in it. Vanished like it was never there."

"What if it was never turned in to police evidence?"

"Then that would mean my prime suspect would be the arresting officer, which was Austin, but I've worked with Austin too long. If it's something as important as proving his friend's innocence, he would've kept it in his office, figuring nobody would be bold enough to break into a police station."

"Well, I guess we're gonna have to surprise him."

"Already beat you to it. Remember that one possible place I was talking about?"

Sydney refocused her sights on the target and looked through the scope. "Well, if Austin doesn't have it, what about Michael? He used to be a cop, maybe he was able to talk his way into evidence and get it himself?"

"It's possible. But if Thatcher was innocent, why not give the tape to Austin or Tessa, since she was the prosecuting attorney? And if he was guilty, where would he have put it? He would've known once Austin discovered the tape was missing, he'd be waiting at Thatcher's front door with a search warrant. He would have to put it where nobody would think about looking for it. And the only place I can think of is Griffin Securities. Leaving the tape at home would be too easy to find, and there was no way he was going back to PremiereTech. As an employee of Griffin Securities, he had full access to the entire facility; he could have hidden it anywhere."

"He could have been innocent and using the tape to blackmail Janocky?"

"It's possible, but he could've also given it to Janocky," he stated. He then pondered the thought, "But after my conversation with Janocky, I don't think he gave him the tape. Janocky seemed surprised to find out that I was on my way to pick it up. In fact, I'm sure he was the one who had me followed this afternoon."

"Maybe he does have it," Sydney stated. "And now he's under the impression that there's a copy."

Derek raised an eyebrow. "That also make sense. In either case, it means I'm going back to Griffin Securities for a little scavenger hunt."

"You mean, we're going back?" Sydney corrected as the loud speaker crackled to life. It announced the score of the third shooter which was a point higher than Sydney and his other competitor.

"I work better alone."

"You don't have a choice in the matter," she said as her body tensed. "I want the truth behind my sister's murder and besides, you need me."

"How so?"

She quickly discharged her rounds, quickly working the bolt like a well-maintained machine. Derek returned to his full height realizing how proficient she was. The loud speaker came to life not only to compliment her proficiency but her accuracy as well.

"Shooter, Sydney Taylor. Round three. Perfect score, fifty points."

She rolled her body and smiled at the detective. "I'm sure I can be useful for something."

"Incidentally," began the investigator. "The sniper you were dating? He is still alive right?"

She smirked in response as the next shooter began his attempts to duplicate Sydney's score. "Are you trying to imply something Mr. Chase?"

Derek chuckled as he quickly shook his head. "No, but I am fascinated at how well you shoot."

Sydney adjusted from her position and sat up, listening to the scores. As she prepared for her departure she noticed that her opponents could not quite match her performance. She checked the weapon to make sure the chamber was empty. "You can thank my father for that. As teenagers, he would take Tessa and me to the country and give us instruction. He felt that women living in the big city should know how to defend themselves. For my eighteenth birthday, he bought me a Walther PPK. You know the gun James Bond has? It matched the one Tessa got the year before when she turned eighteen."

"What about the rifle?"

"This?" she asked as she disassembled the bi-pod from the weapon. She gently placed the items on the ground and then opened the carrying case beside her. "This I bought a few years ago. It's the M91. 7.62mm cartridges with a

Remington 700 trigger configured to Navy specifications.  Carries four rounds plus one in the chamber and only weighs about 14 pounds."

"Perfect for unwinding after a long day at the office?"

"Exactly," she said as she removed the yellow safety glasses from her face. She placed them in the case in their resting place next to the case of extra bullets.  She then cradled the rifle, inspected it one last time and secured it in the case.  She then folded up the bipod and secured that in the case as well.

The third shooter concluded his firing and a moment later the loud speaker was echoing the results.  "Shooter number one, Sydney Taylor, score 148. Shooter number three, John Malken, score 146.  Shooter number two, Fred Dunkin, score 142."

Derek slid his sunglasses on as Sydney closed the long black case.  She stood up, stretched for a moment and dusted herself off before picking the container up.  "I'm sure the guy who taught you how to shoot that thing is still kicking himself in the ass."

She looked past Derek's shoulder at the shooter who scored second place. She smiled and blew him a kiss.  "Especially since I beat him by two points."


**Only a few lights were on when they spied on the building**.  Griffin Securities had tucked in for the night.  They looked on as Janocky and his bodyguards disappeared within the confines of the black limousine.  It started off towards the gate in which the security guard gave a crisp salute before the car rolled out onto the street and into the night traffic.

With his duty completed, the guard went back into his little hut, propped his feet up and began watching television.  Seeing their opportunity, Derek squeezed the wire cutter one last time completing the hole in the chain link fence.  He dropped the tool as Sydney scurried through.  He checked to make sure they were not being watched and then followed after her.

Once inside the perimeter they quickly made their way into the shadows of the parking lot, near the side entrance to Griffin Securities.  His eyes hovered above the fender of one of the logoed company sedans.  He watched a security guard walk by and disappear around the corner.  He then looked up at the camera which had begun its turn away from them.  He ducked back behind the fender and they both looked at the side entrance.  He tapped her on the shoulder and they both sprinted to the side entrance.

Reaching the side entrance, Derek withdrew the lock picking utensil set and started working on the door.  Sydney monitored the camera as it began its turn back towards the side entrance.

"You got about six seconds," she whispered as the lock clicked.  He quickly swung the door open and they hurried inside, closing the door behind them.

Once inside they quickly surveyed the dimly lit layout.  From where they were, they could see the janitor waxing the floor of the front lobby.  He was whistling softly as the machine whirred quietly.  Beside them were stairs leading up and down.  Where would they look first?

They were both startled as a door opened up a few floors above them.  They could hear shoes beginning their descent towards them.  He tapped her on the shoulder and pointed downward.  The decision had been made for them.  She nodded as they began their search within the bowels of Griffin Securities.


**Remaining undetected proved to be quite easy as they searched the basement of Griffin Securities.**  They only had to go down two flights of stairs to reach the dimly lit area that slightly resembled a hospital lobby after hours.  The tile floor had recently been waxed and the surrounding furniture was monotoned and rigid.  The air was chilled and stale allowing for the odor of ammonia to rule over the environment.

Derek's pen light had served its purpose, illuminating the darkness without bringing attention to themselves.  They were able to quickly determine their path and eliminate any paths that would impede their search for Thatcher's video cassette, providing he hid it there in the first place.

The pen light illuminated the plastic sign labeled Locker Room.  He looked over at Sydney, who was continuously checking behind them to make sure they had not been followed. He nodded his head and turned the door knob. They went inside, quietly closing the door behind them.

Unlike the aroma in the hallway, the locker room reeked with the combating stench of sweat and cologne. Derek used the pen light to scan the various lockers. Sydney leaned towards him. "How do we know which one was his?"

Derek had been asking himself that same question. It had been three months since Thatcher had worked for Griffin Securities. He was sure that if Janocky suspected Thatcher had a copy of the video cassette, the locker room would have been torn apart a long time ago. However, he suspected Thatcher was more cunning than he appeared.

"Search them all." Derek answered as he pointed to the far end. "Look for anything that seems loose or out of place."

Sydney nodded as she started at the far end of the locker room. Derek was already at the other end opening a locker. He went through a few uniforms and lightly tapped the back of the locker. He fumbled through a few personal items of the security guard to find nothing out of the ordinary. He quickly closed he locker and moved on to the next one.

He performed the task to four lockers examining the contents in each and making sure their structural integrity had not been compromised. Each locker displayed each security guard's individuality. He realized that two of them had families while the other two remained bachelors.  One of which was a surfer while the other was into heavy metal.  The two family men had mostly pictures of their families with the exception of the one who went to West Point.  He proudly displayed the Army logo throughout his locker.  He glanced at Sydney to find that she too was not having any luck searching through the lockers.

The fifth locker he came across proved to be more interesting than the previous four.  It had a small dent near the bottom and it squeaked when he opened it.  He looked inside to find the uniform neat pressed and hung.  He rummaged through the locker and his hand brushed up against a knot along the side of the locker.  A knot that was not present in the other four lockers.  He moved the uniform to reveal a partially exposed key jammed between the grooves of the lockers.  Scratched above it were the initials MT.  Derek smiled as he withdrew a pocket knife.  Thatcher was indeed a cunning and smart man.

"How clever."  Derek said to himself out loud.

"Find something?" Sydney asked.

After a firm pry, Derek extracted the key from the groove with the pocket knife.  He studied it.  It looked like a key from the Norfolk Bus Terminal.  "I think Thatcher may have left us a clue."

"Thank you Mr. Chase for your assistance," came a voice as the lights came on.  Derek and Sydney turned to find a large man with a white beard standing amongst a trio of Griffin Security guards.  He smiled as he pointed a gun at them. "We've been through this place twice and found nothing." he said. There was a slight hint of an English accent in his voice. "I commend you on your fine skills of observation."

Derek stood silent, but replied with a sheepish smile.

The man with the English accent extended his hand. "The key please?"

The detective nodded over at Sydney in hopes that she would catch on to his next move. She responded with a nod and he returned his focus to the man with the gun. "So, Thatcher did make a copy of the video cassette."

"Mr. Thatcher was a fool to believe he could be able to blackmail Mr. Janocky. It would only be a matter of time before we caught up with him."

"And in the process of hunting down Thatcher," Sydney spoke out, "you murdered my sister."

He cocked the gun as he addressed Sydney's accusation. "I assure you Ms. Taylor, though your sister's death would have eventually been necessary, The Brotherhood's involvement was trivial."

"The Brotherhood?" Derek asked.

"Please, Mr. Chase," the man responded. The gun waved as he continued. "I'm sure that you've already discovered our secret, must I bore you with details?"

"At this point in time, that would probably do neither one of us any good."

"My thoughts exactly. May I have the key please?"

Derek took one last glance at Sydney.  He could see her tensing up.   He then returned his focus to the man with the English accent and tossed the key towards him quickly.  The man reached to catch the key, but Derek had already lashed out.  With his left hand, he grabbed the hand with the gun and pushed it sideways.  He then turned with a spinning back kick towards another oncoming assailant sending him hard against the doorframe.  Derek finished the attack by delivering an elbow to the base of the English man's head sending him to the floor unconscious.

His attention switched over to Sydney as he heard a grunt.  She was sending an attacker into one of the lockers as the other scrambled from the floor to his feet.  However, Sydney was already on an assault of her own.  She nimbly executed a jump sidekick catching the would-be attacker along the jaw.  He limply slammed against a locker and onto the floor.  She glanced over her shoulder to find the remaining attacker trying to climb out of the locker.  She looked over at him and he smiled.  He was impressed.

She smiled back before sending a boot to the face of her opponent.  With a loud clang of metal, he fell back inside the locker slumping to the ground.  Sydney blew a tuft of brunette hair from her face as Derek retrieved the key from the floor.

"I'm impressed." He said returning to his full height. "You're a

marksman and you know martial arts. Your dates must love bringing you home

to their mothers."

She grinned with satisfaction when she responded. "That's why I usually

bring them back to my place."

Chapter Seventeen

**It took thirty minutes to journey to the Norfolk Bus Terminal, which was located on the outskirts of Waterside, Downtown Norfolk.** For eleven-thirty at night, it seemed unusually crowded with travelers. However, Sydney and Derek searched the station for the correct locker number, bumping and stumbling into people rushing to make it to their destinations. In a few cases they could see the people getting frustrated with the scenery of so many patrons in the bus terminal and their excess baggage.

"Hey," Sydney yelled out pointing towards a small yellow square in the myriad of colored lockers. "I think that may be it."

Derek brushed himself past a woman that was arguing with her spouse about his traveling habits. She was concerned that his traveling was more than a business trip suggesting to the detective that the woman was suspicious of an unfaithful husband. The thought of offering his services faded away as he walked over with the key. He matched the crimson number with the number on the locker and quickly inserted the key. The locker clanged as it opened. Sydney reached inside and pulled out a video cassette.

"Voila," she said.

Derek patted her on the shoulder. "I'm sure this has all the evidence to put

Janocky away for a very long time."

"It's unfortunate that you won't live long enough to see it."

Derek cursed silently to himself as he recognized the voice. Twice he had

been distracted and allowed himself to be taken by surprise. He turned to find

Letourneau standing in front of them with his weapon drawn. Derek noticed

that the former sergeant still carried the standard issue revolver, only this time it

was accessorized with a silencer.

"I should have known you'd show up."

Nick smiled at Derek. "Yeah Rookie, you should have." He then turned

towards Sydney. "I apologize Ms. Taylor. Let me introduce myself. I'm Nick

Letourneau. Thanks to your sister, I now work for myself. Please tell her I said

hi when you see her."

A shot rang out knocking Sydney up against the bus terminal lockers.

Derek watched her eyes go wide as she sank to the floor. She fell face down

onto the dusty, tiled floor of the terminal.

"You sonova- " Derek started as he made an attempt to lunge towards

Letourneau. He quickly stopped as the revolver targeted him.

"Now Rookie." Nick said calmly. "Be patient. I'm going to kill you, but

not just yet." The former sergeant, still aiming his weapon at Derek, knelt down and picked up the video cassette.  "I figured we talk a little bit and catch up on a few things.  You know I've been away for a while."

Derek's heart raced as he glanced down at Sydney's body.  He stared at her for a while before returning his attention to Letourneau.  "Catch up eh?  You can start by telling me why.  I looked up to you.  Hell, the whole damn department looked up to you.  Why'd you do it?"

Nick smiled as he started pulling the film from the video tape.  "Ah c'mon Rookie!  You know the answer to that as well as I do.  How many times has the system fucked us over?  Haven't you had enough of seeing the bad guy get a slap on the hand?"

"When I was a cop," Derek interjected.  He tried to restrain the sarcasm in his voice.  "You were the bad guy."

Nick ignored his comment as he continued.  "When the system can no longer support justice, we're there to pick up the pieces."

"You profit from the people you chase.  How are you any different?"

Nick smiled.  "Everything we seize is distributed evenly amongst members of the group and the company."

"And directly into Janocky's pocket.  So Griffin Securities is a front?"

"It serves its purpose." Nick answered.  "It allows us to get into places the police can't.  The private sector of American businesses are more apt to trust a local security firm rather than the police. You'd be surprised at the dirty little secrets they hide."

"So when Thatcher found out what was going on between Premiere Tech and Valkyrie Industries and tried to blackmail Janocky, he needed to be eliminated."

"You catch on fast, Rookie." Nick said with a chuckle. "Thatcher thought he'd take the law into his own hands. He told Janocky that he made a copy of an incriminating video cassette implicating Griffin Securities in some type of scandal. He was bold enough to demand a quarter of millions dollars, or he'd turn the tape over to the authorities."

"And when he approached Tessa Taylor about it, you couldn't take any chances."

Nick pulled one last time before ripping the tape out of the cassette. He placed it in a nearby trashcan, still aiming the revolver at Derek's chest. "I wish I pulled the trigger myself. And then you showed up and started sticking your nose into things that didn't concern you."

"How do you know I haven't sent what I have already to the authorities?"

"Shit. You trust the department as much as I do. Anything you have is locked up in that head of yours. And I intend on keeping it that way."

A low moan coming from Sydney's unmoving body distracted the former sergeant long enough for Derek to crescent kick the gun from his hand.

Letourneau quickly retaliated with a jab to the jaw.  Derek spun in place and sent a back-fist to the rogue cop's head.  Letourneau's face bounced up against one of the bus terminal's locker as Derek sent his foot down on the inside of the former sergeant's knee.  His body buckled and the detective grabbed Letourneau's head and slammed it hard against the locker knocking him unconscious.

Another moan escaped from Sydney's lips as she slowly began to move.  Derek went up to her and helped her to her feet.  She took in a couple of deep breaths before signaling that she was okay.

"Give it a second," Derek began.  "Let your lungs refill with air."

She took a moment before speaking.  "I'm glad you forced me to wear a bulletproof vest," she took one last deep breath.  "But I have to admit I wasn't expecting that."

Derek smiled.  He was relieved that E loaned him the extra vest, that Sydney took his advice, and that aside for some bruising, she was okay.  "I didn't expect it either the first time I was shot.  You may have some bruising, but it's better than being dead."

"You won't hear any complaints from me."

He turned and looked at the strands of tape poking up from the trash can. He walked over and gathered the mess as best as he could.  He was already thinking of the words to say to Jeff without compromising his position regarding

the Ferrari.  Only Jeff would be able to repair the damage caused by Letourneau.

The sound of a bullet ricocheting off one of the metal lockers beside them

quickly forced Derek and Sydney to duck.   Suddenly, people in the bus terminal

began to scurry in every direction screaming for their lives.  The detective

withdrew the semi-plastic pistol from the small of his back and looked towards

the origin of the confusion and the stray bullet.  He found a blonde haired man

wearing a Griffin Securities uniform running towards them.

The detective coughed off a couple of shots.  The bullets missed their

target and shattered pieces of decorative marble instead.  Another spark erupting

from the locker in front him made him spin around.  The detective immediately

found another security guard, a younger one, coming from the opposite end of

the terminal toting a small automatic weapon.  Like an exterminator, he sprayed

bullets as if he was exorcising the bus terminal of unwanted pests.

He handed the excess film to Sydney and withdrew the second Glock from

his ankle holster.  The detective ducked as bullets began bouncing off the metal

frame of the lockers behind him.  He gritted his teeth as he squeezed off shots of

his own.  He looked around to find people scrambling from the fire fight.  Their

scrambling however, made a difficult obstacle for the blonde haired security

guard.  He was trying to look over the people to get a better shot.

Derek focused his attention towards the young man running up with the automatic weapon.  The detective realized that within a few seconds, he and Sydney would be vulnerable.  He turned to face the oncoming assailant and pushed off from his protection.  He fired as he slid across the tiled floor.  The black detective zeroed in on the young man as his finger remained on the trigger.  The first bullet caught the member of The Brotherhood in the shoulder.  The others plucked his chest.  The man's body limply danced backwards.  The automatic weapon clanked against the colored tile when the security guard's body fell into a growing pool of his own blood.

Two empty clips from the Glock fell onto the floor as Derek quickly reloaded.  He glanced over his shoulder to find the blonde haired man swimming through the traffic of panicked people.  He looked over at Sydney who was huddled beside the unconscious Nick Letourneau.

He took the keys for the Ferrari out of his pocket.  "Sydney!"  He yelled.  Sydney turned.  Her face was as pale as a light bulb coming on for the first time.  He slid the keys towards her.

"Get the car!"

"What about you!"

He looked over at the blonde haired man who was slowly beginning to get the best of the obstacle between him and the detective.  "I'm right behind you!  Now go!"

Sydney picked up the keys and scurried towards the exit of the bus terminal. Derek stood and fired above the crowd. People ducked and they scrambled to save their lives. He quickly started towards the exit after Sydney.

He quickly stopped as a metallic ashtray exploded in front of him. He looked up to find another member of the secret society on the second floor landing. He was an older man with gray hair wearing a black shirt. The ominous, black automatic rifle he was carrying seemed like it could outfit a tank. He quickly ducked, hearing a bullet ricochet behind him. He looked to find the blonde haired man had maneuvered through the crowd and was running towards him. He looked up to find the gray haired man steadying himself to take another shot.

He scanned the front entrance to find Sydney had successfully made it out of the bus terminal. He quickly decided it was time for his own departure. He darted off as another bullet from the automatic rifle shattered the metal casing of the terminal locker behind him.

He ran, looking ahead, anticipating freedom would soon be within his reach. His anticipation quickly turned to grief when he was suddenly greeted by a fifth member of Griffin Securities. He was bald with a goatee and the pistol he was holding had taken a hostage.

She had long dark hair and looked like she was Hispanic. With her red blazer and long black skirt, Derek figure her as a corporate executive probably coming from, or going on another dull, company paid for, business trip. Regardless, she would soon be taking a one-way trip to permanent retirement if he did not act fast.

Marble from the column beside him exploded as the gunman with the goatee took aim. While in stride, Derek took aim and fired. The security guard's bald head quickly jerked back and the terrorist fell to the ground with a thud. Now that he was within reach, the detective dove and tackled the corporate-looking woman onto the tiled floor as another metallic ashtray exploded. The force of his tackle caused them to slide a few feet on the tiled floor. Derek wrapped his arms around her and rolled behind a marble column.

Her body laid on top of his as he looked at her. She was still in shock from her ordeal. He took in a deep breath as bullets bounced around them. "Are you okay?" he asked.

She slowly nodded as some of the color returned to her tanned face. Derek rolled her off of his chest and quickly glanced around the side to find the blonde haired man had taken cover behind another marble column a few feet away.

"Good." He replied. "You'll be safe here until the police arrive. Okay?"

Again she slowly nodded.

He heard the familiar roar of the Ferrari as it screeched to a halt in front of the bus terminal. Sydney beeped the horn and yelled for him to get his ass in gear.

"Have a nice day." he said as he stepped away from the protection of the marble column firing at the two assailants.  They ducked behind their protective walls as Derek made his way to the exit.  He ran out and rolled over the roof of the Ferrari.  He quickly scrambled inside the Italian import as Sydney gunned the engine.  White smoke secreted from the ground as the tires clawed for pavement.  The Ferrari screeched off, out of the bus terminal parking lot and into the night streets of Norfolk.

"Are you okay?" Derek asked Sydney.  His body was still generating energy and adrenaline.

She tightly held the steering wheel as she maneuvered the exotic sports car towards the highway.  "Uh huh."  She answered.  "I'm fine."  He could see her quickly gathering her thoughts and regaining her organized composure.  "It's not every day a girl gets to be shot point blank in the chest and chased by men with automatic weapons.  Really Mr. Chase, we must do this again sometime."

Derek raised an eyebrow in amusement.  "Did I detect a bit of sarcasm in that answer?"

**Jeff seemed to be emulating with energy when he opened to door to his home.** Recognizing his best friend, he groaned in disgust and slowly shuffled his way back into the apartment. Sydney and Derek followed him inside as Jeff walked into the kitchen. He opened the refrigerator and pulled out a glass of wine. Both Derek and Sydney noticed the lipstick on the side of the glass.

"This better be good," he said pretending to be groggy. "It's after midnight. I'm just now getting to bed, and I'm looking forward to a great dream."

"Tough date?" Derek asked.

Jeff smiled devilishly as he took a seat in one of the barstools. "She's a gymnast."

"A gymnast?" Derek asked. "What about the flight attendant from New York?"

"Who? Betty?" Jeff began. "It's like I went from a Yugo to a Cadillac. I can't even begin to tell you all the things she can do."

"Good." Sydney interrupted. "I would hate to hear all the sordid details."

Derek smiled realizing his opportunity for introductions. "Sydney Taylor, this is Jeff Tanner. He's a photographer for the Virginian-Pilot and self-proclaimed lady killer of Hampton Roads."

Jeff extended his hand. "Charmed."

Sydney shook his hand and smirked. "I'm sure."

Derek withdrew the heap of videocassette and placed it in front of him. "If there is anybody who can put this thing back together, it's this guy."

Jeff looked at his best friend. "This couldn't wait until morning?"

He shrugged as Sydney answered. "We might be dead by morning."

He could see the confusion sweeping over Jeff's face as the photographer absorbed Sydney's statement. Derek leaned closer to his best friend and offered an explanation. "There are some people out there who are pretty pissed off that we have this tape. We've been chased and shot at already."

"Excuse me?" Sydney stated.

Derek looked at Sydney. "Okay," he surrendered. "I was shot at. Sydney was actually shot."

"He shot me point blank!"

"Who?" Jeff asked.

"Letourneau," Derek answered.

"He's involved in this?" Jeff asked. "The plot thickens."

"May I use your bathroom?" Sydney asked. "I would like to make sure the bulletproof vest did its job."

"It's around the corner to the left." Jeff directed.

He and Jeff watched her walk out of the room. He then re-focused to the task at hand and nodded towards the mess of video tape. "Letourneau pulled out the tape in hopes of hiding whatever is on it. You're the only one I know who can fix this."

Jeff took another sip of wine as he lifted a string of video film. "You know, this is gonna keep me from my dream."

He was about to comment, but a simultaneous chorus of screams reverberated through the apartment. Sydney came hurrying back in the room. Her face was pale and she was gasping for air. She was in shock.

"There's a naked woman in there!" She exclaimed looking back.

Derek's eyes went wide as he looked at his best friend. He gave a devilish smile. "The gymnast?" He whispered.

"Her name is Missy." Jeff whispered back and he made a gesture with his hands indicating her breast size. It was juvenile, but it relayed the message.

"And she's a gymnast?" He retorted only to receive a nod from Jeff.

"Yeah," Derek thought out loud agreeing with his best friend's earlier statement. "That would be a great dream."

***"You can't have it!"***

*"Give it back to me! It's my teddy bear!"*

*"I want it."*

*"Now, now children," she said. "What's all the yelling about?"*

*"Derek won't give me Mr. Sniffles!"*

*He looked at her as she knelt down between her two children. Her long black hair shined and her light complexion accented her angelic face. Her smile was comforting and her voice was soft and loving. "Derek? Why won't you give Crystal Mr. Sniffles?"*

*"Crystal always gets everything!" he whimpered. "I never get anything!"*

*"Ah," his mother responded. "That's not true. Your father and I give you anything you ask for."*

*"I asked for a teddy bear. How come I didn't get a teddy bear and she did?"*

*She rubbed her child's back affectionately. "Well, Mr. Sniffles protects Crystal from all those monsters under her bed. Mr. Sniffles is brave and strong like you. Your father and I thought that because you are a brave, strong boy you did not need a teddy bear. Now, if there are monsters under your bed, we can go to the market tomorrow and get you your very own teddy bear; and you can play with him all day if you like. But, before we do, you have to let me know if there are monsters under your bed. Are there monsters under your bed?"*

*He shook his head.*

*"Do you really think that a big, strong, brave boy like yourself needs a teddy bear to protect him?"*

*He slowly shook his head again.*

*She smiled and hugged him. "I didn't think so either. Tell you what, why don't you give Crystal Mr. Sniffles and you two can come downstairs and help me bake some cookies. Would you like that?"*

*They both nodded and Derek handed the brown bear to his sister.*

*"What do you say?" his mother asked.*

*"I'm sorry."*

*She kissed him on the cheek. "That's my brave son. C'mon lets go make some cookies."*

Taking the time to reflect about his mother allowed him to become complacent and enjoy the night air. He sighed, realizing that he missed her terribly and made a promise that he would redouble his efforts in finding the truth about her death.

He stood on the porch of the apartment overlooking the city streets. A soft breeze caressed his face as he watched the crowds of people converse on the sidewalk. They had been travelling back and forth between the conglomerate of bars Jeff happened to live close to.

Derek turned as the sliding glass door of the apartment opened as Sydney stepped onto the balcony.  "You okay?" she asked.

"Yes," Derek answered.  "I was just thinking about my mother."

She nodded.  "Bad memories?"

"No," he answered.  "Good ones."

"From what I read, it appeared that your mother was forced off of the road."

"That's what I think, but the local police say otherwise.  They think my mother was careless."

"Well, if there's anything I can do to help, please let me know."

Derek turned to her and folded his arms.  He remembered back to the night before when Sydney confessed that she ran a background check on him.  "Can you tell me why the government seems to know so much about my family?  I mean after all, Tessa's background check was sparse; and I'm sure that someone of your stature could have that information readily available."

Sydney gave a smile.  "Not as readily as you think.  During Vietnam, your father was in Navy Intelligence where he served two tours of duty.  After the war, he was stationed in Panama where I understand he met your mother.  When they married, he resigned from the Navy and started working for your grandfather.  All files between then and your mother's accident have been marked as classified and are at Langley in a high security vault  They don't resume until after your mother's accident and even that information is sketchy. From what I read, the Navy sent a forensic team and concluded that your mother's car had been forced off the cliff. There was a list of possible suspects, but that page had been blacked out."

"How convenient." Derek said with a smirk.

She continued. "I'm not exactly sure what happened, but whatever it was, somebody is doing an awful lot to keep it quiet."

"What about your security clearance? Can't you access the information?"

"I tried already. The only people who have security clearance are Admirals and above."

The detective pondered the information. If Sydney was right, his suspicions would be confirmed. He also questioned how Janocky knew about his family. He couldn't imagine an Admiral in the Navy retiring to become a security guard. Janocky's deep pockets had came across a truth Derek was struggling to piece together.

The sliding glass door of the apartment opened and Jeff poked his head out. "Hey D, I might have something."

Derek took one last look at the night scenery and then at Sydney. He would have to address his mother's mystery later. Instead, he diverted his attention to finding Tessa's killer and hoped that the video cassette would provide not only the murderer, but the motive as well.

"I had to do a MacGyver and use some scotch tape in a few places," Jeff began. "But I think I was able to salvage most of it." He gently slid the tape cassette into the VCR and hit play. "I hope."

The television crackled to life as snow filled the screen. Suddenly, the image of Michael Thatcher appeared. He was sitting at a restaurant table. He seemed anxious. He quickly looked up as a figured walked up.

"Mr. Thatcher," came Janocky's voice. "I do hope this meeting proves to be more lucrative than the last."

"It will be." Thatcher assured. "I talked with that cop friend of mine. He's in."

"Is that a fact?" Janocky asked. "Tsk, tsk, Mr. Thatcher. You of all people should know not trust everyone." Janocky's southern drawl was even more prominent on television. "How can you be so sure this cop friend of yours will be partial to our ideals?"

"Because," came a voice from behind the camera. "You can do things the system doesn't allow me to do. Not to mention that someone in my position will be very useful to you."

Derek's eyes went wide when he recognized Austin's face on the screen.

"Mr. Janocky," Thatcher began. "Meet Lieutenant Austin of the Virginia Beach Police Department."

Janocky and Austin shook hands as the Lieutenant took a seat at the table. "Well," Janocky responded. "This may prove to be more lucrative than I thought."

"Oh, this could be lucrative indeed." Austin reinforced.

"This could be even better than Premiere Tech." Thatcher added.

Janocky looked at both men for a long time, unsure of his next move, but a smile came across his face. "Premiere Tech was careless and they paid for it in the end. However, my dealings with them was only the tip of the iceberg. I have many initiatives pending that will be more prosperous than Premiere Tech."

The screen flickered as Austin shifted in his seat. "What could be more prosperous than Premiere Tech.?"

Janocky stared at Austin. He quickly raised his eyebrows and stated. "Forgive me Lieutenant, but I'm still not convinced of your loyalty."

It was Austin's turn to smile. "Mr. Janocky, believe me. I have better things to do. You haven't said anything incriminating. Besides, if I wanted you behind bars, I would have already hauled your country ass downtown, put you in a four by four cell block with the other day-to-day vermin, and wait until it was about dinner time to come up with some lame reason why. And you know that with my reputation, I would get away with it." He then took a sip from

Thatcher's glass of water. "However, I do understand your need for some sort of initiation process, so tell me what you want."

"Impressive Lieutenant," Janocky chuckled. "But I assure you that it'll take more than just threats to convince me."

"What did you have in mind?"

Janocky leaned back in his chair. "I've had some difficulty with Miss Taylor."

"Tessa Taylor?"

Janocky nodded. "She's been snooping around in affairs that do not concern her. What can you arrange?"

Austin again smiled. "I can arrange a lot of things. It all depends on what you want."

"What would you suggest?"

The television screen flickered again as Austin leaned forward. "I can have her arrested and detained indefinitely. Or are you looking for something a little more permanent?"

"Precisely."

Austin raised an eyebrow. "You want something more permanent? Something like -

Janocky held his hands up. "I don't need the details, just make it so."

Thatcher took a sip of his water as he began to whisper. "So you want Austin to kill Te –

Derek and Sydney shuddered briefly as the tape went to static. Jeff looked at the two shaking his head. "Sorry guys. That was all I could save."

The detective placed a hand on his best friend's shoulder. He could feel anger and betrayal welling up inside of him. "That was more than enough."

Sydney folded her arms. "Yes, but it won't hold up in court. All Janocky said was she has been snooping around and do something about it. He didn't come out and say I want you to kill Tessa. We need more proof."

"I have enough proof to know who squeezed the trigger."

"What are you going to do?" Jeff asked as he pulled out the videocassette from the VCR. He handed it to Derek.

Derek looked at the cassette before responding. "I guess it's time to squeeze back."

<u>**Chapter Nineteen**</u>:

**The Ferrari rolled to a standstill on the cobblestone driveway of the beach house next to Elizabeth's car**. Her door immediately flew open as the import's engine quieted. Derek and Sydney slowly removed themselves as Elizabeth walked up with a file. When she saw Sydney, he could see her eyebrow raise and confirm the look of surprise.

Derek quickly introduced them. "Sydney Taylor, this is my friend Elizabeth Companstella, Virginia Beach's finest officer."

She smiled when she mumbled. "Flattery will only save your butt for so long."

"Pleased to meet you." Sydney responded.

"What brings you out this late?" He asked.

Elizabeth held up a file. "I have the ballistics report regarding the security guard."

Derek smiled as he shook his head and looked back at Sydney. "Thanks E, but it's no longer necessary. I know who shot the security guard and it's cool."

Her eyes went wide as the facts started adding up in her head. She turned towards Sydney. "Are you the one who shot the security guard?"

"Yes," Sydney answered. "But I was defending myself."

The file dropped to the ground as Elizabeth reached for her weapon. Her voice became very authoritative and strong. "Miss Taylor, I'm afraid you're gonna have to come with me." she said. Her sidearm remained in the holster, but was poised in case it was needed.

"But," Sydney retreated. "I was defending myself!"

"E," Derek spoke out. "What are you doing?"

Elizabeth used her free hand to withdraw a pair of handcuffs. Sydney complied and her hands slowly went into the air. "The bullet that killed the security guard is the same type of bullet that killed Tessa Taylor. Forensics traced it back to the same manufacturer and gun shop in Massachusetts."

Derek stood there stunned as Elizabeth cautiously walked up to Sydney and began snapping the metal bracelets shut. It seemed to be happening so fast. He looked at Sydney with confusion. "You're making a big mistake!" Sydney began as Elizabeth opened her cell phone and called in the situation. "I didn't kill my sister!" She looked over at Derek, her eyes pleading for him. "You have to believe me. I didn't kill my sister."

He took in a deep breath as his heart thumped against his chest. He watched as Elizabeth began her routine, reciting Sydney's Miranda rights while patting her down. Elizabeth withdrew a Walther PPK and placed it on the trunk of her car. "Is this the gun you used to defend yourself?"

"Yes."

Elizabeth gave a long hard look at Derek before addressing Sydney.  "For your sake, I hope you didn't kill your sister."


**Lieutenant Austin growled as he slammed his fist down onto his desk.** Derek smiled.  He knew the early morning call to the Lieutenant was irritating enough.  Having him in his office pleading the case of a potential murderer was truly frustrating.

"No!" Austin barked.  "You are out of your goddamn mind if you think for one second I'm going to let a prime suspect out on bail.  Geesh!  The courts aren't even open!"

"Austin, until ballistics come back with the report, how can you be sure?"

"It doesn't matter!  Until the forensics tells me otherwise, her ass stays in that cell; and I won't hear another word!"

"Why do you have to be so damn stubborn?  Why would she kill her sister?"

Austin leaned back in his chair.  "You're the goddamn detective, you tell me."

"She doesn't have a motive, you jackass!"

"Everybody has a motive.  You just gotta dig deep enough."

"What about your motive?"

Austin leaned forward. His eyebrows raised with curiosity. "What the fuck is that supposed to mean?"

"You heard me. Everybody has a motive? What's yours? You, Tessa and Thatcher went to the same university, good friends from what I hear. Tell me what you and Thatcher were working on? What was in the file you gave him a couple of days ago at the oceanfront, and what was on the disk he gave you? Maybe Tessa got too close and you had to kill her. And then you killed Thatcher to cover your tracks."

"I can't fuckin' believe what I'm hearing." Austin said to himself. "You were following me? Goddamn you Chase!"

The detective exhaled his frustration realizing the compromising situation he had placed himself in. If Austin was a dirty cop, he would surely go out of his way to kill him. However, the detective played the situation through. "Austin, if I'm wrong about you, then you're no more guilty than Tessa's sister. But if I'm right, I'm going to be all over your ass. Think about that."

"No, Chase!" Austin shouted back. "You think about this! I warned you to stay away from this case! You have done nothing but cause chaos. As far as I'm concerned, we have our suspect and it won't be long before we pry whatever motive out of her. As for you, if you don't get your ass out of my office and back off from this case, I will charge you with accessory and personally get so far up in your ass, you'll think I opened a precinct in there."

He looked at the Lieutenant with defiance. "This isn't over. You know

you got the wrong person."

"Leave goddamn it!" Austin bellowed as he pointed towards the door.

"Leave now!"

The detective gave a huff as he opened the office door. "When this comes

back and bites you in the ass, I'm gonna be right there to make sure you go

down."

"Leave!"

Derek walked out of the office slamming the door shut behind him.

Elizabeth stood against the wall looking at him with apologetic eyes. He smiled

at her. "I know you were only doing your job."

"I hope she is innocent." she said.

"She is." he responded. "Don't ask me how I know. I just know she didn't

kill her sister."

"I called Mr. Garrett like you asked."

"Thanks E. If anyone can get her out this mess, he can."

"I have the day off today," she began. "We can go out and get some

breakfast. My treat."

He smiled at the flirtation. "As nice as that sounds, I'm gonna pass. I have

some things I need to follow up on."

She kissed him on the cheek before walking off. "Maybe next time."

"Maybe next time I'll make you breakfast," he said as he watched her walk off.

He chuckled at the possibilities when she responded. "I'd like that."

**The tapping on the window startled Derek as his fingers tightened around the handle of his Glock.** It took his eyes a few seconds before Slappy came into clear focus. Derek loosened his grip and returned the weapon to the shoulder holster as he rolled down the window.

"Boy!" Slappy began. "You's a crazy fool. What da hell are you doin' sleeping in the parking lot? Don't you know this is da ghetto?"

"I needed to talk with you."

Slappy shook his head. "You could've used the phone. It would have been safer. In this neighborhood your hundred thousand dollar Ferrari sticks out like a buck-bald naked chicken. Might as well get a neon light saying 'come kill me cuz I'm a jackass'."

He silently chuckled at Slappy's comment reflecting on the danger he had placed himself in. "Believe me, I know where I am. And you're lucky I knew it was you, or the hood would have one less cranky old man."

"Cranky?" Slappy retorted. "When I shove my old ass foot up your ass, then I'll show you cranky." He then gave a hint of a smile and nodded towards the barbershop. "Come on inside and I'll make us some breakfast."

**The smell of coffee filled his lungs, giving him a temporary surge of energy, but it quickly passed as he reflected on the previous day's events.** Slappy seemed to had forgotten that he was there. He had been tending to the scrambled eggs and bacon that was cooking on the stove deep inside the "employees only" break room. He seemed content, even though he hummed the refrain from "Amazing Grace".

"Slappy, who do you think killed my mother?"

The humming stopped as he pondered the question. "It could have been any number of people. My guess would be one of Tosillo's men. You know the elders of San Puliero are still upset about your father's actions. I wouldn't put it past them to send Tosillo after him and his family. Why do you ask?"

"It's been on my mind lately."

"Well, watch your back. You never know when somethins' gonna slither out from the grass." Slappy's tone then changed from informational, to concern. "This is just the parent in me, but you may want to reconsider your search for your mother's killer. You may not like what you find."

He looked up at Slappy. His insides were suspicious that the barbershop owner was holding out on him. "What do you mean by that? Is there something you're not telling me?"

Slappy shook his head. "Please boy, you know as much as I do. I'm just saying that sometimes when you uncover the truth; it's more disturbing than the lie. And when it involves the elders of San Puliero and Diego Tosillo, the lie may be what's keeping the shit from stinking."

"Well, the shit's about to get stirred."

The barbershop owner shook his head as he removed the bacon from the stove. He placed the strips on a paper towel and returned the skillet to the burner. He repeated the process with the eggs. He placed the breakfast in front of the detective as he took another sip of coffee.

"Derek, you're like a son to me and I want to find out who killed your mother as much as you do, just be careful okay?"

"I will Slappy." He said, as he took a bite of the scrambled eggs. He chewed for a moment before speaking again. "Tell me about Tosillo."

"He's an educated man originally from the town, but was sent to England where he met his wife Elena. It wasn't until she was accidentally killed during one of the many attempts on your grandfather's life that he became a mean bastard. When everything went down with your father being suspected of your grandfather's death, the local police chief allowed your father to leave. Tosillo quickly caught up with the police chief and expressed his disappointment. He personally beat the living hell out of him in the town square before cutting the man's balls off and setting them on fire. He then executed his wife and little son in front of him. So while the man is crying over his family, Tosillo pours gasoline over him and his family and sets them on fire. Right in the middle of town square!"

"How do you know all of this? Weren't you with my father?"

"I was, but your grandfather still has spies in the local elders' organization that are loyal to your father. They relayed the information to him, which is why he put you with Maria and moved the headquarters to Connecticut. He wanted to make it as difficult as possible for Tosillo to touch him. Your father is so well connected up north that he knows the elders' next move before they do. Tosillo won't fuck with him now, but I'm sure he's biding his time. Snakes are very patient creatures."

Derek stared at the steam rising from his cup. "The whole eye for an eye thing would make sense."

"But it'll never be proven. Nobody is willing to confront Tosillo, and I doubt if anybody ever will."

"Then you don't know my father very well."

"I know him better than you. Your father is more concerned about his children right now and making sure you all are safe. As much as he hates it, he's ignoring Tosillo, because once you chopped the head off a hydra, another one just takes its place; and at least with Tosillo, your father knows what to expect," Slappy took a sip of his coffee before he spoke again. "Besides, your mother would forbid it if she were alive today."

Derek slowly acknowledged Slappy's last statement as truth. His mother would loathe the idea of retaliation. "Slappy, I miss her."

"I miss her too. She was a darling woman and we loved her dearly. She'd be so proud of you and she'd tell you to forget about the past and to move on. You have a life to live."

He swallowed a bite of bacon as he responded. "I try, but it's this case I'm working on. It seems that everywhere I turn, there are subtle reminders of my past. It's hard to stay focused."

"Aren't you the same person who told me whatever you're looking for is usually two inches from your nose?"

The private investigator chuckled. "Yeah, it goes somthin' like that."

"Then follow ya nose!" Slappy exclaimed as he feebly imitated the voice of Toucan Sam, the Fruit Loops cereal cartoon spokesperson. "It always knows!" Derek chuckled and continued to finish his breakfast.



**His cell phone rang as the Ferrari rumbled down Pacific Avenue.** It rang a second time as he observed tourism at its best. It wasn't even eleven o'clock before "The Strip" was littered with people looking to bring a little reminder of their vacation back home. He answered the cell phone as he came to a stop light. Two bikini-clad rollerbladers slowly skated by. His mind wandered to a brief fantasy before realizing he had not greeted the person on the other end of his phone.

"Morning."

"Good morning," came Saundra's voice. "How's your part in the investigation going?"

He weighed the consequences of divulging the details of last night. Realizing that Sydney was arrested for the murder of her sister, when instead the party responsible was a corrupt police Lieutenant, would only put undue stress upon the young apprentice. He decided to be vague. "I'm having my ups and downs. Got any info for me?"

"Not yet. I called Dr. Jared's office and he's been in Maryland for the last couple of days. He gets back later this afternoon, but he's got a tee time of three o'clock at Cypress Point Golf Club. I'm gonna try and catch up with him then."

"Okay, keep me posted."

"Of course," she said with a giggle. "If anything, it'll give me a chance to work on my slice."

"Saundra, I didn't know you golf."

"Yep. I'm pretty good with a shaft."

Derek shook his head as the light went green and the Ferrari eased its way forward. Responding to her last statement would only send the conversation deep into the bowels of sexual innuendos and flirtatiousness.  He needed to

remain focused at the task at hand; go home, shower and take a few moments to

rest.  "I'm not going to comment.  Goodbye Saundra."

Chapter Twenty

**When his father bought the beach house, it was to serve as a summer home away from the day to day reminders of his life and his past.** When Derek dropped out of Ithaca, his father demanded that he take some time to discover himself, and the beach house was the perfect distraction from other distractions. Oddly enough, it was one of the two things they saw eye-to-eye on. The other was the love they shared for his mother and the family she left behind.

He smiled, appreciating his mother's dream. When he was little, she and his father had often talked about a beach house in the Bahamas. She often quipped so many ideas and suggestions that his father would laugh himself to sleep. She even went so far as to sketch a floor plan of what she wanted, and even though she had no formal training, her drawings were vivid and easy to understand.

Soon after they were settled in Connecticut, his father flew down to Virginia Beach where he immediately contracted a local builder. It took two weeks to review his mother's sketches and ideas before they formulated the architectural blueprint. It took another two weeks to find the land that would be suitable. They stumbled across a two and one-half acre oceanfront lot deep within Croatan, a secluded beach development in Virginia Beach. After seven months, his mother's dream had become a reality, right down to the elaborately designed, marble fountains in the dining room and the exotic tapestries throughout the house.

The lock of the door clicked as he turned the knob. He stepped inside the beach house taking in a deep breath when a noise from around the corner startled him. It sounded like one of his desk's pictures had been knocked from its resting place. Someone was inside the house.

His body tensed in anticipation as he withdrew the Glock from the small of his back. He quietly cocked the weapon as he began to ease around the corner. He trained the weapon on the intruder as they came into view. Derek immediately recognized the security company's logo on the intruder's shoulder.

"You picked a bad time. I'm not up for visitors today."

"Too bad Rookie," came a familiar voice from behind as he felt a hard thump across the base of his head. His scenery quickly went blank.

**A slap across his face brought the blurred images slowly into focus.** He could feel the tightness of the handcuffs digging into his wrist. His mind had instantaneously begun to assess the situation. His home had been invaded by the very people trying to kill him. Other than Letourneau, two other security guards were in the house. From what he could hear, one was upstairs and the other was in the den which was off of the living room. They were rummaging through the house in search of something.  He had been captured and handcuffed.  He sat in the desk chair from the den in the middle of his living room, defenseless.  He looked up to find Letourneau circling around the chair like a predator determining the right moment to pounce upon his prey.  Derek quickly began to ask himself why he was still alive, while silently thanking the angels that kept him that way.  His mind promptly began to construct different scenarios to escape from his perilous dilemma.

"Rookie," Letourneau said with a chuckle.  "You got a lot of balls!  I can't believe you were crazy enough to break into Griffin Securities.  Man, if I wasn't going to kill you, I'd offer you a job."

"And I'd tell you to take that job, and shove it up your ass."

"Defiant to the end, eh Rookie?"

He smiled as he shook his head.  "I've been meaning to tell you that I hate it when you call me that.  It's so juvenile."

Letourneau withdrew his weapon and screwed the silencer on the muzzle.  "Oh, believe me when I tell you that you won't be hearing that much longer."

Derek's heart quickened.  "What do you want Nick?  If you were here to kill me, you would have done it by now."

The former police sergeant smiled.  "You don't know how close I came to doing just that.  I could have easily told Janocky that you put up a fight and I had no other choice, but he wants to know what you did with that video

cassette.”

"What video cassette?” Derek smirked. “You pulled the tape out,

remember?”

"Yeah. I also remember that I owe you one for slamming my head into a

locker.”

"Aw,” Derek taunted. “Did you get a little boo boo?”

Letourneau growled as he sent a fist across Derek’s jaw. “Keep it up

Rookie. I got all day.”

He could feel the warmth of blood running down through his goatee to his

chin. “I hope that wasn’t your best shot.”

Letourneau cocked the weapon and aimed it at his head. He grabbed onto

the chair as an opportunity presented itself. “Where is the goddamn tape?”

"Up your ass!”

Letourneau turned to the side as he took in a deep breath allowing Derek to

seize an opening. Because his feet were not bound, he was able to stand and

shove the former police sergeant backwards with his shoulder. He then turned,

sending the wheels of the chair towards his frustrated interrogator, knocking the

gun out of Letourneau’s hand. He then swung the other way catching the rogue

cop square into the chest. The blow caused Letourneau to stagger and fall onto

the glass coffee table. It exploded it into tiny shards of glass. He released the chair and quickly dropped to the floor. He curled up into a ball and brought his bound hands up under his feet and in front of him.

He glanced over at Letourneau who was now trying to get up and reach for his weapon. Derek quickly picked up a picture that had been thrown off of the sofa table and hurled it at his former partner, hitting him in the arm. Letourneau looked at him angrily as he hurried to retrieve his weapon.

Derek stood to his feet as the tips of Letourneau's fingers began to wrap around the handle. But before Letourneau could get a firm handhold and take aim, Derek kicked the weapon further from reach. He looked down at the disgusted face of Letourneau and smiled.

The light beside him exploded from gun fire above. Letourneau rolled out of the way as Derek dove for the discarded weapon. Bullets strafed the carpet as the investigator secured the pistol. Derek took aim to find the security guard zeroing in with a sub-machine gun. Derek squeezed the trigger catching the man in the chest. The hitman took a step backwards as Derek coughed off another quiet shot. The bullet spun the hitman sideways and he fell slumping over the railing.

The detective immediately spied the second security guard coming from the den and fired the pistol. Bullets slammed the assailant up against the wall, allowing him one last breath before he slowly fell to the floor.

Derek then turned sideways and took aim for Letourneau, but he was gone. One of the exotic curtains flapped in the gentle summer breeze. Letourneau had escaped to the patio.

*This isn't over.* He thought. *Not by a longshot.*

Weapon taut, he went over to the patio door. He cautiously peered through it. Finding it clear, he stepped outside onto the patio just as a foot kicked the gun out of his hands. He turned to find Letourneau reeling for a punch. Even with handcuffs, Derek was able to block the punch and send an elbow to the mid-section and a back hand to the nose.

Letourneau staggered backwards regaining his breath. "I've been waiting for this day for a long time, Rookie." He raised his hands ready to fight.

Derek couldn't help but chuckle. "You come to my house and expect to whoop my ass? Oh, you gotta anutha thing comin'."

The rogue cop sent a fist and Derek easily avoided it and retaliated with an elbow to the chin. Letourneau quickly sent another fist catching Derek along the cheek. The black detective took a step back as Janocky's enforcer lunged for another attack. He quickly sent a roundhouse kick into Letourneau's mid-section. The rogue cop buckled. Seeing his opportunity, Derek went for a front kick, but the former sergeant was able to block the attempt. Letourneau slowly rose to his feet as the detective sent a spinning high kick catching him across the base of his jaw. The force of the kick slammed him against the glass of the patio allowing him to look into the living room. He slowly turned to find Derek already sending a back kick. It connected with his chest sending him up into the air against the railing of the wooden deck. The railing buckled under his weight and permitted the sergeant to fall a few feet down onto the beach sand.

The detective could hear a low moan come from the former cop's lips as he walked down the stairs. He stood over his once mentor and taunted. "C'mon Nick! You've been waiting for this day for a long time! Get up!"

Letourneau growled loudly as he threw sand towards his tormentor. Derek turned sideways to avoid the attack. The burly attacker took that moment to rush the detective and tackled him onto the beach sand. They rolled around trying to gain the upper hand. However, Derek had the experience of different grappling techniques and maneuvered into a position where he was able to get behind Letourneau and wrap his bound hands around the discredited officer's neck. He tightened his hold as Letourneau clawed for freedom. Derek gritted his teeth as he continued to apply pressure. He could hear the struggle for air from his opponent. It would only be a few moments more before Letourneau's body went limp.

"Derek!" He looked up to find Elizabeth standing on the patio above them. She was already coming down the stairs. "Derek, don't do it."

"I'd….. listen to her." Letourneau managed to choke out.

Derek ignored their comments as he continued his stranglehold.

"Derek, please." Elizabeth begged.

"Don't you….." Letourneau gritted. "want to find out……who killed…..your mother?"

"I can do that without you." Derek answered.

"If you kill me…" Letourneau gagged. "…..then… you're no diff...er...ent….than me."

He growled as Letourneau's last statement echoed in his ears. He loosened his grip and sent the former police officer face first onto the ground. Letourneau coughed as his tried to regain his breath. Elizabeth quickly went over to Derek as two uniformed police officers took Letourneau into custody.

"Are you okay?" Elizabeth asked as she withdrew a key from her pocket. She knelt down and unlocked his handcuffs. "You're lucky I live close by. When I heard there were shots fired at this address, I came as quickly as I could."

A tear rolled down Derek's cheek as a reminder that the encounter with Letourneau was as emotional as it was physical. He had been tormenting himself since the day he had to turn his mentor in. During his confrontation, he realized that Letourneau was able to hide it better, but the former cop was no different than anybody else. He was just another person corrupted by their own greed. He understood it now and was relieved that he could close that chapter in his life.

"I should've accepted your offer for breakfast." he said to E.

She smiled and then her eyes went wide as a shot rang out. She fell forward into his arms. He looked past her shoulder to find Letourneau wrestling with the two police officers. He saw the Berretta in Letourneau's hand. Derek quickly reached for Elizabeth's holster and withdrew her weapon as Letourneau broke free from the two cops. He took aim at the private investigator.

"Time to die Rookie."

Derek squeezed the trigger and watched Letourneau's head jerk back. His body slowly fell to his knees as his eyes rolled to the back of his head. He fell face first onto the sand.

*Not today.*


**He sat in the waiting room with his heart in his throat.** Elizabeth was undergoing surgery to remove the bullet from her back. He was thankful that she had worn her vest; otherwise she'd be the first in her family to die in the line of duty. The vest also helped in deflecting the bullet away from her spine. The doctors said her situation was serious, but reassured him that she would make a full recovery.

"You okay?"

He looked up to find Steele standing above him. His response was silence.

"I know she's close to you, but she's a tough cookie, she'll be alright."

"I should have killed him when I had the chance."

"If what they told me is correct," Steele interjected. "You did kill him."

Derek looked up at the life-size Ken doll as he held his hands up in defense.

"Hey, I'm just making sure my facts are right."

Derek took in a deep breath reflecting on what he could have done

differently. His mind re-played various scenarios, but each had the same

outcome. Again, he swallowed the lump in his throat. He had feelings for

Elizabeth. He had made love to her. His mind and his heart quickly reminded

him of his past. First his mother, then Tessa and now Elizabeth. It was through

Elizabeth's own diligence that she was still alive. He took in a deep breath

silently vowing to keep love at arm's length. It would be a lonely road, but a

safe one for his heart.

"Mr. Chase," came a soft voice. "I didn't expect to see you back here so

soon."

He looked up to find Dr. Gellar. When they met for the first time, her

scrubs were green, today they were blue. Her hair was thrown into its usual

ponytail and her stethoscope hung loosely around her neck. She folded her arms

around her clipboard.

"A friend of mine was shot in the back. They're operating on her now."

"The female police officer that was with you the other night?"

He nodded.

Dr. Gellar smiled. "She's in good hands, there's no need for you to worry." She then caught a glimpse of his wrists. "My word, look at your wrists!"

He looked down to find that his wrists were red from the grip of the handcuffs. In fact, one hand was still handcuffed. He ignored her concern.

"She'll be fine, I promise." Dr. Gellar restated. "Let me take care of you," and she gave a head nod towards Steele. "Do you mind removing the handcuffs?"

Steele snapped out of his stupor and fumbled for the keys. He quickly reached for the handcuffs and unlocked them. "The doc is right; you probably should go with her and get checked out."

"I'm okay, really." Derek replied.

"Listen, Chase. Austin is on his way here and he's already worked up about this whole shit storm. I don't think it'll do any good for the two of you to be in a pissin' match. I'll stay here and get you as soon as I find out something. I promise."


**"You really care about her, don't you?"**

Derek nodded as she rubbed ointment on his left wrist. Her touch was soothing and gentle.

"She's lucky to have a guy like you in her corner."

"It's more of a curse."

"Listen, Derek," she said. He could hear her unsureness in calling him by his first name. "You need to stop beating yourself up about this. You're only one man and you can't do it all. Your friend is a police officer. She did her job and would do it again without question. It's what she does and she accepts that. Why can't you?"

"Because, everyone I care about sooner or later winds up dead. It's a miracle E is still alive."

"You can't mean that."

He took in a deep breath. "Look Doc, there's a lot you don't know about me. My life is very complicated."

"So, everybody's life is complicated."

"Not like mine."

She took another glob full of ointment and began treating the other wrist. "What makes you so different?"

"Doc, it's a long story."

She looked at him with a smile. "I don't think I'll be going anywhere soon."

He looked at her debating if he should divulge his life's story to another person. "My grandfather was the overlord of a South American cartel." he began. "My father worked for him and fell in love with his daughter, my mother.  When my grandfather fell ill, my father took control of the cartel, much to the dismay of other cartel members.  They attempted to kill my father, but murdered my mother and my four month old brother.  When the local police tried to investigate, the other cartel members discredited my father with false rumors that he was responsible for my mother's death and the attempted murder of my grandfather.  Fearing for his family's life, my father moved us to Virginia.  Shortly after, my grandfather died from the virus that attacked him.  Upon hearing the news, the cartel's replacement for my father took the opportunity to solidify my father's tainted reputation and vowed revenge for the death of "San Puliero's Patriarch".  My father evacuated us from Virginia and we globe-hopped for three years before he placed us with the family maid in Connecticut."

He watched her reaction as she stared at him.  "You miss them."

He nodded.  "Yes, I do."

"Good, because they are a part of who you are.  You will never be able to run from it.  It will always be there."

His nose took in a deep breath.  "You know, my father sent me to Ithaca to become a lawyer.  Thought it would be a great idea to have a lawyer in the family.  I never knew what my father did for a living until my second year of college."  He shook his head.  "Putting everything in perspective, I swore I wouldn't be like them.  So, I moved back to Virginia and became a police officer.  But because of my past, that eventually went to shit.  So here I am, a private investigator, investigating the murder of one of the two people who believed in me and gave me a second chance.  In that process I almost killed the second person."

"I want you to think about this." Dr. Gellar directed.  "What's the point if we stop caring?  You need to stop blaming yourself for what happened."  She smiled as she cupped his hands.  "If it's any consolation, I believe in you."

"You'll be safer if you don't."

"Can't help it." she smiled.  "Call it doctor-patient privilege."

The door slammed open as Austin stormed in.  He look angrier than a bull with his balls kicked in.  Steele quickly followed behind him and grabbed him as he lunged towards Derek.

"Words can't even describe what I'm feeling right now!" he bellowed as Steele struggled to hold him back.  "It's bad enough she's an acquaintance of yours, but to bring her into all of this is just fuckin' irresponsible!"

Derek sat in silence.

"Chase," the Lieutenant began as he shrugged free from Steele.  "This is the very last straw.  Your ass is mine!"

"Get him outta here!" Dr. Gellar yelled.

"Your ass is mine!" Austin repeated as Steele grabbed him.

"Get him outa here!"

Steele escorted Austin out of the room as Dr. Gellar refocused her attention to her patient.  She chuckled.  "You enjoy pissing him off don't you?"

He took a moment and thought about the many confrontations he had with Lieutenant Austin.  A brief chuckle came across his lips as he answered.  "Yes, I do."

Chapter Twenty-One

**He was there when her eyes fluttered open.**  She smiled.  "Hi there."

"Hey.  How are you feeling?"

She groaned as she tried to move.  "Like I've been shot in the back."

He smiled as he held her hand.  "You had me worried there for a moment."

Her thumb caressed the contours of his palm.  "You're not going to get rid

of me that easily Mr. Chase.  What time is it?"

"Six o'clock."  He then took in a deep breath as he began his next sentence.

"Elizabeth, I think-

"I know Derek," she interrupted.  Her voice was still weak.  "You don't

have to explain.  I know."

"E. It's not that I don't want to."

She pretended to smile.  "But you won't.  It's how you survive."

He kissed her on the forehead.  "I will always be there when you need me."

"Just remember that it's a two-way street."  She forced a smiled as she

squeezed his hand one more time before shooing him away.  "You better get

going.  Don't you have a job to do?"

"Are you going to be okay?" he asked slowly moving away from her.

"I'll be fine.  Are you going to be okay?"

He smiled as he searched for another answer, but there wasn't. "No, but that's not gonna stop me now."

**For the second time, police officers were at his beach house.**  The crime scene van was pulling out of his driveway as Steele's unmarked cruiser rolled to a stop.  Plain clothes detectives with latex gloves were ensuring that they had gathered all the evidence available.  Derek watched.  It was a little unnerving to have his home invaded and him taken hostage.

He opened the door of the Crown Victoria.  "Thanks for the ride, Steele."

"Whoa!" Steele bellowed.  "You're not going too far.  I have strict orders to bring your ass down to the precinct.  Austin wants you in his office in an hour.  He'll kill my ass, if I don't bring you in."

He conceded.  "Can I at least go inside and call my lawyer?  I need to let Kevin know everything that's going on.  Besides, I might need him at the precinct."

Steele mumbled under his breath and shook his head.  "I'm so going to regret this.  Go on and make your call.  If you're not back here in five minutes, you won't have to worry about Austin!"

He slapped the police detective on the shoulder as a gesture of thank you before removing himself from the police car.  He trotted up the cobblestone driveway towards the Ferrari. The exotic import sat amongst the scenery unscathed, as if it were invisible.

As he drew closer, he saw the light on his cell phone flashing. Someone was trying to call him. His trot quickened as he reached the door. He opened the car and yanked the phone out of its resting place.

"This is Chase."

"Derek, it's Saundra." There was static in the background. "I'm just now leaving the golf course."

"Did you find out anything from the doctor?"

"He said when Tessa hadn't called him back, he emailed the results to her. I told him about Tessa and asked if he could share the results with me, but he gave me a firm no and continued to play the tenth hole."

"Where are you now?"

"On my way to Wesleyan. I'm going to see if my friend can break into Tessa's email at work. I'll call you if I find anything out."

"Thanks Saundra," he said as he slid into the Ferrari. "Keep digging."

"Any luck on your side?"

He smiled as the engine of the Ferrari roared to life. He shifted the gear in neutral. "There will be if I can force Tessa's killer to confess."

"How are you going to manage that?"

"By pissin' him off even more," he said disconnecting the call as he

stepped on the accelerator.  The tires squealed as the import hastily backed out

of the cobblestone driveway.

*He bounced out onto the street catching a glimpse of Steele's face.  It was*

*a look of surprise and anger.  He hit the button on his automatic window as he*

*came to a stop next to the Crown Victoria.*

*"Tell Austin that I know about his deal with Janocky.  If he wants me, he's*

*gonna have to do it himself.  I'll be at Buzz Cutts Barbershop in Norfolk."*

*Derek then saluted with a smile as the Ferrari emitted a white smoke and*

*launched forward down the street.  If Austin was teetering on the edge of a*

*conniption, this stunt would surely push him over.*


**The dance version of a new song from Salt 'N' Pepa blared loudly in

the background as he walked into the barbershop.**  The smell of urban hair

spray and grease seeped into his nostrils.  Many of the chairs had been filled

with patrons who had came in for a last minute haircut.  Slappy's barbers

worked feverishly to accommodate them all.  Normally, they too had last minute

errands before they went home.

He found Slappy sitting in a corner.  He was reading the local newspaper.

Derek smiled, realizing Slappy was the only barber not cutting hair.  He walked

over and sat down beside his old friend and father figure.

"Punchin' out early?" the detective asked.

Slappy turned the page of the newspaper. "Why shouldn't I?  I helped build this place with my bare hands and have worked here ever since.  Don't you think I deserve to punch out early?"

The detective chuckled.  "Oh, you deserve it alright."

"Besides," Slappy continued as he nodded over to his young co-workers. "They're the ones wanting their gold chains, designer clothes, and fancy cars. Might as well let them work for it.  They'll come to appreciate the value of a dollar."

"Hey Slappy!" came Paxton's voice.  "Anything good playing at the movies tonight?"

"Why?" Slappy started.  "You gotta hot date tonight?"

"Don't I always?" Paxton responded.  "Look who you talkin' to.  You talkin' wit G-Love man."

"Ya keep goin' out wit all these floozies, you'll be G-Dead."

"Ah, Slappy," Andre started as he trimmed the hair around his customer's ears.  "Ya just jealous."

"Jealous of what?"  Slappy responded.  "All I see is a boy trying to prove his manhood.  Back in my day, women wanted a true gentleman."

"Back in your day," Paxton started.  "women were still getting hit over the heads with stone clubs."

The barbers and customers chuckled at G-Love's jab at Slappy.  The owner of Buzz Cutts non-chalantly turned the page of the newspaper.  Derek was enjoying another friendly confrontation between mentor and students.

"Keep it up."  Slappy warned.  "Or I'll get up and slap you upside the head with a club."

G-Love laughed.  "Slappy, did you say a club?  Or did you mean your cane?"

"Paxton, I suggest you focus on cuttin' that boys hair before you give him a reverse mohawk!"

The barbers chuckled as G-Love withdrew the electric clippers from his patrons head.  G-Love smiled as the customer stared at him.  "Don't mind him. He's not wearing his glasses.  You know how the elderly are these days."

The customer's dark, coffee-colored face was wide.  He looked like an unfed Rottweiler employed by the Military Police.  He even growled as he spoke.  "I don't want a reverse mohawk."

"A reverse mohawk?" G-Love started.  "C'mon man.  Give me more credit than that."

It was Slappy's turn to chuckle.  "Never let a customer doubt his barber." He said to the private investigator.  "No one wants a messed up haircut.  If they think they're on the verge of getting one, the end result will always be unsatisfactory."

Derek chuckled along. "I always said you were the best."

"You damn skippy." the older barber responded. "And don'tcha forget it either." He then returned to reading the articles in the newspaper. He took in a deep breath and folded the paper. "Did I ever tell you about the first time I met your father?"

He shook his head.

"I was in Army infantry during Vietnam and my platoon was on recon when we were ambushed by the enemy. Man, we were getting our asses handed to us on a silver platter. I got shot in the leg and in the chest. Damn near thought I was gonna die, but out of nowhere, these two Huey's come swoopin' down and level the place. Well, the next thing I know, I see this big ass black man, your father. He carries my ass to the chopper as what's left of the enemy regroups. He places me in the chopper and do you know what that crazy sonovabitch does?" Slappy starts laughing. "He takes the M-60 mounted on the Huey and starts runnin' towards the enemy screaming, like he's Rambo on crack. Man, I never seen people run away from a nigga so fast, I 'bout peed in my pants."

Derek gave a humpf. "I never knew that story about my dad."

Slappy chuckled. "There's a lot of shit about your father that you don't know. I tell you one thing; your grandfather liked him a whole hell of a lot."

"Yeah," Derek said. "Papa did like my father."

"Well after the war, your grandfather brought him into the family business. He was only a few years older than you are now.  When he met your mother that first day, it was love at first site.  Hell, your grandfather like your dad so much, he practically married off your mother to him.  When I caught up with your father a few years later, I had the chance to meet your mother and the Denteveron family.  They made me feel welcomed, and in this day and age that goes a long way.  I owe your father my life, so when you decided to stay here and live, I promised him I would watch over you."

"It's a debt you've paid a thousand times over."  Derek replied.

"Have you talked to your father lately?"

"No," Derek replied.  "I don't know what to say to him.  Ever since I dropped out of law school and went into the police academy, we've been kinda distant."

"Well, I'm not gonna tell you that he wasn't upset by your decision.  He really wanted a lawyer in the family and not for the reasons you think.  I will tell you that he respects you for being honest with him and he is proud of you."

"I guess his way of saying it is by buying a two hundred thousand dollar sports car?"

Slappy chuckled.  "Bribe must've worked, coz' I don't see you complaining when you're driving around in that two hundred thousand dollar sports car. Betta check yourself. Besides, your mother would want the two of

you to be close."

"I know Slappy," he replied. "I know."

Slappy took in a deep breath as he unfolded and returned to his newspaper.

"By the way, what brings you to this neck of the woods this time of day? It's

almost closing time."

The black investigator reflected on Slappy's words before answering the

aging barber. "I'm looking for Titus actually. I figured you had the 4-1-1 on

everyone in this neighborhood."

"You got that right," Slappy replied. Derek could hear the sarcasm in his

voice. "I'm Bell fuckin' Atlantic."

"Not to mention, word on the street is that he's cuttin' hair for you now."

"Yep." Slappy answered as he flipped through the newspaper. "Not a bad

boy either. Just a little misguided. Felt sorry for him, so I'm givin' him a

chance to change his ways and make somethin' of himself."

Derek looked around the barber shop to find an empty barber's chair in the

corner. The other barbers did not resemble the former gang leader. "Ya know

where he is now?"

Slappy looked over the newspaper and also saw the empty barber's chair.

He then leaned back and returned to the newspaper. "He's probably in the back

room wit his hoodlum friends."

Derek stood up and straightened his outfit. "A little misguided, eh?"

"Just a little."

The black detective placed his hand on Slappy's shoulder in a gesture of appreciation and friendship. "Take care of yourself Slappy."

"That's all I've been doin'," the barbershop owner replied. "You need to start worryin' more about yourself."

He nodded in agreement and walked off towards the back room, leaving the barber engrossed in his newspaper. He went past the sign labeled "Employees Only" and peered around the corner to find a bald-headed Titus with two of his associates from the "Park Place Posse". He recognized them both instantly. One was the Mike Tyson look alike and the other was Titus's secretary, the posse member with the gold cappings. They were conversing quietly around a box of KFC. When Derek walked in, their chatter ended.

His eyes met with Titus's and then focused on the other two Posse members. They seemed apprehensive about his intrusion. "Listen," Derek began. "I'm just here to talk with Titus. We can make this easy, or we can do it the hard way."

The Mike Tyson look alike was about to stand, but was stopped by Titus. "Chill man." Titus ordered. He nodded towards Derek. "No more Kung-Fu shit. Tell me whatcha need Homey?" he asked as he picked up a chicken leg.

"I need to talk with you about the night your car was impounded."

"What about it?"

"Do you remember the cop that bullied you?"

Titus swallowed and took a fork full of mashed potatoes. "I don't remember his name if that's what you mean, but I damn sure won't forget his face."

"Could you identify him if you saw him again?"

"What's in it for me?"

"You might get your car back for one thing. And, I'll owe you one."

Titus took a swig of his soda and looked at the detective. "You'll owe me one?"

"Scout's honor."

Titus chuckled. "Yeah. I bet you were a scout." he continued chuckling as he bit into the chicken leg. "Okay man. That's cool."

A voice bellowed from the barbershop. He immediately recognized it as Austin's. "Chase! Get your ass out here now!"

Derek nodded towards Titus. "Come tell me if this is the guy that took your ride."

Titus took another swig of his soda before following Derek out to the barbershop. The other two "Posse" members continued with their dinner.

"Yo," Titus said as he looked back. The two "Posse" looked up like startled dogs. "Betta be anutha leg waitin' for me when I git back." He continued to follow the detective out from the break room.

All work in the barbershop had came to a halt when Derek came out of the back room. Austin stood at the front door. His face was red with anger. "Chase, you are under arrest for obstruction of justice, and I hope to hell you make this more difficult than what it is."

"Why don't you arrest yourself?" Derek yelled.

"What the hell are you talking about?" Austin bellowed.

Derek leaned towards Titus. "Is that the cop that impounded your car?"

"Naw dawg. Never seen this slice of whitebread before."

"You sure?"

"Positive. It ain't da muthafucka."

"Chase." Austin began as he walked deeper inside the barbershop. "What the hell are you talking about?"

Derek took in a deep breath as he divulged his story. "I know you're a dirty cop Austin. I can prove it. I also have evidence linking you to Tessa Taylor's murder."

Austin chuckled. "That's absurd! So Thatcher, Tessa and I went to the same college? So what? So you followed me to the oceanfront and saw me exchange information with Thatcher? Big deal?"

"I have the videocassette of your meeting with Janocky."

Austin shook his head. "Is that what this is all about?  Damn it Chase! You're stirring the shit and don't have the slightest idea.  That so called meeting with Janocky was an elaborate sting operation.  Tessa was secretly working on the necessary court documents and Thatcher was working at Griffin Securities as an insider for me.  We would have had him when everything went down with Premiere Tech, but it did not go cleanly, hence, my meeting with Thatcher. When Tessa was murdered, Thatcher got scared, so he came to me with everything he had and was going to leave the country, but you had to stick your nose into everything and fuck it all up.  Because of you, I'm almost back at square fuckin' one!"

"You signed for the release of an impounded car.  It was used to run Thatcher off the road."

"Chase, I sign my name a hundred times a day.  How the hell should I know what they're for?"

"Fact of the matter is," came a voice.  Derek looked over Austin's shoulder as the police Lieutenant whirled around.  Sgt. Steele stood behind them with a big smile and a .44 Magnum. "You shouldn't."

<u>**Chapter Twenty-Two**</u>:

**"Yo!" Titus yelled as he pointed towards Steele. "Dat's da muthafucka who took my ride! Dat's him!"**

Derek smiled as he shook his head. The pieces were slowly beginning to fit together. "You played me all this time?"

His grin was sinister. "Like a fiddle." He motioned for Austin to back away from him. "You see, Janocky was suspicious of Austin from the get-go, so he called me. Offered me a hundred thousand dollars to keep tabs on him. Then as the Lieutenant said, you stuck your nose into things and Janocky asked me to take care of it. Who would thought you'd be wearing a bullet proof vest that night? Then you stumbled across Thatcher and I thought having you around might be more of an asset than a deterrent. Man, we've been looking for him for a while. I knew Austin had him tucked away somewhere. It was only a matter of time before I caught up with him. Thanks for doing my legwork."

"You sonovabitch." Austin snarled.

"So you killed Tessa in your process of eliminating loose ends."

Steele shook his head. "Nope. I can't take credit for that, but I'm glad someone did. The bitch's death is what scared Thatcher out of hiding in the first place."

"You'll never get away with this," Austin vowed.

Steele laughed. "Who's gonna stop me? A washed up P.I., a hot headed police Lieutenant and a barbershop of unarmed degenerates. Please."

"Fuck you man!" Titus yelled. "I should've popped a cap in ya ass da night you took my ride!"

"Threatening a police officer?" Steele responded as he aimed the weapon at the reformed gang leader. "Oh we can't have that can we?" and Steele squeezed the trigger to the .44. Everybody flinched from the loud boom echoing throughout the barbershop.

Derek watched as the newest member of Buzz Cutts lifted backwards in the air. Titus landed hard against the arm of a barber's chair and fell limply to the floor. A pool of blood began to mix with the discarded hair of the patrons.

The detective refocused his attention to the muzzle of the six shooter now aimed at his chest. It became apparent that Steele's agenda was to kill anybody who stood in his way. He looked to the right of the gun to find Omar slowly moving closer to the rogue cop like a wild panther stalking its prey. He had to think of something quick to give Omar that extra second of surprise. Then suddenly, it hit him and a chuckle escaped from his lips.

"What's so goddamn funny?" Austin asked.

"Yeah," Slappy added. "What's so goddamn funny?  Somebody just got shot in my damn barbershop.  Shit!  Do you know what kinda of bad publicity that brings?"

"Shut up!" Steele yelled.  "Everybody shut the fuck up!"

Derek's chuckle turned into a slight laugh.  He pointed towards the security camera mounted to the wall.  "I almost forgot.  I was going to get Austin to confess to everything on camera, but I guess your testimony and murder of an innocent civilian will have to do."

Steele looked up at the camera that had caught the entire scene as it unfolded.  "Fuck me," he said, mumbling softly.

The discredited police detective gave a frustrated yell as he fired a shot blowing the camera to bits.  Omar took his opportunity to rush the burly Ken doll.  He tackled Steele into a barber's chair and fought to wrestle the gun out of his hand.  Austin and Derek saw their opportunity to assist Omar while the rogue cop was on the defensive.

Before they could get to the two men grappling for position, Steele quickly sent a knee into Omar's groin.  Omar buckled as the rogue cop drove the butt of the large revolver across his jaw.  Omar fell to the floor with a thud.  Steele turned, took aim and fired at them.  Derek dove to the floor just as a yelp came from the police Lieutenant beside him.  He looked up to find Austin falling backwards onto the tile floor.  He quickly looked back at Steele who was taking

aim at the private investigator.

Bullets ricocheted off the wall beside Steele before he could get off a shot.

Derek looked over his shoulder to find Titus's gang affiliates had joined in the

firefight.  Steele covered his head as he retaliated.  He backed out of the

barbershop's entrance coughing off two shots of his own.

The black investigator took in a deep breath as he looked over at the

Lieutenant fearing that he joined Titus in "The Afterlife", but was relieved when

a low moan came from the cop's lips.  He began opening the Lieutenant's bullet

holed shirt.

"Austin!"  He yelled as he ripped the shirt open.  He raised his eyebrows in

amazement.  Embedded in his bulletproof vest was the .44 slug.  Austin started

coughing as he slowly regained consciousness.

The Lieutenant sucked in a deep breath of air as his lungs re-filled.  He

slowly began to pull himself up.  "I'm okay," he coughed out.  He started

waving off the detective.  "Go catch that bastard!"

The detective concluded Austin would soon recover from his almost point

blank shooting.  He silently thanked the cop for risking his life and quickly

stood up.  Determined to see this through the very end, he took after the

renegade cop.  It was time for retribution.

**Steele glanced over his shoulder to find the detective coming out of the barbershop after him.** He ran down a crowded street, bumping into people and attractive store stands, hoping the obstacles would slow his pursuer down.

Derek saw how the sergeant was trying to slow him down, but he was not to be denied. He side-stepped and hurdled the obstacles in front of him and seemed to will himself to run faster as he gained on the aging sergeant.

The sergeant stopped and turned, firing. Derek stopped and ducked behind an illegally parked car. Steele went to take another shot, but only heard the click of his gun. He threw the six shooter to the side and resumed his retreat, disgusted in his failure of detouring the investigator.

He glanced around the bumper as people scurried around to avoid being shot at. He looked through the crowd to find Steele running across a four lane intersection towards another shopping plaza. He continued his pursuit, crossing the intersection filled with the busy evening traffic of Norfolk. Cars quickly jerked to a halt and blared their horns as he followed after the sergeant.

The plaza seemed unusually crowded. The people who did not have their arms littered with shopping bags were either roller blading or riding their bikes. The summer atmosphere made the perfect scenery to do whatever. Derek's engagement with Steele would soon make ripples in their tranquil environment.

*"I don't get it Officer Chase," Tessa began. She went back to her table and picked up a file. She opened it as she continued her observation. "When*

*you fired your weapon, you hit the suspect in the shoulder. Why not his chest or his head? I reviewed your academy files. You were the head of your class in marksmanship, both with a pistol and a rifle. You could've nailed him easily. If you felt your life was in danger, why not put the suspect down?"*

*"I was taught by my instructors at the academy that my sidearm and my badge are only tools to enforce the law. It was unwritten, but outwardly known that our law, above all else, is to serve and protect. How I used those tools would determine how well I enforced that law."*

*During his pursuit, he quickly gained on the sergeant. He was behind him by three steps before directing his momentum in a jumping side-kick. He planted his foot across the Sergeant's back causing the fleeing cop to move faster than what he could handle. Steele fell forward onto the pavement and rolled to a stop.*

Derek fought to quickly catch his breath. "Tell me you're not gonna make this easy," he taunted.

Steele quickly scrambled to his feet and took off his trench coat as he taunted back. "On the contrary," he said as he assumed a martial arts pose. "I'm gonna make this as hard as hell."

Derek recognized the Tae Kwon Do stance. He raised an eyebrow in amusement. "Steele? You can't be serious."

"Fifth degree black belt in Tae Kwon Do." Steele said with a smile. "What's the matter Chase? A little bit out of your league?"

Derek brushed off the sarcasm. "Not a chance."

Steele yelled as he attacked and charged at the investigator. Derek moved to his left and straightened his right arm catching the sergeant full in the throat. Steele landed on his back with a thud. Derek turned and sat in a defensive pose as the rogue cop slowly rose to his feet.

"What's the matter, Steele? You fight like you're up for retirement or somethin'. I'm not moving too fast for you am I?"

Steele growled as he sent a punch. Derek leaned back as the sergeant's fist missed its target. Derek countered with two punches of his own, catching the renegade cop in the face. Steele staggered backwards clutching his jaw, laughing.

"Not bad Chase. Not bad at all," and he yelled as he charged again. Derek could not move quickly enough, and was tackled against the thick, steel railing corralling a herd of shopping carts. Steele sent a flurry of punches into Derek's mid-section. The detective buckled as Steele recoiled for a strike to the face. The martial arts training reacted and Derek blocked countering with his own strike to the face. Again it caught Steele in the jaw.

The sergeant stumbled backwards as the detective sent a crescent kick. It caught the other side of the police sergeant's jaw. Steele slowly returned to his full height as the detective balanced himself on one leg.  In rapid succession he sent round house kicks connecting with the side of Steele's head.

The traitor of the police department buckled as Derek closed in for the kill. He tightly clenched his teeth as he sent a punch downwards.  It knocked Steele onto the pavement, flat on his face.  Derek followed after him, rolled him onto his back and pinned him to the ground.  His hand lashed out and wrapped itself around the sergeant's throat.  Steele quickly sent his leg up and flipped Derek onto his back.  Both men scrambled to their feet.

Steele cracked his neck as he resumed his fighting stance.  "You're better than I thought, but now it's my turn."

He lunged towards Derek and faked with a punch, but sent a spinning back-kick connecting with Derek's gut.  Derek buckled as another foot came across his jaw.  Derek fell to the ground coughing.

"Fighting like I'm up for retirement, eh?" he mocked.  He grunted as he sent a foot into the private investigator's ribs like he was trying to kick a field goal for some football team.  "Didn't you learn anything from Nick?" he asked as he sent another kick to his midsection rolling Derek onto his back.  "Rookies should obey their superior officer!"

*The courtroom illuminated like the Fourth of July as newspaper photographers fought each other for that one picture that would summarize the entire trial.  Sheriff's deputies locked the metal bracelets around the Sergeant's*

*wrists and began to escort him out.  Derek watched him as they escorted him
past the prosecutor's table.  They stopped in front of the rookie police officer.*

*"You did good Rookie, but it doesn't stop with me.  This is bigger than
anybody could imagine.  My advice would be to watch your back.  Be seeing you
around Rookie."*

*Sergeant Letourneau chuckled as the two deputies revived their efforts to
take him into custody.  His chuckle turned to laughter as he exited the
courtroom with photographers and reporters hounding his every step.*

*The rookie officer fell back into his chair, relieved that the ordeal was
coming to an end, but was now questioning the Sergeants parting remarks.
Several ideas were beginning to formulate in his mind.  His thoughts were
interrupted when Tessa placed her hand on his shoulder.  It was a comforting
gesture.  She smiled as if she understood what he was thinking.*

*"Sometimes when you win, you also lose.  You gotta take each battle as
they come, and grow from them.  It's how you survive when you do what we
do."*

Derek's ribs burned with pain, reminded of the earlier encounter with the
red Lexus. He coughed as his lungs re-filled with air.  He struggled to ignore
the pain as Steele came in for another attack.  Derek caught his foot and twisted,
spinning the rogue cop off balance.  Quickly rising to his feet, he glared at the
turncoat.

Derek wiped his mouth and looked at the blood on his hand.  He then turned his attention towards Steele.  "You forget.  I'm not a cop anymore."

Steele threw a punch towards Derek and the black investigator caught the attempt and twisted his arm.  He stepped inside and kneeled sending an elbow below Steele's rib cage.  Derek completed the maneuver by flipping the detective who looked like Sam Spade onto his back.  Derek returned to his normal height and was poised for another attack.

Steele got up and charged for another attack.  Derek stopped him in his tracks with a crescent kick and a spinning heel kick to the temple.  Steele staggered sideways as Derek continued to attack.  The black investigator took two steps before leaping in the air with a jump sidekick.  His foot caught Steele square in the nose slamming him hard against the steel railing of the shopping cart gate.

The renegade cop fought to secure his footing as he reached around his back.  "You're so fuckin' dead!" he yelled in anger and he spun around towards Derek with a small revolver in his hand.  His eyes went wide when he found the muzzle of Derek's Glock 9mm aimed at his head.

"I don't think so." the private investigator replied and he calmly exhaled as he squeezed the trigger.

Chapter Twenty-Three

**Dr. Gellar sighed as she re-wrapped Derek's rib cage.** "If I didn't know any better, I'd say you have thing for hospitals."

He flinched as she smoothed the tape against the gauze. "No. Although, I do have a thing for cute doctors."

"Still trying to get me to go to dinner?"

He gave a low groan as he answered. "I know a great place on the oceanfront."

She gave a humpf as she begun to add a third layer of gauze. His muscles checked in from all parts of his body. He could picture them complaining about being sore from his encounter with Steele. His mid-section was probably the most vocal. If he twisted slightly, or took in a deep breath, it felt like somebody was squeezing him like a sponge. He looked over at a smiling Lieutenant Austin who watched the episode unfold as she taped the final strip of the protective barrier. Again, the detective winced in pain as he took in a deep breath.

Derek could see the Lieutenant's glee. "Did I ever say thank you for saving my life?"

Austin folded his arms as he leaned against the wall of the Emergency Room. "No," he answered. "I don't believe you did."

Derek smiled as Dr. Gellar nodded at her handy work. "I'll be back in just a moment." With that, she opened the door and left the room.

"You know this doesn't change anything between us," Derek said. Austin nodded his head in agreement. "I still think you're a pompous jackass."

"And I still believe you're a reckless endangerment to society."

"Mortal enemies to the end?"

"Agreed."

The two of them laughed as Derek's cell phone rang. He groaned as he dropped from the edge of the bed. He picked up the phone that was next to his other belongings and answered it on the second ring.

"This is Chase."

"Where the hell have you been?" Saundra asked. "I've been trying to call you for over an hour!"

"I've been preoccupied." Derek said as he reached for his shirt. "What did you find out?"

He could hear Saundra taking in a deep breath before she relayed her information. "Kevin is the father of Tessa's baby."

"What?"

"It didn't take long for my friend to break into Tessa's email and pull up Dr. Jared's test results.  It was 96.8 percent positive.  Tessa was having Kevin's baby."

He took in a deep breath absorbing the results of Saundra's inquiry.  He thought about it for a moment.  So they had an affair.  Many people nowadays were sleeping around with someone other than their partner.  He thought back to the woman that hired him to follow her husband, who only a few days ago, not only confronted the shocking reality of her husband's infidelity, but partook in its deceitful allegations.  So Tessa and Kevin were more than just business partners.  It would take a lot more to convince him that the co-founder of Garrett and Taylor had anything to do with Tessa's death.

"Good work Saundra.  I'll touch base with you later."

"What was that all about?" Austin asked as Derek disconnected the line.

Derek shook his head.  "Just tying up some loose ends."

Dr. Gellar walked back in with a large manila file.  She cocked her head to the side shuffling her brown hair to the side.  She smirked.  "The X-rays came back.  You are very lucky.  Besides the hairline fracture you suffered earlier, your ribs are just bruised, so you'll be sore for a few days.  I am asking you to please give them a chance to heal this time."

"Dinner at Isle of Capri tomorrow night would ensure a speedy recovery."

She giggled giving in to the suggestion.  "If it will keep you out of trouble."

Austin coughed interrupting their conversation.  "That's bullshit!  Nothing will ever keep him out of trouble."

Derek looked over towards Austin and smirked.  Dr. Gellar smiled, ignoring their banter.  "Just so you know, I don't normally have dinner with my patients."

He smiled.  "I'm not your typical patient."

"Got that right."  Austin interjected.

Dr. Gellar collected her clip board, placing it with the manila folder.  She turned as the door to the room opened allowing a uniformed police officer to walk in.  He handed a manila envelope to Austin and then walked out.  "Well then, until tomorrow night."

"I'll call you with the details."

It was her turn to smirk.  "Unless they bring you back in here on a stretcher between now and then.  Goodnight Derek."

"Goodnight Doc." he retorted and Dr. Gellar left to attend to other patients.

Austin opened the manila envelope as he began to speak.  "I'm sending a squad car over to Mr. Janocky's residence.  It seems he and I will be up for the rest of the night.  Thanks to Steele's videotaped confession, I'm sure we'll have a lot of things to discuss." Satisfied with the contents he handed the manila envelope to Derek. "This is for you."

Derek took the envelope as he slid the black shirt over his body. "What is it?"

"It's the results of the ballistics report Officer Companstella did for you." he continued as Derek reviewed the sheet of paper. "The bullets that killed Tessa are the same bullets that killed the security guard in her office. Same manufacturer and stock number. However, the bullet that killed Tessa wasn't fired from Sydney Taylor's gun. According to the report, the bullet friction doesn't match. It's slightly off. Tessa was killed by a different gun."

"A different gun?"

"Yep. Looks that way."

*Sydney adjusted from her position and sat up, listening to the scores. As she prepared for her departure she noticed that her opponents could not quite match her performance. She checked the weapon to make sure the chamber was empty. "You can thank my father for that. As teenagers, he would take Tessa and me to the country and give us instruction. He felt that women living in the big city should know how to defend themselves. For my eighteenth birthday, he bought me a Walther PPK. You know the gun James Bond has? It matched the one Tessa got the year before when she turned eighteen."*

He could not believe the implications his mind was making from the information he was getting.  The bullet friction was slightly off.  Killed by a different gun, but the bullets used are from the same manufacturer and stock number as Sydney's.  Could Tessa have been shot by her own gun?  If she was, was she defending herself?  And who was she defending herself from?

*He could hear Saundra taking in a deep breath before she relayed her information.  "Kevin is the father of Tessa's baby."*

"What's on your mind?" Austin asked.  "You look like someone just kicked you in the balls."

He shrugged off Austin's comments sustaining his attention to sorting all of the information in his mind.  Theories were presenting themselves and he did not like what he was concluding.  *Could Kevin have killed Tessa?*  He asked himself.

How was that possible?  Kevin was at dinner with the Commonwealth's Attorney that night.  He had dinner reservations for 7:00 that night and Derek did not drop Tessa off at her apartment until 7:20.  It would have taken Kevin thirty minutes just in driving time alone.  There wasn't enough time.  But what if he was already there?

*The apartment had been torn apart.  It was as if a tornado had been born in the middle of the living room and unmercifully displayed its insatiable appetite for destruction.  The burgundy couch and love seat had been ripped* open like gutted fish.  The glass coffee table separating them, were now many little islands of glass splinters.  Looking past the living room through the breakfast bar, he could see the refrigerator door and the kitchen cabinets had been thrown open and their contents exhibited across the counters.  He suspected much of the same throughout the apartment.  There was an oak desk in the far corner by the kitchen.  It had been toppled over, its desk drawers strewn across the floor with their contents emptied on the carpet.  The awards and framed pictures that were once on the wall above the desk, sat on the floor cracked open.  A computer monitor with a busted screen had somehow managed to travel to the other side of the room where it positioned itself next to a plant that had been uprooted and discarded.  At the far wall leading to the bedrooms were the remnants of an aquarium.  It had been emptied out onto the carpet, soaking it with a variety of fish and aquarium toys that the detectives were still having a hard time avoiding.  In the center of that mishap was a large black bag as the sum of one's ill-timed actions and a sad reminder of how precious life was.

"Listen Chase," the Lieutenant interjected.  "You may not have gotten it in that mule head of yours, but you're no longer a cop and this is a police matter.  I don't need you turning this into a three ring circus.  As far as I'm concerned, this is a simple breaking and entering case.  Tessa Taylor came home, found a prowler, there was a struggle and he shot her in the chest."

*Derek walked over to the Lieutenant. "Austin, I hate to shatter this perfect scenario; but if this was a simple breaking and entering, why didn't the prowler take her diamond tennis bracelet or the money in her wallet? I found an unsigned credit card on the table. What prowler in his right mind would turn that down?"*

*"He was scared."*

*"Bullshit!" Derek exclaimed. "Somebody was looking for something."*

There were too many coincidences beginning to formulate in his mind. He had to be sure. He looked over at the table near Austin and nodded towards it. "Will you pass me the phone book please?"

Austin followed along as the detective picked up the hospital phone by the bed. He watched as the detective opened the book and started to quickly flip through the pages. "What are you doing?"

He ignored the Lieutenant's question as he found the number that he was looking for and started dialing. He looked at Austin as he waited for an answer. He could see the frustration building in the police officer's eyes. The phone rang four times before a man answered.

"Le Chambord. How may I assist you?"

"Good evening. I'm calling from Garrett and Taylor Law Firm and I'm auditing their expenses for the month and need the confirmation of a receipt. The amount is kind of smudged and unreadable."

"Do you know the date sir?"

"Yes.  It was under the name of Kevin Garrett for last Thursday at 7:30."

"Please hold."  Soft jazz immediately started playing in his ear.  He took in a deep breath as his heart thumped against his chest.  He hoped his suspicions were wrong.  "I have a Mr. Kevin Garrett, party of two for 8:00 last Thursday."

"8:00?"

"Yes sir.  I seated them myself.  If you don't mind, it'll be just a moment to pull that receipt."

Derek shook his head.  "No, that won't be necessary.  Thank you for your time," and he hung up the phone.  "Damn."

Austin gave a huff.  "Will you please tell me what the fuck is going on?"

He could feel his face turn pale as he realized what he now knew.  "It's time for me to go pick up Tessa's killer."

"What?"

"Kevin Garrett killed Tessa."

"Her partner?"  Austin asked.  The confusion in his voice was more distinguished.  "But why?"

Derek hurried to gather his things.  "I'm not exactly sure, but this is what I do know.  Tessa was pregnant with Kevin's baby."

"Huh?"

"Tessa and Sydney were given identical, well almost identical, Walther PPKs by their father for their eighteenth birthdays.  That would explain the same bullets from two different guns.  The night Tessa was murdered; Kevin said he had reservations for Le Chambord at 7:00.  I just got off the phone with the maitre'd and he confirmed that their reservation was for 8:00, not 7:00."  He still couldn't believe the words flowing from his lips.  His heart was sinking to the pit of his stomach.  "That would have given Kevin plenty of time to commit murder."

"I still don't understand.  If she was pregnant with his baby, why kill her?"

"I don't know."  Derek answered as he thought back to Kevin's tour of Lynnhaven One.  He hardly displayed the characteristics of someone willing to take another life.  "We can ask him that before you arrest him," and then Derek stopped as he remembered another important detail.  "Oh shit."

"Now what?"

Derek did not respond as he quickly picked up the receiver to the hospital phone and dialed.  It rang four times before a woman's voice answered.

"Hello?"

"Hello?  Mrs. Garrett?"

"Yes, this is she."

Kevin's wife sounded like she had been sleeping. "I'm sorry to disturb you this evening. My name is Derek Chase and I work with your husband. I have an urgent matter that I need to discuss with him. Is he in?"

"I'm afraid not," she answered. "He called earlier this evening and said he'd be working late. He said he had to finish some paperwork with Tessa's sister."

"So, he is at the office?"

"I believe he is."

"Great. I'll swing over there and talk to him personally. Again, I'm sorry to disturb you Mrs. Garrett. Good night."

"Good night."

Austin looked on with curiosity. "Will you please tell me what's up your ass?"

"When Sydney was arrested, I had E call Kevin to bail her out. She's smart, so I'm sure she has figured out that the bullet that killed Tessa came from Tessa's gun. She may not know who pulled the trigger, but if she tells Kevin what she knows, she may be in more trouble than she thought."

Austin raised his eyebrows as Derek went for the door. "Oh shit."

<u>**Chapter Twenty-Four**</u>:

**The air seemed chilly for a summer night as Derek and Lieutenant Austin stepped out onto the observation deck of Lynnhaven One.** They found Kevin and Sydney standing across from one another with the lights of the Chesapeake Bay Bridge serving as a lighted backdrop. However, the detective's attention was not focused on the night lights, but the trembling hand of Kevin Garrett. The lawyer was holding Tessa's Walther PPK and had it aimed at Sydney. Austin immediately withdrew his weapon and pointed it towards the armed attorney.

"Drop the gun Mr. Garrett!"

Kevin looked at the two intruders and then back at Sydney who was backing away from him. His hands trembled even more. "She doesn't understand."

"Drop the gun now!" Austin ordered.

"Can't you see what she's doing to me?"

Derek placed a hand on Austin's shoulder as he took a step forward. "Kevin? What is she doing to you?"

He could see a tear roll down the cheek of the hostage taker. "She wouldn't listen to me! She's gonna ruin everything! Heather wouldn't understand!" He pointed towards Sydney. "She and I spent every waking moment together.  I loved her!  When she told me she was pregnant, I didn't

know how to handle it.  I went bezerk!  I went over to her house to look for her

medical records and she came home early.  We got into an argument and I.....I

hit her.  She got scared and pulled out her gun."

"And you shot her?"

"It was an accident!" Kevin said as he broke down into tears.

"I know it was an accident and I know you loved Tessa."

"But....Heather?"

"You still love her don't you?"

Kevin nodded as a few more tears rolled down his face.

"And she loves you?"

The attorney nodded again and shook the gun at Sydney.  "But I can't let

her ruin everything!  I just can't!  You hear that Tessa?  I won't let you ruin

everything you selfish bitch!"

Derek drew closer realizing that Sydney's resemblance to her sister had

Kevin walking a fine line between past and present.  It was become an

increasingly volatile situation.  He took another step closer to the gun toting

attorney.  He could almost reach out and take the gun.  "Look at me." Derek said

calmly.  Kevin turned his head as the gun shook wildly.  "It's over Kevin.  Tessa

can't hurt you anymore."

"She can't?  But-

"It's over." The private investigator said softly as he reached up and lowered the gun in Kevin's shaking hand. In one quick movement, his reverted back to his police training and put Kevin in an arm lock and forced him to the ground. Austin ran up, re-holstering his weapon and unveiling a pair of handcuffs as Derek slowly pried Kevin's fingers away from the gun that killed his business partner.

He looked over at Sydney who was beginning to shake like a leaf. Austin knelt down and snapped the metallic bracelets on Kevin's wrist and began reading him his Miranda Rights. "Kevin Garrett, you are under arrest for the murder of Tessa Taylor. You have the right to remain silent."

Derek stood as Sydney ran up to him. Tears were welling up in her face as she wrapped her arms around him. He did his best to comfort her. "I still can't believe he killed Tessa," she cried. "When he told me-

"Shh…" he comforted. "It's gonna be okay. It's all over now."

He looked over at Kevin who was still having his rights read to him as Austin hoisted him to his feet. His tears had stopped, but his face was still glazed over. The police Lieutenant yanked him forward and began towards the door exiting the observation deck.

"No!" Kevin yelled as he resisted. "You can't!" and he snatched himself away from Austin's grip and ran away from him.

"Goddamn it!" Austin said mainly to himself as he took chase. "Come back here!"

Derek and Sydney watched as Kevin ran full sprint towards the ledge of the observation deck with Austin quick on his heels. They stared in horror as Kevin dove head first over the railing. Austin reached out for him, but the expression on his face confirmed his failure. The Lieutenant lowered his head in pity.

He took in a deep breath as the lump in the base of his stomach settled. He could feel Sydney nestling her head deeper in his chest as she began to finally grieve. Now, it was over.

**The sun was beginning to rise over the ocean as Derek stepped up and propped himself beside the successor of Garrett and Taylor.** He handed her the morning paper which he had already perused. He was happy to read that Janocky had been indicted on felony charges, including conspiracy to commit murder. There was also a brief paragraph praising Tessa Taylor and her work prior to her unfortunate demise. He was satisfied to see that the reporter omitted the facts leading up to her death and left it to the reader to speculate. It was a justifiable ends to a means.

He looked around the observation deck and saw the small memorial of flowers in honor of Tessa and Kevin. One of the metal picnic tables had been set aside to serve as its staging area.  From the many people that frequented to observation deck, a few had actually stopped to pay their respects.  It had been three weeks since Tessa's death and things were slowly getting back to normal. He looked out across the way towards the ocean.  A sailboat had just hoisted its sail and was beginning to set adrift.

Sydney took in a breath of morning air and started the conversation. "Have you found out anything else about your mother's death?"

Derek shook his head.  Janocky's and Letourneau's admission of knowing who was responsible for his mother's death inspired him to do some further investigation of his own.  He latest search resulted as the others, and was unsuccessful.  "No, not yet.  But I'm sure something will turn up."

"Well, if you need anything from me, don't hesitate to ask."

Derek smiled.  "Thanks."

Sydney sighed as she looked out towards the blue canvas of the Atlantic Ocean.  The sail of the small craft was slowly filling with wind.  She smiled. "You know, I've always wanted to go sailing."

The private investigator said nothing as he watched the boat slowly move across the water.  It seemed so peaceful all alone making its way across the blue water.  He maintained his site on the boat as he listened to Sydney continue on.

"There's something so peaceful about it.  Just you and the big blue ocean."

"Well, maybe one day you'll get a chance to. That is if you decide to stay."

She looked at him with a smile. "Actually, I submitted the final paperwork regarding my hardship discharge from the Navy. It should be approved sometime next week. After that, I start filling my sister's shoes at Garrett and Taylor Law."

"You're still keeping the name?"

She nodded. "Despite what happened between them, they still represented truth. My sister believed in this firm and the good that it does. I don't want to take that away from her." She then nudged him with her shoulder. "Hey. By the way, I could use a good, seasoned investigator."

His attention diverted from the sailboat to Sydney. "Are you offering me a job?"

"Yes," she said moving her brunette hair behind her ear. "I am."

He raised an eyebrow and leaned back to take a look at her ass. He chuckled quietly to himself. "Definitely no underwear."

Sydney's eyes went wide as she glared at him. She didn't know whether to laugh or slap him across the face. "Did you just look at my ass?"

Derek laughed as he returned his gaze upon the sailboat. He could feel the wind picking up. "It's a joke that I had with your sister. I'll tell you about it sometime."

"A joke with my sister?"

"Yep."

She shook her head with a sigh and left the potential for a flirtatious conversation alone.  She turned and refocused her gaze on the sailboat as well. Her long hair slightly flapped from the breeze.  "I can't believe I'm filling her shoes."

Derek smiled.  "You'll do a good job."

"I miss her."

He nodded as a feeling of sorrow returned for only a brief moment.  He acknowledged the sentiment when he said.  "Yeah.  I miss her too."

She took in a deep breath and one last look at the scenery around her.  "I'm going to go downstairs and see if Saundra can bring me up to speed on everything. You comin'?"

He shook his head still watching the sailboat as it turned into the wind. "No."  He answered.  "I think, I'll stay out here a bit longer."

"Okay," she retorted and she leaned towards him and kissed him gently on the cheek.  "Thanks again Derek," and she pushed away from the railing and walked off.

He watched her exit the observation deck before returning his sights on the sailboat going farther out to sea.  Its journey was just beginning.

*"By the way, I enjoyed my tour of Lynnhaven One," he said attempting to change the subject. "You can see for miles from the Observation Deck. It's absolutely beautiful."*

*"That's what I hear."*

"Well, maybe I can talk you into going up there for a cup of coffee."

*"Thank you Derek, but I'm not too big on heights. Not to mention, every time I go up there, it's cloudy and I can't see much. Can I take a rain check?"*

*"Sure."*

The sailboat disappeared along the morning horizon. He looked around noticing that the day was going to be another day of sunny skies and warm, mild weather. Despite a touch of soreness from his mid-section, he invigorated his lungs and took in another deep breath of morning air. It was sweet. He exhaled slowly and smiled.

Tessa would have enjoyed the view

# END